The Switch

The Switch

J. Boyett

SALTIMBANQUE BOOKS

NEW YORK

Typeset by Christopher Boynton

Saltimbanque Books, New York
www.saltimbanquebooks.com
jboyett.net

ISBN: 978-1-941914-13-7

For Leo and Mary.

For Chris Boyett, Pam Carter, Dawn Drinkwater, and
Andy Shanks.

Acknowledgments

As usual, many thanks to Kelly Kay Griffith for her help with the manuscript.

The Switch

One

To ordinary New Yorkers, the shop on Thirty-Seventh Street between Eighth and Ninth Avenues was nothing but a dingy fabric store. But it would have given any denizen of the Shadow World pause, for fabric plays a central role in the lore of that silent society.

Beth entered the store with Dolan. He used his own key—dawn hadn't yet come, and the store was still closed. He held Beth's elbow in a pinching grip as he steered her between two cloth-crammed shelves, toward the bolt of red fabric hanging against the back wall. Beth looked fifteen years older than him; gray sullied her red hair. She was almost but not quite heavyset, and seemed like she'd been aged by something other than just time. Her green sweatshirt had a hole just past the neckline and had grown dark under the armpits. Her blue jeans had crusty patches and stains. She stank.

She snuck a meek glance at Dolan's smirk. He was dark-skinned, taller than six feet, and he walked with a rolling, thuggish gait that Beth had trouble matching her nervous steps to. "So, um," she said, "is this the front way? I've never come in this way."

"*Shut* up," said Dolan, mouth twisted. He spoke with impatience and contempt, but was plainly enjoying himself.

The heel of a baguette was in Dolan's hand. Then the whole thing disappeared into his mouth, leaving both his hands free to hold her. Lithe and hard as he was, rarely was Dolan seen without food.

The two proprietors were there already, despite it being before dawn on a Sunday: an Asian man and woman, with gray in their hair and drab gray clothes. They seemed composed of dust. Beth tried to catch their eyes, but they kept their gazes down—their refusal to look at her was the only sign they knew she was there.

It hurt, their refusal to give her even a kind look. Of course Dolan was going to hurt and mock her. But these were mere little people, like herself.

She and Dolan slipped behind the heavy red fabric, Dolan yanking her in after him.

In the blood-colored gloom Dolan slipped a key into a hidden door and opened it. He pushed her ahead into the dark passage before shutting the door. She nearly fell down the unexpected stairs. Before she had quite regained her balance Dolan's hand was between her shoulder blades, shoving her ahead, and her legs had to scramble to keep up with the momentum of her body. Whatever Mannis wanted from her, it wasn't important enough for Dolan to be worried about breaking her neck before he got it.

The only illumination came from faint yellow bulbs sparsely placed along the walls. Beth clung to the cold metal bannister, struggling to keep ahead of Dolan's careless, clattering footsteps. The winding black-painted concrete steps were hard for Beth to see, but they seemed to give Dolan no trouble. Like he could see in the dark, like a cat.

Behind her she heard a familiar clicking sound. That would be Dolan, taking out a toothpick. He had a little metal box he kept in his breast pocket, full of solid silver toothpicks. Beth didn't see why anyone would need a whole box of solid silver toothpicks—it wasn't as if one would ever wear out.

This was the only time she'd ever actually seen an entrance to Mannis's lair. On the few occasions she'd been taken to meet Mannis in his sanctum sanctorum, Dolan had put her in a car, blindfolded her, driven around for what felt like miles, then led her, still blindfolded, to an elevator that plunged deep, deep down under the city. After those interviews Dolan had smushed a chloroformed rag to her face. She'd woken hours later on the street way out in Brooklyn, head pounding.

Did the fact that she'd been allowed to see this entrance mean nobody was worried about her living to tell of it?

Dolan gave her another shove that almost knocked her down the stairs. "*Move*, bitch," he said, but without sounding excited about it; like pushing and berating her were just things to help pass the time.

The steps spiraled down, and down, and down. Sometimes the passageway filled with the rumble of a subway train passing, perhaps only a few feet away behind the walls. Once in a while pipes traversed the stairway, running from one wall to the other—once Beth came close to tripping over one of them, a couple times she whacked her head into one. Then they were deep enough underground to be past the city pipes.

Beth began to make out the hint of a glow less dim than the stairwell's. She quickened her pace, hungry for light. When the stairs abruptly ended she hurt her knees with her first few steps on the level floor, because her legs were still expecting to descend. They turned a corner, into the room the light came from.

And saw Mannis, sitting and waiting a few feet away, in the cool, dim fluorescents. Beth ducked her head.

He was like a cat too. It was his widow's peak, his satanic eyebrows, whose V-shapes were mimicked by the lines etched into his forehead; his dark obsidian eyes; and the grace of his movements. For instance, as she rounded the corner, he had just taken a drink from his plastic water bottle, and she came upon him as he was wiping his mouth gently with the back of his wrist, a gesture of feline tidiness.

Beth knew she herself was not at all cat-like. More like a rodent, with her matted graying auburn hair, her wild eyes, her hunched-up body. Her front teeth felt prominent because of the missing back ones.

The bare room was empty, except for her, Dolan, and Mannis. The weak light didn't fully penetrate the gloom, as if the air were thick enough to provide resistance, and Beth couldn't clearly make out the edges and contours of the space.

Mannis was fiddling with the cuff of his white button-down shirt. The button was still attached, and Beth couldn't imagine what else could be wrong with a cuff besides a missing button. Of course, she knew he was only pretending not to notice her presence, so as to fuck with her. She tried to stand still and wait it out. But she kept fidgeting and shifting her weight from one foot to the other—the chronic pain in her shoulders and lower back made it hard to stand still—and pretty soon she broke down and said, "Hey, Mannis." She heard herself trying to fake a cheerful, jaunty tone.

"Beth," said Mannis, still devoting the bulk of his attention to his cuff. "You owe me money."

"Yes, yes, that's true," she said, switching to a grown-up, mature tone.

Mannis kept studying his sleeve. Beth tried to take heart. Mannis was trying to psyche her out. Well, he might be a sadist, but he didn't like to waste time. If he'd wanted her dead, he could have already had Dolan do it. He wouldn't pencil her in to his busy schedule merely to freak her out before killing her. The only reason to soften her up was that he wanted something more from her. And if he wanted something more, he couldn't kill her first.

Then again, she couldn't think of anything she had left to give.

And Mannis was a sadist, after all.

"A lot of money," murmured Mannis, his attention having moved on to his manicured nails. Actually it was only ten thousand. True, that was an astronomical sum for Beth, but she didn't think it was so much to Mannis.

"I know," she said. "I'll get it to you, Mannis."

"How?" He looked at her at last, with those glittering eyes just a shade too dark to be natural.

Beth's mouth sputtered past various answers, all of them too fantastical to actually say out loud. Including the one she wound up using: "Friends."

"I don't think you have any friends. You have family. That daughter of yours. She lives in Williamsburg, yes? Without

6

a roommate. So she might be rich enough to raise twelve thousand, in a pinch." Beth said nothing about the increase in the tally. "Would she give it to you, though?"

"Probably not," said Beth. Her gaze seemed to depart her surroundings, seemed to be dwelling on some distant, equally unpleasant prospect.

"Thereby hangs a tale, I suppose, but actually I couldn't care less. I'm sure there are countless reasons why a child burdened with you for a mother would prefer not to be reminded of the fact. That leaves me needing money, though. Now what do you propose?"

"I, I don't know." Although she hated herself for it, Beth hoped Mannis's diabolical plan was to extort the twelve grand from her daughter. Farrah possibly *could* raise it, just barely. It would have to be Mannis who went after it, though. Beth couldn't imagine anything she could say that would make Farrah give it to *her*.

Mannis said, "You don't know?"

Beth didn't want to grovel. Not because of her dignity, but because she sensed that begging would be an invitation to hurt her. She cleared her throat, and tried to sound brisk and business-like: "Well, you know, my original hope in borrowing the five thousand to go to the cleansing center up in Ithaca was that, you know, that it would help me get back to the way I used to be. And that definitely would have helped me pay you back the five grand I already owed you for the, you know, to help me get by this past year, on top of the five for the center."

"Five and five—that doesn't add up to twelve, does it? You owe me twelve."

"Right, I, uh, I mean, uh … I mean, I *know* I owe you twelve, *now*, but...."

"Anyway, the cleansing didn't work. So now we're right back where we started. Except that then you owed me five, and now you owe me thirteen. So what do you suggest?"

"Well. It didn't work this time. But I, you know, that doesn't mean it'll *never* work."

Behind her Dolan laughed, a quick guffaw. Mannis looked at her with an unreadable expression. "Beth. Are you asking me to pay for a second treatment?"

"Not at that cost. Not at, at any cost. There's other cleansers, right? Maybe you even know someone, who could do it as like a favor."

"Now you're asking me for favors."

"Not a favor to me, a favor to you! Because I'd work for you after, for as long as it took. I bet one of your spellcasters or mages could do a better cleansing job than those Wiccans. They're too gentle, but what I feel like I need is just a really good scrub, you know? They were gentle, but your guys could...." Not for the first time, it flashed through her mind that the Sisterhood up in Westchester could probably do the job if they wanted to. Anyway, they'd have a better chance than the hippie Wiccans. Of course, she could never suggest that to Mannis; he and the Sisterhood were natural enemies. "I mean, even if it hurt me, I wouldn't mind, as long as it got me back in the game. You know? I mean, you could hurt me."

"I could hurt you," he repeated.

Something about his tone, about the anticipation she felt radiating off Dolan behind her, suddenly convinced her that she really was going to be killed. "I had powers!" she cried, and tried to throw herself at Mannis's feet, but Dolan caught her shirt and held her in place. "I had powers, before I fucked myself up with the drugs, with the meth and all the rest of it. Mannis, you never knew me when I was really good, you have no idea, *no idea*. If I could get back up to full strength, oh, I'd make it worth your while, there's so much I could do for you. Like, you have a meeting with a guy you don't trust? I could read the guy's mind for you."

"I'll tell you what," said Mannis, "let's see if you can read minds. I'm going to give Dolan a signal. And afterward you tell me if you were able to read our minds and see what it meant."

Mannis looked past Beth's shoulder at Dolan and nodded. Something exploded in her lower back. She felt something

8

slam into her face—it was the floor—a high croak escaped her. She writhed, fighting to suck in gulps of air, agony and nausea rippling through her.

Above her, Mannis's voice: "Amazing, you guessed it—that signal was for him to kidney-punch you."

They really were going to kill her. She craned her neck back to raise her head, trying to make eye contact with Mannis. It was hard, what with being on her belly. But even if she'd been physically capable, standing up would only be an invitation to get knocked down again. Rolling onto her back would give her a better chance of seeing Mannis's face, but she feared exposing her middle. She wound up curling halfway onto her side, still tilting her body so as to protect her abdomen. "Please!" she said.

Mannis rose to his feet. "Please what?" he asked mildly.

"Please. I know it sounds like I'm just asking for one more favor. Like I'm not grateful for everything you've already done. But I swear, all I'm asking is for you to make it so you can use me, so I can pay back what I owe."

"Oh, I'll find some way to use you, Beth." Craven relief washed through her, since if she was to be used then she couldn't be killed. "The only question is how. There's not much you're good for anymore."

"I'm telling you, if I could just get some solid treatments...."

"I think you're downplaying the role of entropy in all this—you're not a girl anymore, Beth. Although it's true, you've made plenty of bad decisions that have ruined you before your time. Now I wonder if the only use that can be made of you isn't one involving straws."

At first the remark seemed cryptic, and once it sunk in she started trying to scramble up onto her knees. "Oh, no, please, I'm better than that!..." A foot stomped down on her back, driving her to the floor again and pinning her there. Behind and above her Dolan said, "Bitch, you ain't better than *anything*."

Her cheek was on the rough, cold concrete floor. All she could see were Mannis's feet, as he stepped closer. "It's true, Beth," he said. His words seemed to come down from the

9

heavens, because she couldn't see his face. "Do you remember the first time we met? Or were you too high? You came to buy some crystal from one of my street dealers when I happened to be making some rounds. I felt your power, even then, already stifled though it was. I took the trouble to introduce myself, to tell you that while I had no problem taking your money you did have something still more valuable, if only you wouldn't squander it. But you always were an addict, Beth, and one can't reason with an addict."

"It's true," Beth wept. "I regret it, I regret it."

"Yes, I imagine you do."

Dolan's foot shook her roughly. "You got a face that isn't even worth sticking a dick into anymore."

"True." Mannis's voice lowered, to a pitch Beth associated with lust. "There's only one way left to get pleasure from that face, now."

She saw his right foot, already so close, slowly rise; then she felt the sticky sole on her cheek. It didn't merely rest there, but pressed down, gradually adding weight till it began to hurt. Beth was afraid she would see the left foot rise as well, that he would put all his weight on her face. That would break her jaw or cheekbone, she supposed. She waited, submissive, trying not to provoke him with any complaints. In the end she couldn't keep a whimper from squeaking out. That must have been what Mannis was after, because the pressure eased, a bit.

He did leave his foot on her face as he said, "Do you know why I didn't have Dolan bother to blindfold you this time, Beth?"

She assumed the question was rhetorical, but when she let a moment pass without answering he pumped his foot impatiently. "No," she tried to say. It came out as a smushed blob of sound.

"Because no one's worried about what you may or may not tell anyone. You have no one left who trusts you, no one who wants to sit through your addled tales. No one cares if you've gone six months drug-free. You're a stinky bag lady who has nothing left, least of all her word."

10

Beth wasn't sure if she was supposed to reply to that or not; anyway, she didn't. There was nothing to say.

"We're having a party tomorrow," he said, "at about eight. Best try to get here early. If you haven't got my fifteen thousand, you're going to be one of the main attractions."

Two

Tim's wife Ann was an operations manager at a financial consulting firm, and worked nine-to-five in downtown Manhattan. Tim was a free-lance marketing consultant, who worked from home in their Cobble Hill apartment in Brooklyn. There were trees, there was a pretty view of the river only a block away, there was a little park where yuppies took their kids. Ann was out for her walk and he was hanging out in his underwear, debating whether to get dressed and go out to the local sandwich shop, when the buzzer rang late on Sunday morning. He had a premonition that it might be his half-sister Beth buzzing, even though he hadn't seen her in a couple months, a premonition strong enough that he was tempted to ignore the bell.

But he threw on some pants and a T-shirt and buzzed her up. Even if he'd known for sure who it was, he would have done the same thing. She was his sister, after all. Half-sister.

Tim and Ann lived on the third floor. Their intercom was broken, but when he opened the apartment door he was able to smell that it was Beth before she even made it to the first landing. He silently listened to her trudge her way up. It took her a long time to climb all those flights, like an old lady, even though she was still a year away from forty.

He didn't hug her when she appeared, partly because of her stench and partly because in recent years she would shy away when he tried. There were bruises and lots of little scratches on the left side of her face. "What happened?" he asked, appalled, as he closed the door behind her.

"I fell!" she lied, and laughed maniacally.

He switched off the air-conditioner and started opening windows, trying to be discreet about it.

Once he had the windows open he noticed the way Beth was eyeing the sofa, as if unsure whether she should sit on it. It had clearly been a long time since she'd bathed, and her clothes were filthy. But he made himself gesture at the couch and say, "Please, please, sit."

Luckily she sat in the wooden chair by the window instead. Wood didn't hold scents the way fabric did. Tim took the sofa, sitting catty-cornered from Beth and making himself lean toward her into the smell, elbows on his knees and hands clasped before him, a grin pasted on his face. "You look *great*," he said, ridiculously.

Beth let her gaze flutter to the floor in embarrassment. Tim looked down too.

The moment stretched on till Beth said, "Can I have a beer?"

Tim grimaced. "Well, I mean, I don't know…are you sure?…"

"I was addicted to meth, Tim!" she shouted. "Crystal meth! Not alcohol!"

"Okay, okay," he said, hurrying to the kitchen nook.

As he was getting the beer out of the fridge she kept going: "And even that I haven't taken in half a year! I'm clean! I can have a beer like anyone else if I want! Anyway, I never had a problem with beer!"

"All right!" The exchange upset Tim so much that he had trouble popping the cap off the bottle. "I'm sorry," he said as he rushed it to her, "don't get offended, I didn't mean anything by it."

She stayed sullen. "Aren't you going to have a beer, too?"

"No. I don't feel like one."

"Oh." Now she seemed self-conscious at being the only one drinking, and looked at the cold bottle in her hand as if she would have liked to get rid of it. Tim almost did go back and get himself one, just to make her feel better, but he was afraid that would be silly.

His eyes returned to her face. It would be useless to ask Beth again how it got banged up. She'd just keep insisting she'd fallen

14

and laughing that laugh of the damned. "Are you sure you're all right, Beth?"

"Oh, you know," she said, and scowled at the floor again.

"Would you like to take a shower?" he asked; a little hopelessly, because it wasn't like it would do her any good to bathe and then get right back into those soiled clothes. There had been a time when he'd kept outfits in Beth's size, for surprise visits such as this. But over the course of a few guest showers, Beth had walked off with all of them. And because Ann had never been thrilled with the practice, he hadn't bought replacements. He was thankful that Ann was so much smaller than Beth that there was no temptation to give away his wife's clothes to his sister.

Still, even if she did have to change back into the same reeking outfit, Tim thought a shower might feel good to her. But she only shook her head, as if such luxuries were things of her distant childhood. "No, I can't. I have to run, I can't stay long."

Ah. "Does that mean you're here for something specific, Beth?"

"Well. Kind of, yeah."

"Well. Tell me what it is."

"I just, I kind of need some help."

"Okay. You know I'm always happy to help you. And I've told you what kinds of help. Like, if you need help enrolling in some sort of program. Or if you'd like to go out on some job interviews, I'll take you out for a make-over and buy you some new clothes and you can use our place for the address on your job applications...."

But she was already shaking her head in that familiar, impatient way. Tim hardened his heart; he felt a shriveling in his guts, a vomitous taste in his mouth.

He said, "I can't give you money."

It was like he'd said, *I can give you money.* Her face burst into a funhouse travesty of liveliness; she set the beer on the floor so she could have both hands free to hold out to him, and said, "It's kind of a lot that I need. But don't worry, I don't need *all* of it from you. If you could help me with part of it, I could find the rest someplace else."

Where else? Tim knew this was her ploy for being able to mention the whole amount to him, without scaring him off right away. Then, once she'd gotten him to agree to pay for a part, it would be easier to get him to spring for the whole kaboodle. The tactic had been effective the first couple times.

Even though he wasn't going to give her any money, he asked, "How much is it?," telling himself he was merely curious.

In the tone of a used-car salesman about to explain why a price is actually a much better deal than it seems, she said, "Fifteen thousand."

"Fifteen thousand!" Tim shot out of his seat. He gaped down at her, then clapped his hands onto his cheeks and paced in circles around the room.

While his gaze was off of her, Beth allowed her own face to go slack and dead. No need to expend energy animating it, if no one was looking.

Tim came to a halt and stared down at her. His hands migrated up from his face to bunch themselves in fists in his hair. "Beth, I find it very difficult to believe that you owe someone fifteen thousand if you haven't been into something you shouldn't be!"

"It wasn't for drugs, Tim.... Or, well, part of it was. But not most of it! And that was a while ago. It's an old debt."

"So at least part of it is a debt to a drug dealer. You're asking me to give money to a drug dealer.... How did you manage to accrue a debt of fifteen thousand?!"

"A lot of it was interest," she said bitterly.

"You have to go to the police," said Tim. She laughed. "Beth, you have to! They can protect you from these people. That's what the police are *for*, is to protect us from drug dealers."

"It's not a drug dealer...or, well, mainly that's not what he is...."

"What, then?"

Instead of answering she got that look that always infuriated him, that look like there was some massive secret about the scumbags she surrounded herself with, something he wouldn't be able to comprehend even if she explained it. Sure enough, she said, "You wouldn't understand. And if you mess around and try calling the cops on them, who knows what they'll do."

At that, the insides of his belly went soft and wet with terror. "So they're not just regular drug dealers. So they're what? Gangsters?"

"That's a little closer."

If Beth had been just trying to bilk him out of some dough, he felt sure she would have picked a lower, more achievable sum. So she probably really did need it. "What's going to happen to you if you don't get it?"

She only flinched.

He couldn't just give her that money, though. Certainly not in cash, and he couldn't imagine who he'd make a check out to (Beth didn't have a bank account to deposit it in). Besides, Ann would flip. "I can't give you that much money, Beth."

"Then I'll die," she snapped. Not exactly true, but close enough. She stood and started for the door.

"Wait!" cried Tim, blocking her way. She stopped, glaring at him.

Helplessly, he said, "Aren't you going to drink the beer I gave you?"

"I don't want to drink alone. I thought we would both drink together. It's embarrassing if it's just another gift someone's giving me."

"All right.... If you don't get this money, they're really going to ... *kill* you?"

"Worse, probably."

"What's the deadline?"

"Eight o'clock, tomorrow night."

"Jeez.... Okay. Look, calm down, we'll work this out. Okay? Now, just sit down, I'll go get a beer...."

She sat on the sofa after all. Tim turned toward the kitchen nook in time for her not to see him wince—Ann would be able to smell that Beth had sat there.

He came back with his unwanted beer. Beth's was still on the floor beside the wooden chair—she seemed to have forgotten it. He sat on the sofa, his body angled toward hers. "Beth," he said, "you're my sister and I want to help you."

"Then there's only one way."

"We've talked about this before. With the money. I've given you a lot of money over the years. It isn't that I care about the money. But, Beth, it never seems to make things better."

She gazed into space with a defeated, angrily grieving look. It scared Tim, because even during her very bad times he'd never seen anything quite like it. She said, "I guess things won't get better this time, either. But if I don't get that money, they sure will get a shitload worse."

Tim stared at her. She was telling the truth, he realized. There was no con here. She wasn't even exaggerating.

He reached out and gripped her wrist. The touch startled her, and her eyes shot to his face like an animal's, preparing to fight.

He said, "You're my sister. I want to help you. And if what that means is...."

The rattle of a key in the lock cut him off. His stomach plummeted, and Beth's face closed up even tighter. He twisted around to see Ann enter the room, her face already puckered in bewildered repugnance at the smell, her hand on the swell of her belly as if she wanted to protect the unborn child from the noxious fumes. When her eyes lighted on Tim's sister, her confused expression vanished. "Hello, Beth."

"Hey, Ann." Beth dropped her eyes and squirmed. She snuck a look at Tim, to see if he would continue along the same lines, now that his wife was present. Tim stared at his quietly fidgeting hands. Beth huffed and hauled herself upright: "I was just going," she said.

"You can stay," said Ann. She really was trying to be gracious and welcoming, but her effort was audible.

"Nah, fuck it," said Beth, already halfway to the front door, "I better go."

18

Tim stood. "Wait, Beth!" He turned to his wife. "Honey, Beth is in trouble."

Ann's face got harder and more vivid as she saw that yes, Tim really was about to throw yet more money at his homeless junkie half-sister. "Then maybe she should get help from someone who can *actually* help her. With her *real* problems, not her symptoms."

"What do you know about real problems?" demanded Beth.

Tim waved frantically at Beth to be quiet, and to Ann he said, "Okay, well, I agree with you. Now what? It sounds like she still has a big, immediate problem, that has to be solved first."

Ann turned to Beth, and, keeping her tone civil, said, "I wish Tim and I could have a chance to discuss this alone, without having it sprung on us all of a sudden."

"Yeah, well, they kind of sprung it on me, too."

The way she said it, as if Ann's objections were just tiresome quibbles that Beth had to sit through, tipped Ann over the edge. "I don't see why it's always Tim and I who have to cover your little 'expenses'!" she snapped. "Don't you also have a daughter? Farrah has a job, why don't you go ask *her* to help you out!"

Beth's face burned bright red, and something about her bulging eyes made Ann take a step back. Beth stormed past her, out the front door and down the stairs. She didn't bother to close the door, and when Tim stood at the top of the stairs calling her back, she wouldn't turn to look at him.

Three

Even though Eli was in the bathroom, leaving her momentarily free of him, Farrah couldn't stop checking her eye makeup, couldn't stop worrying about how far back her shoulders were and whether she was too obviously poking out her breasts. Even when she was alone in the apartment she worried over what she looked like, even in the dark; she got way more compulsive when there was an actual guy over. And she was doubly self-conscious because, now that he'd seen her real boobs, he knew how much she padded.

But she told herself again to relax; Eli had seemed to enjoy the goods. True, he was a little distant and ironic, but he was a Williamsburg hipster. Low affect and a noncommittal vibe were part of his whole thing.

And it wasn't like he was nervous about *his* body. Once they'd gone down on each other modesty had become superfluous, as far as he was concerned. Ever since then he'd been walking around buck-naked, scratching his hairy, not super-developed belly, his hairy but otherwise almost nonexistent ass, his beard, his hairy chicken legs. Right now she could hear him blowing his big schnozz, lustily honking the snot out without a care for what she might think. More power to him. Farrah still thought he was cute, but she made a tally of his imperfections just to demonstrate to herself that her own didn't necessarily need to matter, either.

No use. The problem was not that she thought this or that specific attribute of her body would disgust Eli. It was that she herself found her body globally hideous. She hated catching glimpses of it in the various mirrors around the apartment, and if she'd been alone she would have covered it up with more than the T-shirt she had on now. She was afraid, though, that Eli would think it was weird if she got dressed again while he was still naked. Like, maybe he would take it as a reproach to his own nudity. Too bad he wasn't a pervert who would be into fucking her while she wore a burqa or something.

A flush resounded in the bathroom, and Eli emerged without washing his hands, scratching himself. They couldn't avoid crowding each other. Farrah didn't own much, but thanks to the apartment's cramped dimensions her belongings gave the place a squeezed feeling. There was the living room, so narrow that her worn, maroon sofa seemed to have been jammed almost all the way up to the big-screen TV and stereo. Off that was a narrow kitchen nook. Then, behind a door, a bedroom just big enough for her double bed. The walls were a somber blue; there was a window in the kitchen but it was high and narrow, and the place didn't get a lot of light. Regardless, living alone even at the outskirts of Williamsburg, Brooklyn was big enough of a status coup that Farrah didn't let herself be bothered by details.

Eli came and sat beside her on the couch, and started to slide his hand up under the hem of her long T-shirt.

Farrah laughed as she shoved his hand away. "If you're wondering if I'm a real redhead, you won't find out from down there," she said, "it's all waxed. As you know."

He quit trying to stick his hand up between her legs, but continued to stroke them. His eyes rested on her, in that weirdly blank way he had.

His gaze freaked her out. It was like he was waiting for something, but was in no hurry to get it and so didn't feel the need to tell her what it was. Unable to stand the silence, Farrah said, "But, anyway, yeah. Real redhead. Got it from my mom. About the only thing I *did* get from her," she added, and produced an embarrassed laugh.

He didn't seem interested enough in that comment to follow it up. Farrah found that off-putting; on the other hand it wasn't like she wanted to talk about her mom, so she was relieved, she guessed.

They hung out. Farrah hooked her iPod up to the speakers and played him some of her favorite music. None of it seemed to impress him, but maybe it was just that flat affect again. She got him to tell her about the bands he was into, but she'd never heard of them. They didn't seem to be bands one would just naturally *hear*; they were all people Eli personally knew, whose shows he went to.

Farrah didn't know anything about the hipster scene; she wasn't hip enough. She just had a thing for hipster guys.

After a while he said, "You have kind of an accent."

She rolled her eyes and grimaced. "That's the *other* thing I got from my mom, I guess. She had me in Tennessee, I didn't come to New York till I was seventeen."

Farrah thought maybe he would ask why she'd moved here. But no. She wasn't sure he was even looking at her anymore, exactly; his head was pointed in her direction, his eyes were too, but it seemed to Farrah like they were unfocussed, like he had completely spaced out.

If someone had asked her why she was so keen to hold Eli's attention, she wouldn't have known how to reply. All she knew was that it was imperative she hold it, that she prove she wasn't just the boring, useless, ugly girl she knew herself to be.

Trying to think of something interesting and funny to talk about, her loser mom was the nearest thing she found to hand. "She lives here now," she said, "my mom. New York, I mean. Like I said, I moved up here when I was seventeen. Basically I ran away, except not really because I came and stayed with my Uncle Tim and Aunt Ann, and Uncle Tim helped me get enrolled in college at Hunter and all that. Also, it wasn't like my mom was looking for me, so it wasn't a very dramatic runaway experience.... I stayed with Uncle Tits and Aunt Ass a few weeks, but then my aunt started getting weird about having me there all the time, so my uncle helped me get set up in an apartment with a bunch of other girls...."

"Uncle Tits and Aunt Ass?" repeated Eli. It was the first proof that he was listening.

23

"Oh. Tim and Ann, T and A. That's just what I call them—not to their faces. It isn't super-nice, I guess.... Anyway, then my mom followed me up here.... New York's not a natural place you would expect her to be, because she's a big meth-head. That's more, like, a Midwestern drug."

"Oh, yeah?" A kindling of interest in Eli's eyes. Squalor and scandal were always a draw, when interest in everything else flagged.

Actually, as far as Farrah knew her mom hadn't smoked meth till she moved to New York. Digressing to make the clarification didn't seem worth the trouble, though. "Yeah," she said. "She's totally fucked up. She's homeless, as far as I know. I haven't seen her in almost a year."

"And, so, like, you don't care? It doesn't bug you that your mom is a drug addict and she's out on the street and everything?"

There was no sign Eli had intended his words to cut; he merely gazed at her with bland curiosity. But Farrah felt betrayed, as if he'd taken the mockery intended for her mother and turned it around on her, switching her and her mother's places, making it seem like *she* was the ugly unloved loser.

"Of course it *bugs* me," she said. "I mean, I wish her all the best. I hope she gets cleaned up or whatever. But there just isn't anything I can do to help her. Believe me, I've had years to learn that."

She squirmed her legs up onto the seat and in close to her, pressed her palms together and squeezed her hands between her thighs. "I mean, she's always been fucked up, my whole life. It wasn't easy, being a kid and growing up all alone with this crazy mom who had me when she was only fifteen years old."

She fell silent, staring at a spot on the floor. A pop song jangled out from the speakers and into the silence. It was from her collection, yet she didn't recognize it.

"I mean, do you want to know how fucked up she was, even when I was a kid? She used to swear up and down she was a witch. Like, a real one, who could cast spells and shoot fire and fly...."

She didn't check Eli for any reaction, she just kept staring at that spot on the floor.

She said, "And that kind of thing can really fuck a kid up. You know? Because we're so impressionable. Like, I have all these false memories she must have sort of implanted in me by just talking. Like, memories of blocks floating, toys flying...."

She heard what she was admitting and, flinching in embarrassment, turned to look at Eli. In his flat, dull gaze there was no hint of judgment, surprise, mockery. No hint of anything else either, though. She found herself having to fill in the blanks. And she had nothing very nice to fill them with. It was like looking into that disdainful gaze she always imagined emanating from every mirror. Except it was all the more painful, coming from another person's face this way, and she, hasty and confused, had to let her eyes drop from his.

Four

Kris jolted awake, her head recoiling from the rattling window. The dream broke up and floated away. Wisps of it clung to her mind; she brushed them off.

She was riding the Greyhound to New York. No pious member of the silent society would have taken an airplane, except in a dire emergency—commercial flight (as opposed to levitation, flying carpets, and so forth) tended to cancel out the experience of physical distance, one of the aspects of reality sacred to the Shadow World. She'd taken a cruise from Europe to Canada, then hopped onto a bus to New York. (Twenty years ago she would have probably worked her way across by posing as a Merchant Marine, but she'd earned some luxuries here and there.) Small glamours cast upon her passport had taken care of visa issues. Of course, she could have taken a cruise directly to New York, but she'd preferred to make her final approach to the city via ground transportation. One got a better idea of the lay of the land. Lines of power. Centers of force.

When they were still more than twenty miles north of the Bronx, she felt a big tug. That would be the Sisterhood, their commune and its compound—rather, the tug would be from the Stone that provided their commune's strength but which they'd founded the commune a respectful distance from. The Stone of Pellerian. She'd been expecting to sense it along her route, but was still impressed by its power.

This was her first trip to New York. As they arrived she took in the city's skyline with interest, but only a mild one—she wasn't here to sight-see.

At Port Authority she got her rucksack and figured her way out of the building. The place was one part homeless shelter, one part cave, and one part mall. She wore a jacket and jeans in matching blue denim, steel-toed boots, and a white T-shirt tucked in. Her oval face, with its big eyes and dark shoulder-length curls, was pretty enough that a couple of guys on the bus had tried chatting her up, till she'd given them the look she used for defusing such attempts.

The signage in the paradoxically fluorescent gloom of Port Authority was straightforward enough that she never felt tempted to use a guiding spell. Then she was out on the broad, crowded sidewalk a block from Times Square, letting the jostling crowd flow past her, taking it in and ignoring the taxi drivers shouting their offers of a cab.

Kris allowed herself twenty seconds to be wowed by New York. Then she got down to business.

She'd studied maps of the city; maps, guidebooks, photos, blogs. Despite having never been here, she could find her way around. The trick was picking the destination. She had to figure out where the person she was looking for was. For that, she'd use a spell.

First she wandered around a bit, getting a deeper feel for the terrain. She walked a couple blocks south and then stopped and gazed a few blocks still further in that direction, towards a faint emanation. That would be the local yokel, the little warlord they called Mannis. She'd learned about him in her research, too. If this had been her turf, he was the kind of scum she would have stamped out, especially now with the new coven behind her. But she had sworn an oath not to do anything heavy-duty here in North America.

She strolled another couple blocks, leaning forward under the rucksack's weight. The rucksack wasn't too big, considering that she never knew how many months she'd have to live out of it. It contained the necessities: clothes, weapons, soap, a grimoire; plus small pieces of intricately embroidered fabric tucked here and there, the sort of thing you would expect to see in the luggage of a witch in service of the Light, with a pious respect for the Warp and Weft of Destiny.

And Kris Bouts was indeed a pious witch. She believed with a child's faith that each soul would one day take its place upon a thread laid down in the cosmic Great Tapestry, except for those entered into the Black Book and cast for all eternity into the Black Ice. Except in matters of life or death, she never violated any of the annoying strictures that hampered life in the modern world: against mechanized air travel, for example, or using a telephone in any but the most strictly defined contexts. She was an exemplary knight errant, her faith her lodestar.

She'd planned to find a quiet spot, but soon realized that there were no quiet spots in the streets of midtown Manhattan. So she stopped, put the bag down, leaned against a wall, and meditated.

She'd worried that standing still and spacing out would attract attention. But even as she slipped into the trance she could sense the crowd rushing heedlessly past her. Good—New York was living up to its reputation for public anonymity.

She cleared her thoughts. Quicker than she'd hoped, the living spark of her quarry formed itself in her mind. Kris had to concentrate, lest her happy excitement shake loose the vision.

What she was seeing was not the person herself, but a sort of imprint. Kris realized with pleasant surprise that this was quite a recent trace—she'd been afraid that any trail her friend had left through this particular neighborhood might be weeks or months or years old, depending on her routine.

As Kris probed deeper her mood sombered. The beginning of the trail was scrambled and garbled, diffused, the way such trails got when the person leaving the spoor was distressed. And it wasn't lost on Kris that the origin of this trail, its point of greatest distress, was a blob of pain that seemed to encompass the headquarters of that little turd Mannis.

Never mind that for now. What mattered was finding her.

After a couple minutes of concentration, Kris saw a kind of energy thread in her mind's eye, that she could overlay atop the

29

physical world around her. She opened her eyes. It felt like the energy thread went underground very nearby. Peering around the corner, she saw that it did indeed lead to a subway entrance. She started walking to it.

The invisible line she held in her mind seemed like it went south-southeast once underground. She lost sight of it after about a mile, but was confident that as long as she concentrated she would be able to keep following it.

South. South was Brooklyn, she remembered from all those maps.

The trail led all the way to a particular block, and then a particular apartment in Brooklyn. But it radiated more and more anxiety as it neared that point, till by the end it was fuzzy and scrambled and almost as difficult to read as at its origin, back near Mannis's, and it took all Kris's concentration to keep the thread clear in her mind. In its departure it exploded out in anxiety, pain, and fear. It was too distorted by distress to easily follow it from this point on, and Kris would have to spend some time getting a lead again. So she may as well drop in and see what she could find out.

On the stoop she paused and concentrated, and felt how the thread terminated this leg of its journey on the third floor. She looked at the buzzers. It was a four-story building, and there were eight apartments. The apartments on the third floor must be numbers five and six. Five came first, so that was the one she tried.

She bore in mind the terrible distress that had been provoked in this apartment, not long ago. She would have to be on guard against whatever awaited her.

Meanwhile, upstairs in number five, Tim kept planning to strip back down to his underwear but seemed to lack the strength. When the buzzer rang again he was lying in bed with the lights off. He leaped up to go buzz in whoever it was.

He was sure it was Beth. She had nowhere else to go; there was no way Farrah would give her mother money. It still made Tim angry, the way Ann had so cavalierly suggested Beth humiliate herself by groveling to her child. Shortly after Beth had stormed out Tim had silently resolved that he would give his sister the money after all, if only he got another chance. Ann had gone to a movie, since the only thing likely to come of their brooding together in the apartment was a fight. Tim hoped to write Beth a check and get her out before Ann got home. He didn't know how a drug dealer would deposit a check, but he didn't have access to fifteen grand in cash tonight so he hoped that either it would be okay, or that Beth would be able to get an extension. He'd gone online and transferred enough from their savings into their checking account to keep the check from bouncing. He was trying not to think how Ann would react, after the check cleared and he had to confess to blowing such a big chunk of their savings.

But when he opened the door, it wasn't Beth at all. It was a nice-looking brunette in some kind of denim get-up, with a big rucksack. Like she was backpacking through Brooklyn. Once the door was open, they both stood still, he frozen by the mild surprise of not finding his sister there, she looking like she was sizing him up. Finally, she smiled at him. A cold smile.

"Um," he said. "Hello?"

"Hello," she said. "Is Beth here?"

In theory, a five-foot-six brunette might not have seemed threatening. But the intensity of those big eyes, combined with Beth's earlier terror, made Tim wary. "Why?" he said.

"I'm a friend."

"As far as I can tell, Beth doesn't have any more friends," he snapped, and slammed the door.

Slammed it on her foot, anyhow. Tim looked down at the steel-toed boot blocking the door, then nervously back up at the woman's face. It had softened.

"Of course," the stranger said. "You must be Tim."

Five minutes later, Kris was sitting in the living room while Tim brewed them both some tea. He was still nervous, but now it was because he was worried Ann might have picked a short movie and would get home in time to catch him with this hot woman, and see how her hotness discombobulated him.

Kris watched him fumble around with the tea bags and the kettle. She could tell that she turned him on, and also that he wasn't going to do anything about it. A harmless guy. Same father as Beth, but, Kris imagined, a far drabber mother.

He seemed all right. A little straight and narrow for Kris's taste, but then most people were. When she looked closely, she could see the resemblance to Beth. Maybe. His hair was a lighter, weaker version of Beth's auburn, and his nose seemed kind of similar.

Not the eyes, though. He didn't have Beth's eyes.

But she could tell from the apartment's vibe that decent folks lived in it. It was a bland and anonymous space that had been warmed by long, constant contact with Tim and Ann.

All these observations were filtering through in the background. What she was really paying attention to was this story he was telling, about how Beth needed fifteen thousand "or else." Tim assumed that the "or else" was death. Considering that she'd come to her brother directly from some traumatic experience in Mannis's neighborhood, Kris suspected something different, but not necessarily better.

Tim brought two steaming cups over from the kitchen. Kris occupied the wooden chair Beth had sat in earlier; Tim took a seat on the sofa. That homeless-person smell still clung to it, under the air freshener that had been sprayed around. "So, you see the kind of trouble she's in," he said grimly, and blew on his mug.

"It's all right," Kris reassured him. "I'll take care of it, as soon as I find her." She blew on her tea once, then took a sip.

"Well, yeah, but how?" said Tim.

"I'll give her fifteen thousand dollars," said Kris.

"By tomorrow? In cash?"

"Sure."

"Wow." Tim eyed her rucksack, as if wondering just how much money she had in there. "Okay, I guess that would work. You guys must be pretty good friends."

Kris took another sip of her tea. Certainly, she and Beth were friends. There wasn't even any need to say so, even now, when it had been nearly twenty-five years since they'd spoken.

He tried to drink his tea, but recoiled as soon as his lips touched the liquid. "Gah! How can you drink it while it's still so hot?"

She took another sip. "Tim. Something happened when Beth came over, didn't it? She was upset when she arrived, but it was worse when she left."

Guilt clouded Tim's face. "Sure," he said. "Because I turned her down. For the money. Probably she was counting on me."

"No. I'm sure that's part of it, but there was something else. Something specific, and something stronger than just disappointment."

He frowned. "How would you know?"

"Please. Did something set her off?"

"Well ... my wife came home and found her here. Now, Ann is great, Ann is compassionate, but, you know, she was less than thrilled. We've helped Beth a lot, Ann and I both. And I guess Ann feels like no matter what we do it never seems to do any good, it's just money and emotion down the drain."

Kris forced herself to stay patient. "Okay, your wife and Beth don't get along. But there was something more. Did something happen?"

"Nothing except what I just said."

But he hadn't actually said much, only given a vague summary of the visit. "What were Beth's exact words when she left?" tried Kris.

"Well, she didn't actually say anything, she just stormed off. Ann inadvertently pissed her off by suggesting she ask Farrah for money, and Beth didn't like that.... Farrah's Beth's kid, you know. Have you met Farrah?"

"No, but I know about her," said Kris, thinking, *Ah, naturally—the kid.*

Five

One reason Beth had no phone was that she had no money, no credit card, and no fixed address for anyone to mail a bill to. Another reason was that if she called anyone to ask them to meet, they would just try to avoid her, so it was better simply to show up.

Not having a smartphone had kept her relatively sharp when it came to remembering phone numbers and addresses, more so than one might expect given her history of drug abuse. She definitely remembered where her own daughter lived, though she'd only been to her current apartment twice, neither time by invitation, and it hadn't been easy to learn the address in the first place.

The name card under Farrah's intercom button bore her father's surname, Davenport, instead of Beth's, which was Weaver. That was insane, because Farrah had only ever met her father twice, and anyway the guy had been a statutory rapist. Not that Beth had complained at the time.

Beth glowered at the name card, till one of the building's residents came out and seemed mildly freaked to see her looming there in the vestibule. Beth shied back. The resident was a twenty-something who'd come home from work to change into her stylish black outfit, and now was heading back out to burn off the excess energy of youth. It jarred Beth that someone so young could be flowing through the world so competently.

The girl's surprised stare and then her carefully averted gaze as she hurried by reminded Beth that she was a homeless person, and wouldn't be allowed to stand in this vestibule indefinitely. She pushed the button above the card that read, "Farrah Davenport," and waited.

Soon her kid's voice crackled through the speaker. "Yeah?" she said. "Who is it?"

Beth knew better than to identify herself. Farrah wasn't likely to just let her in—she might even prefer to call the cops and have them remove her. Instead of speaking, Beth pressed the button again.

Her daughter's voice said, "All right, you can stop buzzing, I hear you! Just tell me who this is."

Beth waited a moment, then buzzed again. Hopefully Farrah would decide the intercom was busted, like Tim's was, and just give up and buzz in whoever it was.

Frustrated, her daughter exclaimed, "I can't just buzz up some stranger! You've got to tell me who you are first!"

Beth said nothing. Merely waited, then pressed the button again.

"Hello?!" demanded Farrah, exasperated. There was a pause. Though it was impossible for Beth to know what Farrah was doing—she'd lost her powers, after all—she could imagine her hesitating, her thumb on the intercom button, trying to decide something. Sure enough, the distorted voice from the speaker said, "Is this...?"

But then the voice faltered. Beth knew her kid well enough to know she'd feel stupid if she asked some stranger if he or she was her mother, and that fear of looking stupid would prevent her from acting on what her intuition told her. After a moment the door buzzed to signal that it was unlocked.

Beth hurried upstairs, hoping to avoid the looks she was bound to get if any of Farrah's neighbors bumped into her. She knocked on Farrah's door and saw her daughter's shadow fall over the peephole, then heard her say "*Fuck*" to herself and, to her mother, "Go away!"

"Just let me in a minute, Farrah."

"No! Go away! The reason you wouldn't say who it was on the intercom was because you *knew* I wouldn't want to let you come up!"

"Were you trying to talk to me? I didn't hear anything, the intercom must be busted."

"Mom, *please*," Farrah begged. "*Please* just go."

Beth's mouth twisted at how desperately Farrah wanted to be rid of her. "You have to talk to me first," she said. "Then I'll go."

The door clattered as Farrah undid the locks, then it cracked open. Beth slipped her foot into the gap.

Farrah's aggrieved face glared out at her. It had been at least six months since they'd seen each other. "You changed your hairstyle," Beth said.

"*Seriously?!*" hissed Farrah, more appalled by the second. "Mom, just tell me what you want and get out!"

Beth noted how low Farrah was keeping her voice. Not only did she find her mother repulsive, she feared being overheard, having their drama made public. Good. If she wanted to get rid of Beth, the quickest way was to help her. "I'm in trouble," she said.

Farrah snorted. "When have you ever not been?"

Touché. "It's worse this time...."

"It's always worse than it was the last time."

"That's true. Jesus, is that true." Beth knew how unlikely, how well-nigh impossible it was that Farrah would give her enough money for it to matter, or even any money at all. Even enough for a coffee. Yet the bare slim infinitesimal possibility of salvation intoxicated her. "But I just need help or I'm fucked. See, there's this party...."

"A party? Where? *You* got invited to a *party?*"

"Yeah, I'm 'invited.' It's tomorrow at eight, under this fabric store at Thirty-Seventh and Eighth...."

As the door opened down the hall Farrah shushed her. Farrah's neighbor stepped out, wrinkled her nose at the smell, glanced over, saw Beth in her stained and torn clothes, and quickly looked away as she hurried downstairs.

"You're making a scene," accused Farrah once the neighbor was gone.

"Me?! I just want to talk! You're the one who wants to do it in the hall!"

"Shhh!" Farrah twisted her neck to look back over her shoulder. "All right, come in, come in, just get out of the hallway. And keep it down!"

Farrah stepped back to make way for Beth, who closed the door behind herself. The tiny entry hall was decorated with a few knick-knacks and funny magazine pictures; no family photos. Beth assumed they would keep walking into the living room, but instead Farrah halted a few paces in and turned round to face her. Apparently they were going to do all their talking here. Like Farrah was afraid Beth would infect the rest of the apartment.... Well, she did stink. In case she happened to forget, there were spasms of disgust rippling across her daughter's face to remind her.

"All right, fine," said Farrah, still speaking quietly as if they were still out in the hall. "So you're going to some party at a fabric store and you need, what? A bath?"

"I need money."

Farrah laughed. "Yeah, well, it's a recession, so you're fucked."

"I need fifteen thousand dollars."

"Fifteen thousand dollars!" Now she wasn't keeping her voice down. Shock momentarily burned away her anger. "Are you fucking crazy?! Why would I have fifteen thousand dollars?!"

Beth was flustered. "I don't know, I thought you might have, you know, savings...."

"Oh, and you just figured you'd take them all, is that it?! I'm a receptionist for a dentist, Mom. More than half of what I earn goes into rent for this stupid apartment."

Beth had no clear idea anymore of how much per year normal people earned, or what percentage of that went into rent. Blinking, she said, "You, you wouldn't have to pay all of it, if you could just help me out I could get the rest from other friends...." Bullshit. She'd made a mental list of people she was calling prospects, but she didn't even know where to find most of them anymore. And none of them would give her money.

"Why should I give you *anything*? I'm your daughter, what have you ever given *me*?"

38

"Farrah, please. It's life or death."

"Oh, please, you are so full of bullshit."

"No, really."

"Fine, then. At least I'll be rid of you once and for all."

There was the sound of a door opening around the corner, deeper in the apartment. The bedroom door. Farrah winced, and blushed bright red. Ah, Beth realized, it wasn't only the neighbors Farrah wanted to keep from hearing them—she had someone in the apartment.

Over Farrah's shoulder a hairy bearded skinny boy with a big nose emerged, rubbing sleep from his eyes and scratching his chest. He looked at Farrah and Beth in the doorway, with no apparent self-consciousness over the fact that he was wearing only his boxers. "I must've dozed off," he said.

Farrah tried to recover her poise. "Eli," she said, "this is that person I was telling you about. My mother." She turned to face Beth again. "Earlier I was telling Eli all about you."

From her smirk, Beth could guess some of the unsavory bits Farrah had told. Not that there were a whole lot of savory ones. Rage, humiliation, and terror at what was going to happen all smothered her vision. "You're lucky I'm not the woman I used to be," she growled. "There was a time I could have fucked you up so bad for talking to me like this."

"Haven't you already fucked me up enough?"

Beth's fists bunched, but at the same time she cowered away. Farrah wasn't doing anything threatening—it was just that Beth suddenly felt as if all people were threatening, as if the whole world was.

And there was that little shit staring at her with his blank eyes. They were so flat and unreadable that Beth had to fill in for herself what they must see. And the list of contemptible things she could dredge up about herself was never-ending.

She said, "I wish we could switch places just for one day, so you could know what it's like to be me."

"Well, I could still become a meth-head, but it's too late for me to get knocked up at fourteen so I guess I never will be able to follow in your footsteps. But don't worry, I think I can pretty much tell what it's like to be you by the smell."

Beth stood there, fists clenched, frozen, glaring crazy-eyed.

"Good-*bye*!" shouted Farrah. "We're done here! There's nothing you can say to me, and there's nothing you can *do* to me because you're weak and pathetic and you've spent your whole life wasting it! So now get out, unless you want me to call the cops on you!"

Beth did not want the cops called on her. She struggled to make her feet move, and finally, they did.

As she backed out of the apartment, she growled, "You're gonna regret it."

She turned and started clambering down the stairs, so that her daughter slammed the door on her back and not in her face.

Six

So she wasn't going to be able to raise the money. Beth made herself accept that. Once she left Farrah's, there was nowhere left for her to go and beg. No direction she could set her feet to march in, with the hope that at the end of that line she might find some sympathetic, monied friend. Or even someone to share a last toke.

But not getting the money didn't mean she had to go to that straw party. Fuck that. Let Mannis come and catch her, if he wanted. The worst he could do was torture her to death, and nothing better awaited her at that party of his.

Who knew, it might not even be worth it to him to chase her. Maybe no one would ever bother with her again.

For her to have any chance of slipping under Mannis's radar, she would need to leave town. Fine by her. When she'd come to New York five years ago she'd had the rather naïve idea that being around her kid and half-brother would bolster her spirit, or whatever. And then she'd started smoking crystal meth—smoking it enough to fuck up her thaumaturgical abilities. Mannis had hired her out for the last strangled gasps of her power, and then once it had finally sputtered away, strangled to death by her chemical abuse of her own body, she had clung more desperately than ever to the petty tyrant in the hope that he might help her undo the damage.

That was when she'd finally managed to kick crystal; when she'd realized with horror that she really had killed the magic within her. Physical cravings remained, but their aching tingles only filled her with disgust and revulsion.

To be fair to Mannis, he had tried to help her get those powers back. But he'd sent her to that hippie coven up near Ithaca: lots of insistent smiling and chatter about everyone being part of the Great Mother, plus some chants Beth suspected they'd gotten off the internet. In hindsight it was no surprise they hadn't been able to clean her pipes.

What she really wished was that she could find some way to get the attention of those ladies in the Westchester compound. The ones who drew on the Stone of Pellerian. The Sisterhood. Back before the crud had clogged up her thaumaturgical channels, Beth had been able to sense the tug of their power from as far away as the South Bronx.

Of course, they were serious ladies. One could tell that simply from the flavor of their aura. They weren't likely to be interested in piddling shit like playing den mothers to little lost witches—at least, not for money. Power like that was too precious to be for sale.

But that was exactly why Beth felt that they would have been able to take care of her, if only she had ever attracted their notice.

Anyway, that was all moot now. She would get on the subway and just take it as far as it went into the Bronx—the Bronx, so that when the New York subway came to an end she would be on the mainland and could conceivably just walk out of Mannis's sphere of immediate influence. Or hitchhike out, if anyone would stop for her. To get on the subway she would have to beg a swipe from some passerby's metrocard, because she had grown too fearful to risk jumping the turnstile and having a cop materialize and arrest her.

But the stress of her day had exhausted her; her flesh felt like heavy sodden towels draped over the thin frame of her skeleton. Maybe the smart thing would be to start running now, on the cusp of dusk before night fell. But Beth knew that once she was sitting down on the train she would doze off, and as a hunted creature she feared sleeping while exposed to public view. If only she could get a couple of hours' rest someplace relatively hidden, then she would have the strength to stay alert through the first leg of her journey. So when she came to a dark overpass with nobody already under it, and nice deep shadows where she could remain unseen by passersby as long as they didn't look too close, she wedged herself into the corner of the sloping floor and the slanting ceiling. As her cheek came to rest on her folded arms, the drone of traffic overhead lulled her to sleep.

In the millisecond before sleep she had time to think of her kid. Who did she think she was? Had Beth ever given Farrah shit about the way she lived her life? Take for example that little fucker at her apartment. Did Beth try to make her feel like a slut for sleeping with the guy? No, of course not.... She couldn't stop thinking of that little shithead, of his flat dead eyes. Beth could well imagine all the despicable stories that Farrah had filled the head behind those eyes with.

She slept hard, with dreams that she couldn't remember and which were best left in oblivion. Something startled her awake, and when her eyes snapped open she saw that a person was approaching. It was almost like a sixth sense had warned her someone was coming, but that was impossible, she didn't have a sixth sense anymore.

She blinked away the grogginess and watched the person. It was real nighttime now, Beth had probably slept a couple hours. The approacher was a woman, smaller than herself. She was under a streetlamp but was about to step into the shadows of the overpass. Her huge rucksack made it look like she was carrying around all her belongings, which at night was the kind of thing one associated with homelessness. On the other hand, the denim outfit she wore looked clean, so maybe this was a regular person. Plus she was a woman, therefore possibly compassionate. Beth hauled herself upright and staggered on her still-numb legs into the woman's path. The woman looked at her; it was a strange look, though she didn't seem afraid. Beth held out a hand: "Hey, ma'am, please, if you could just spare me enough so I can get something to eat."

"Beth," said the woman.

When Beth heard her name, the pieces of the woman's face assembled themselves. "Kris?" she said, trying to figure out the trick.

"Beth," said Kris again, and embraced her. At first Beth panicked at being grabbed, and tried to squirm out of the hold.

43

But once it sunk in what was happening, she brought her own hands up to wrap around Kris's back and squeezed her hard, maneuvering around the rucksack. For a while neither said anything.

The first thing Beth did say, pulling her face back from the crook of Kris's neck and shoulder, was, "I shouldn't be hugging you, you'll smell bad."

Kris acted like she hadn't heard. "You hungry?" she said. "Come on, I'll buy you some dinner."

Beth suggested that people at a restaurant might not like having her there. But Kris said that in that case they could all go fuck themselves, and since Beth was starving she didn't argue.

Kris hailed a cab, and told the driver to stop at the first restaurant they came to. During the ride, they didn't say a lot; mainly just sat in the backseat, holding hands and staring at each other. It had been a long while.

At one point Beth said, "Kris, what?..."

Kris said, "I'll tell you. There'll be time."

The first restaurant was a diner, but there was a fancier-looking Italian place a couple blocks down and Kris directed the cabbie to take them there instead.

The fancy Italian place intimidated Beth. But when they went inside she was grateful for its lighting, which was dimmer than the diner's. The host was all smiles at first, but while leading them to their table he frowned over his shoulder. He'd caught a whiff of Beth. If she had tried coming in here on her own, they would have kicked her out—but Kris looked like someone who could pay her tab, and the place wasn't busy, so he went ahead and gave them a table in a dim corner and washed his hands of them.

Kris beamed at Beth. Yet there was a tension in her smile, too, something caused by the gap between her feelings and her ability to express them. "Everything's on me," she said.

"It'll have to be," laughed Beth.

"Right, right," nodded Kris, and looked down at the tablecloth, rubbing her fingertips against it as if she wanted to test its texture. "I know things have been hard, Beth."

44

"All my own fault."

"I don't give a shit about fault. I'm here to help you."

Beth could have cried with relief. Still, even though she would never turn down aid, memories of old obligations did prompt her to say, "Of all people, you're the one I would most hate to put out."

"What the fuck are you talking about? You're in trouble—I can tell. And it's *me* who owes *you*."

Again Beth felt tears crowding the backs of her eyes: a mixture of shame and gratitude. "It's been a long time. Maybe you don't know me anymore."

"I still know you. But if you want to tell me how it's been since I left, I'd like to listen."

"No. Not yet. Tell me about you, instead. About the last twenty-five years."

Kris gave her a brief sketch of the last quarter-century: the paths her training had taken after they'd lost touch, after she'd relocated to Europe and then Asia and then back to Europe; the mentors, the secret academies, the shadow battles. Some of it Beth had heard rumors of, back before she had fallen out of the loop completely. But she'd known nothing for certain, and found herself stunned by some of the names Kris mentioned, half-legendary generals for whom she'd served as adjutant, scholars for whom she'd been amanuensis.

Beth felt a pang of sad awe upon learning that the legendary mage Old Sullivan was dead, but the sadness was balanced by amazement that Kris had actually fought at his side. Soon Beth realized that Kris had been right in the middle of one of the biggest mage wars of the last hundred years. Kris's part had had to do with an enemy named Lefebre, whom she called "the shitty Frenchman," who'd betrayed and tried to murder his old teacher Old Sullivan, ten years ago. Old Sullivan had bested and humiliated him, with Kris's aid. Not for the first time it struck Beth how surreal it was that this kind of shit never got reported on the news.

"Did you kill Lefebre?"

"No. But a time will come. Meanwhile we put his name in the Black Book." Kris spat into her palm, then wiped it on her jeans. Warriors of the Light customarily spat when they mentioned the Black Book, but it would have been uncouth to just aim it at the floor.

Kris grew somber at the mention of Lefebre being inscribed in the Black Book, because it meant his soul would be imprisoned in the Black Ice for all eternity after his death, expunged from the Great Tapestry's design. No doubt his crimes had been horrific enough to deserve it, but still. Kris still really bought into all the pious stuff, Beth saw; although her parents had been warriors, they'd kept her ignorant of the Shadow World, and she'd stayed that way till she'd been placed with Beth and her mother. Since then she'd always had a touch of the zeal of the converted. Unlike Beth, who'd been fed this stuff from birth, and had her doubts about its more woo-woo, New-Agey aspects.

Kris continued her stories. She seemed almost embarrassed by how impressed Beth was—on the other hand, they were pretty boss stories, and she enjoyed telling them. There had been a flying-carpet battle over the Pacific—Kris had knocked some bad-ass dudes and dudettes into the drink. Soon Beth had half-forgotten her own troubles, so exalted was she by Kris's stirring tales. She was on the verge of asking what Old Sullivan had really been like, when Kris said "Excuse me" to the passing waitress.

The waitress kept walking like she hadn't heard. Something about the set of Kris's jaw prompted Beth to say, "Hey, Kris, it's no biggie...."

Kris's hard eyes stayed on the waitress. "Ex*cuse* me," she repeated.

This time Kris spoke loudly enough that the waitress couldn't pretend not to notice. A few customers glanced over, as well. The waitress granted the other tables an apologetic, exasperated glance. "Yes?" she demanded.

The waitress was a young pretty brunette who managed to smell like perfume despite running around all day with food.

Beth lowered her gaze to the tabletop. There was a candle in the center. Suddenly it hurt her eyes, so she blew it out.

Kris glared at the waitress until the girl dropped her gaze. "We'd like some waters," said Kris. "And a couple of beers."

"Okay, I'll get to you as soon as I can, but I have other tables."

"Bullshit. You just asked that table over there what they wanted to drink, and we've been here way longer."

"Ma'am, there's no need to curse at me. If you keep that up my boss'll ask you to leave." She glanced down at Beth, and her lips crumpled tightly with disgust.

"Hey." When Kris spoke the waitress gave a quickly-stifled cry and nearly fell to one knee before catching herself on the table. People looked over in alarm, as if the waitress had been attacked—but no, Kris and Beth were just sitting there, their hands nowhere near the younger woman, Beth not even looking at her.

The waitress, gasping, looked down at her left knee, the one that had given out. She touched it, as if expecting to find that it was bleeding, or that her kneecap had slipped out of place. Nope. She gaped at Kris.

Kris's mouth stayed a hard line. "Be nice to my friend," she warned. "Two waters and a couple of beers. Whatever the fancy ones are."

As the waitress scurried off, Beth said, "Hey, Kris, maybe we could just go to a bar. Or even just, whatever—I'm not even really that hungry...."

"Are you kidding? I know you're hungry. We'll have a few beers, we'll eat dinner, I'll pay and they can all fuck off. Like I said before."

Beth nodded, but the waitress's contempt had taken much of the savor from the coming meal. Not that she wasn't going to wolf it down. But it did seem cruel that she should be lucky enough to have dinner in a nice restaurant without first being lucky enough to have a shower and a change of clothes, so that she could sit there without grossing out all the real people.

Kris kept trying to get Beth to talk about herself. Beth kept squirming out of it. Kris apologized for not having come to Beth's mom's funeral. That had been right after Kris had been taken overseas. Listening to her, Beth was surprised to realize Kris had been craving absolution for that the past twenty-five years; she was even more surprised to remember how angry she had been at Kris for her absence. Of course there would have been no way for Kris, still a novice, to leave her temple. Beth reassured her that it was all perfectly all right. She was even tempted to confess that on the day of the funeral she herself had been too high to show up, but in the end she couldn't say it.

She decided she at least owed her friend the sad gist of her life story, so she spat it out. How she'd started drinking and snorting coke soon after Mom's death, with a break to give birth to Farrah. By some miracle she hadn't fucked the kid up in the womb, with her drugs and alcohol.

How had she wound up like this? After her mom had died, she'd wanted nothing more than to get away from her mom's friends, that band of hippie-dippie witches who'd wanted to sit her down for heart-to-hearts about the Great Circle and about how her mom had been worried by the path Beth was taking. Beth had been driven to seek out people as different from that as possible. The ones she'd found drank and snorted a lot of coke. They never talked about the Great Circle and didn't know shit about her mom's fears for her. She'd eked out a living with fast-food jobs and increasingly shady, shitty mage-for-hire gigs. Soon her mother's old circle had begun to shun her. A few years ago, she'd finally decided to clean up her act: quit the booze and blow and move to New York City, where she could reconnect with Farrah and Tim and make a place for herself in the local Shadow World, where her reputation hadn't already been tainted. Hardly had she arrived in the city when, ironically, after spending her whole life in meth country without ever trying any, she got hooked on it. She'd been given her first, fatal toke by some stranger at a party before she'd even called on Tim or Farrah. Now she was homeless and had to be careful how she held her mouth muscles in order to hide that she was missing some of her back molars. Her half-brother and sister-in-law had once bought her some dentures, but she'd managed to lose them, who the fuck knew where.

Kris held her face carefully still as she listened.

They each ordered the lasagna just so they wouldn't have to stare at the menus forever, deciding what to get. When it came it was so good that Beth nearly cried.

Kris watched her eat. Beth could tell it gave her a sad pleasure to see how much Beth enjoyed the food. She tried to hide the fact that it made her uneasy to be so closely watched; she had to chew with her mouth in what she felt were funny-looking positions, to compensate for the missing teeth.

"Beth. You haven't asked me why I'm in the States."

"I thought it might be secret business."

"Not secret from you," Kris reproached. "Nothing will ever change that, no matter how long we've been apart."

Beth thought that Kris had an optimistic view of the stability of things. "You can tell me whatever you want whenever you want," she said. Then, hopefully: "You're not moving back here, are you?"

"No. You're the one who's moving. To a quiet, green little spot in the Hungarian boonies."

Beth laughed.

The laugh disconcerted Kris only a little. "I know you have family here that it might be hard to leave—your brother, your daughter...."

Beth threw her head back and laughed hard enough to draw more looks.

Kris smiled. "Well, then. If there's no reason to stay...."

"Definitely no reason to stay. Problem is, you've got no reason to take me."

"Don't say that."

Beth saw that her napkin was still crumpled on the table beside her plate. It had been so long since she'd used one that she'd forgotten it was supposed to go in her lap. She took it now, twisting it in her hands. Before the meal was over she was going to ask Kris for help, either for fifteen grand or for her to kill Mannis. She dreaded the look on Kris's face more than she had that on Tim's or Farrah's. Kris didn't yet realize just how far she'd fallen, and Beth was going to have to watch as she figured it out.

Still looking down at the napkin, she said, "I'm certainly not in a position to say no to charity, but even so...." She trailed off. She'd been about to say there were limits to what she would ask for, but then realized there weren't.

"Charity?" said Kris. "Charity? What could I ever do for you that would count as charity? How could I ever do so much that it wouldn't be just a fraction of what I owe, if not to you then to your mom?"

"My mom's not here anymore."

Kris leaned forward over her forgotten lasagna. "It's the chance to start over, Beth. Some big ladies are putting together a new coven in Hungary, and they've invited me in. It's a chance to do real good works, all over eastern Europe. It'll blow your mind when I tell you who some of the founders are—true old-school shitkickers. We'll give the dark powers a run for it."

"That sounds like the kind of outfit we always used to dream of," said Beth; a little wistfully, but truly happy for her friend. "But, you know, I'm not exactly unaligned with some dark powers, myself. Could really screw up your cred with the new posse, bringing me around."

"I'll explain to them about your wrong turns."

"You don't know about all of them yet. Anyway, it's moot. I'm no good to your coven. The meth burned me out and dried me up."

"With a good strict cleaning...."

"No. One of the reasons I'm currently fucked is that I borrowed dirty money to go upstate for a cleanse. I keep pretending it just wasn't thorough enough, but who am I kidding? Those bitches had the power. If they couldn't clear me out, it means there's more than just internal scarring. It means the thaumaturgic endocrine sacs have been crisped.

It means the sorcerer's synapses are totally scrambled. Even if there *is* any water left in the well, the dirt has collapsed in on it."

Beth wished for Kris to contradict her and tell her there was still hope. But her friend's face only held itself more still, as if she were concentrating on not betraying her own sudden grief.

Her hand came across the table to grab Beth's. "Even if that's true, it doesn't change anything for me," she said. "I love you, and I owe you. I'm not leaving you like this."

"I keep telling you, you owe me nothing. It was Mom who took you in."

"And you, who made me feel welcome. Who became a sister to me. And who taught me, as well. Your mom was one of the greats, and so are you."

"Was one. Could have been one." She took her hand back, and returned to twisting and scrunching the napkin. She stared at it, as if this were some real task that she actually had to pay attention to. "You know, there is one thing that ... I mean, you don't owe me anything, but if you did want to help me out...."

"I know you're in trouble." Beth could feel how Kris was trying to keep her face blank, to hide her own embarrassment at noticing Beth's humiliation. "Is it that guy Mannis?"

Beth blinked in surprise. How had Kris known? She'd only just gotten to town. "Yeah."

"Don't worry about him. His reach won't extend over the Atlantic."

"I know he's small fry, but I'm not sure I'll ever relax as long as he's around."

Kris nodded her understanding. But she said, "I can't k—." Just then the waitress crept over to gingerly refill their waters. Kris waited till she'd gone, then started over: "I can't kill Mannis for you, Beth," she said. "I swore an Oath of Constraint."

"Ah." Beth smiled bitterly down at her lap.

"It's part of joining the new coven. Just a procedural hoop, but they take it seriously."

A moment passed. Finally Kris said, "If I thought the only way to keep you safe was to break that oath, then I would do it. But I really think we can keep you safe in Hungary."

"Ah, what good could I do you in Hungary?"

"Lots. It would be good for you, too. This could be your crossroads." She started pushing the debris of her lasagna around on her plate, as if that might make her next question seem casual: "So what's supposed to happen if you don't give him the fifteen thousand?"

Beth held onto her beer bottle so tight she had to make herself ease up before she shattered it. She answered, but she was barely audible and Kris had to ask her to repeat herself. She did: "Straw party," she said.

Something happened to Kris's face that scared even Beth. Her voice was lower as she said, "I can't kill him this trip. But I'll come back someday, and do it then."

Beth waited. That was all very fine, but she was hoping for something a bit more immediate.

"And I'll get you that money," Kris added. Now that everything was settled, she began shoving food in her mouth with renewed energy, chewing the pasta like it was Mannis.

Beth hardly dared hope. "You have that much cash on you?"

"No."

"Oh," said Beth, deflated.

"Tomorrow I'll rob a bank," Kris said.

"Oh, no, Kris...."

"Don't worry about it. I can probably disguise myself with a teensy glamour—if it's small enough an energy-output, the oath shouldn't apply."

"I don't think I can let you do that," said Beth, though she knew she *would* let her do it, and for that she loathed herself.

"Fuck it," said Kris. "Why shouldn't I? Do you really believe I'd let you go off to a straw party?" She added, "Anyway, I probably won't even have to use any of my own bio-thaumaturgy for the glamour. I've got my grimoire."

"Oh?"

"Yeah. One I inherited from Old Sullivan. I loaded it with an independent charge before I left, so my Oath of Constraint won't apply. None of my essence'll be involved. Anyone can

52

use it, if they know what they're doing. Even someone with no personal bio-thaumaturgy."

"Oh." It was weird that she'd mentioned the independent charge. Beth waited to see if Kris would say more, but she didn't.

During the silent interval Beth started looking around the restaurant again. Once more she noted the wrinkled noses, the stares that were quickly averted when her eyes crossed theirs. Plus a few starers who didn't bother to avert them. Who didn't think enough of her to avert them.

She looked back down at the dregs of her lasagna. When the pretty waitress had brought it out it had seemed like such a luxury. Now it was just as disgusting as everything else. "I don't want you to rob a bank for me," she said, and this time she meant it. "It's not worth you risking that kind of trouble."

"You're worth it. But okay, if you don't want that, we can try something else."

As far as Beth could see, there wasn't anything else. But whatever. "I went out and ruined myself, with all the drugs. Now I've kicked them, but I don't know why I bother since it's too late to do any good. I should have been more disciplined, I guess, but whatever. How could I have known that when I was a kid? Who was there to teach me, to train me? Was I some sort of soldier? I was just a kid."

Looking up, she saw the reply in Kris's face, even as Kris refused to say it, struggled to not even think it. Bashfully, she dropped her eyes again. "Of course, *you* made it. And we came from the same place, except you had it rougher than me. So I guess the lesson is that I've got no excuses and it's all my fault."

"That's not the lesson I meant for you to get out of this."

"Yeah, well. It's not you talking. It's all of fucking creation."

Another silence. They sat without moving. Finally Kris squirmed in her chair, to break the spell.

"Wanna go get drunk?" she said.

Seven

How many hours later was it that they staggered back to Kris's hotel room? Beth had no idea. Maybe Kris was better at holding her liquor, but then again she'd had more shots. So they were probably even.

It was a fancy hotel room, fancy by Beth's standards anyhow. Kris had ducked into the place while tracking Beth and asked for a room; "A big one," she'd specified, and handed them the card that charged to the coven account.

Now it was the middle of the night and they stumbled and rolled around, hunting for the light switch until they gave up. Beth couldn't tell if they were talking or shouting. When they laughed, she couldn't gauge their volume.

It was a big queen-size bed. Kris tumbled into it and laughed at how obscenely soft and fluffy it was, and invited Beth to feel for herself. But Beth didn't want to get in the bed, because she stank. Kris vehemently denied that Beth smelled bad ... but in any case, she was welcome to use the shower. When had been the last time Beth had had a shower?, she demanded, giddy at being able to offer such a treat.

A shower did sound pretty nice. But Beth still didn't want to sleep in the bed, because all she had to change into after the shower were these same smelly clothes.

So sleep naked, Kris told her, exasperated. Hadn't Beth's mother bathed them together when they were little? Hadn't they skinny-dipped together the whole time they were growing up, off in the woods?

That was all true. But Beth found it surreal to remember that there had been a time when she hadn't been too repulsed by her own body to show it to anyone, anyone at all. The memories were there, but it was like they'd been imported from someone else's brain.

To keep Kris happy, she agreed that sleeping in the buff would be fine, though actually she had no intention of doing so—she would just get dressed again after her shower and sleep on the floor.

But then she collapsed onto the floor and realized that she couldn't make it to the bathroom at all. She started to doze off, but Kris complained again. She said her whole reason for getting the room was so that Beth could have the chance to sleep in a bed again, and if Beth didn't want to sleep in one with anyone else then Kris would be the one to sleep on the floor. All right, all right, Beth said, and struggled upright and fell into the bed. She lay there on top of the sheets, hyper-aware of the reeking grime that coated her like rotting moss. Once Kris's breath deepened and grew regular with sleep, Beth climbed back down onto the floor.

Trying to ignore her nausea, Beth dragged herself to a corner of the room. She curled up in a ball and shut her eyes and pretended the room wasn't spinning. No doubt she'd nod off soon.

Except she didn't. All sorts of memories had been stirred up today, and now they buzzed around like flies in a swamp, with swamp and flies both sealed up inside her skull.

Weirdly, most of the memories weren't about Kris, even though seeing Kris again must have been the main thing that had knocked them loose.

Not that images of Kris weren't in the mix. Like it had been just this morning, she felt herself a child again, her mother crouching down to her level and explaining that a new little girl was coming to live with them, and Beth was to treat her as a sister. Beth hadn't been jealous. She'd been such a lonesome kid, the idea of getting a sister had sounded wonderful to her.

And for a long time she'd stopped being lonesome. There had been the woods to play in, even though the encroaching developers were shrinking them all the time and they really weren't isolated enough for skinny-dipping. Best of all, there had been someone to share the secret of Momma's powers. And someone to join in the lessons Momma gave. They'd each used the other to push off of, a little friendly competition to keep spice in the game, to prompt themselves to new heights.

There were lots of such memories of Kris, memories that should have been happy but had turned bittersweet. But most memories were of her daughter. And none of those were happy.

It seemed like there ought to have been happy ones. But what leaped out from Farrah's infancy was that moment at the hospital, when they'd put the red wet shrieking thing in her arms for the first time. *Why are you giving it to me?!* she'd wanted to cry, but had known she wasn't allowed to. Still, shouldn't they have known better, all those adults? What had she been: a fifteen-year-old with a newly dead mother and a newborn whose father had skipped town. They should have put Beth in foster care and put the baby up for adoption. Instead Beth's paternal aunt had taken her and the baby in. She'd done so only out of a sense of obligation, and she'd made that fact plain enough till Beth had taken the baby and moved out on the eve of her seventeenth birthday, without provoking any complaints.

Now she had trouble remembering why she had even taken the baby with her. Because it had been *hers*, she supposed. One of the few things that were.

It was a wonder Child Services had never taken the kid. Maybe because she'd moved around too much for anyone ever to get a bead on them. Then, when the kid had finally grown up enough to leave, Beth had suddenly missed her. And when Beth had moved to New York she'd actually been looking forward to seeing Farrah again, though she certainly had not been chasing after her the way Farrah accused her of having done.

Bits and pieces of their lives together popped up from the depths of Beth's mind. None were pleasant. But the cat shit was the worst.

That was the last time she'd ever spent the night in the same place as her kid. It had been nearly four years ago, during Farrah's senior year at Hunter College, and right around the time that Beth was tipping over the line into homelessness. It was during one of her big major pushes to quit meth, before it fucked up her magic completely. To escape from Mannis's influence, as well. She was trying to get a job, and she needed an address to write on applications and someplace where she could change clothes and take a shower. Tim and Ann were off on a cruise, so Beth had cajoled Farrah into letting her crash for a few days on her sofa.

It hadn't been easy. For one thing, Farrah's roommates were peeved. For another, Beth was allergic to Farrah's cat. After a raucous sneezing fit, she made the mistake of complaining to Farrah.

"Are you crazy?!" Resentment had been building inside Farrah for days—years—and Beth's comment about the cat made her blow a gasket. "You want to know the difference between you and the cat?! The cat lives here. The cat was invited here."

"Okay, okay," said Beth, with a fake laugh, trying to make light of it, partly because she was too tired and harried to fight and partly because she was afraid her kid would get mad enough to really kick her out. "I'm just allergic, is all. But it's no big deal! Really!"

"I know you're allergic. Do you know what that cat's supposed to be? A Mom repellent."

Beth laughed, high and loud, like that was a good one. "Well, hopefully I'll get that job and then I'll be out of your hair! I've got an interview this afternoon, you know."

Farrah rolled her eyes. "You're *not* going to get that job, Mom. In New York, people like their office workers to still have all their own teeth."

Beth kept a grin locked in place. "No one can tell I've got dentures." Only her back molars had rotted. When Beth had realized what was happening, she'd cast a preservation spell on her front teeth, to protect them from full meth-mouth. Now, here in this hotel room, at the end of this process of personal disintegration, her teeth's recent yellowing and the recent mild but constant hum of incipient toothaches told her that the spell was starting to wear off—she tried not to think about it.

But she'd had a decent enough smile for the interview.

She'd blasted that decent smile at Farrah with defiant cheerfulness. Privately, she told herself that she was absolutely going to get that fucking job.

And as a matter of fact she did great at the interview. Her outfit looked smart, her smile held up to scrutiny, and she gave no hint of desperation, homelessness, or drug addiction. About halfway through, sensing how much the interviewer liked her, she was euphorically telling herself that she might just have to go and thank Farrah for having kicked her ass into high gear. Then the interviewer's pen ran out of ink, and Beth opened her purse to helpfully fish out one of her own.

Her fingers brushed against strange objects. The shadow of a frown passed across her face. Looking in her bag didn't clear up the mystery, not at first. Grainy lumps, most of them hard but some of them a little soft. The granular surface was actually made up of tiny rocks, the grains too big to be sand. Teensy pebbles, blue and gray and white. As she stared into the dimness of her bag it finally came to her: after Beth had complained about her cat allergy, her kid had fished the cat's turds out of its litter box and slipped them into her purse.

"Anything wrong?" the interviewer asked.

It wasn't like he'd seen the cat shit in her bag; it wasn't like she'd taken shit-smeared fingers out of her purse. Theoretically she could have kept her cool and continued the interview like nothing was wrong. But a sudden huge weight of exhaustion descended upon her. Her vision was cloudy, she started stammering. Her purse fell out of her lap, seemingly of its own accord. Some of its contents spilled out onto the floor. The turds didn't, but Beth didn't know that at first, and she lunged to snatch everything up and shove it back in her bag. Her seemingly unmotivated panic was not lost on the interviewer.

When the interview was over she didn't go back to Farrah's. In her purse there were still twenty bucks left over from a big wad Tim had passed her. She wandered, zig-zagging back and forth and up and down Manhattan for hours. Her interview had been down in the Financial District, but after it had been night for a while she looked around and found herself on the edge of Harlem. She was still wearing the classy business get-up, but fuck it—she lay down right on the sidewalk to sleep, curling up against a brick wall. For her pillow she used her purse. New York was safer than in the movies, so maybe it would still be there when she woke up.

Someone took it, though. At some point in the night she woke up to the sensation of it being yanked out from under her and her head hitting the concrete. Fuck it. She went back to sleep.

The weirdest thing was, the next day and every once in a while after that, she missed having the purse simply because she had the urge to open it and look at the cat turds. Like she wanted to make sure they were really there, that the whole thing had really happened. More than the twenty bucks, or any of the other junk in the purse, what she really missed were the turds.

She just stayed out on the street. Begging got easier as her outfit decayed to match her status. Soon she was craving a high. She couldn't afford one, but she went back to doing little odd jobs for Mannis. Beat sucking dick. It was months before she saw Tim again, longer till she saw Farrah.

Now, lying in the dark, she told herself that it would be ridiculous to blame everything since then on her daughter. Beth had simply continued down a path she'd already been traveling. Even whether Farrah had given her a shove was debatable. Probably she would have wound up the same way—possibly with more delay, was all.

Still, it had been a shitty thing to do, slipping those cat turds into her purse just before the big interview.

Beth sat up and looked at the dark clump of shadow that was her friend. Kris really would rob a bank for her, even if it risked her place in the new coven, even if it risked her reputation and career. Beth knew she didn't have enough pride to refuse Kris's help, but it hurt anyway. It didn't exactly boost her sense of self-worth, knowing that the mere fact of having gotten back in contact with her was going to wreck the life of the one remaining person who wanted her around.

More memories floated through her mind. All those lessons from her mother, that Kris had shared. All that friendly competition—sometimes fierce, but always loving. That was a feeling she had difficulty even recalling.

Back in those days she never would have asked Kris for help, not first thing. That would have been like throwing the race. But back then she had her own powers.

Beth eyed Kris's rucksack, where she'd tossed it to the floor. Her eyes flicked to Kris again, then back to the rucksack. Trying not to breathe, she crept toward it.

Keeping her breath almost silent was one thing, but there was no way to open the rucksack and go through it without making some noise. At the first rustlings she froze and checked again on Kris, but her friend still didn't move. She must have been really drunk. A thin rhythmic snoring was leaking out of her. Beth went back to digging through the bag, now trying harder to be fast than to be quiet.

The thing she sought wasn't hard to find: packed in near the top, a blue, battered, college-ruled wire notebook. Beth flipped through it and confirmed that it wasn't merely a journal or anything like that, but Kris's grimoire. The writing might have been done in ordinary ballpoint ink, but there was nothing ordinary about what filled the pages: diagrams, runes, cuneiform, spells in Latin, Greek, medieval French, Assyrian, sorcerors' tongues.

And like Kris had said: it bore its own charge. Beth could feel it pulsing, could almost hear its whispers at the frontiers of her imagination. She didn't need her own bio-thaumaturgical wells for that; only enough experience and training to know how to listen. And how to talk back.

One last time she looked up at Kris's sleeping form, with the crazy impulse to wake her and apologize for stealing her book.... *Not stealing,* she corrected herself, *borrowing. Borrowing it so she doesn't have to do anything that would get her in trouble.*

Even as she formed the thought, she knew it was only half the truth. The other half was that it would feel good to handle this herself. It would feel fucking great. Before she slipped out of the hotel room, she thought, *Thank you,* in Kris's direction.

After Beth had left, Kris's snoring ceased. She rolled over and looked at the door.

"You're welcome," she said.

Eight

Farrah started to drift up into wakefulness—but then that felt so awful, she tried to will herself to sink back down into the dark. She didn't even have the strength to whimper. She started to root herself down deeper into her bed, but whatever she was lying on had no give to it. Must have passed out on the floor.

She remembered when she'd started drinking—after Eli had left, she'd gone to the fridge and cracked open one of her beers, one of the few he'd left. After her mom had barged in and woken him up from his nap, Farrah had spent a few minutes trying to keep him engaged before finally realizing that, actually, she didn't want him around. From there it took nearly another hour of sullenly ignoring him before he left—what finally did the trick was when he'd opened the fridge again and she'd sharply asked him to please leave her the rest of her beers.

I guess the pussy wasn't worth it without the beer thrown in, she thought. Hangovers always made her feel a little like dying.

This one was particularly fierce. And that wasn't even the floor underneath her, she realized; it was a hard, granulated surface. Concrete. And there was something like a breeze, and what felt like sunlight leaning hard against her eyelids. The noise of the city was crowding her. Had she gotten trashed and then headed upstairs to pass out on the roof? Lucky she hadn't fallen off.

As she started trying to piece together last night, she realized she must have gone on a bender extreme enough to make her black out. Her last memory was of drinking the second of her two beers in front of the TV. It was almost like she'd fallen asleep then and sleep-walked to wherever she was now, except that somewhere in the middle she'd done something to earn this monster hangover.

She accepted that she wasn't going back to sleep. Painful as it was, it was time to open her eyes and get off this roof. And drag herself to her shit job.

Except she wasn't on the roof. She couldn't tell through her smeary vision where she was, but it definitely was not her roof. Blurred cars were passing by a few yards away, as well as foot traffic. Overhead, the bored roar of traffic—looking up she saw that she was near an overpass. It was not merely her hangover sickness that made the city noises louder—they were louder because she was right in the middle of them. She'd gotten so wasted she'd wandered away from her apartment and passed out in the street.

Now Farrah was scared. On top of everything, her body didn't seem to be working right—she sat up, leaning on her left arm, then fell over when she tried to raise the arm to rub her face and eyes, as if her torso couldn't support itself anymore.

She started trembling. All this from alcohol? Had she gotten drunk and wandered off and tried some sort of new drug? That was the kind of thing she was secretly scared of, that she would wake up one morning and discover she'd turned into a druggie like her mom.

Her blurry, shaky eyes crept back to the passersby. Dreading the embarrassment that would come when one of them realized she was in distress, she tried to pull herself together before anyone approached. She didn't manage to pull herself together, but the point was moot because no one was rushing over to help.

She tried to laugh at herself ruefully and say something like, *That's New York,* but she was too freaked out.

No matter how hard she blinked, squeezing her lids shut and popping them open, her eyesight stayed smeared and blurry. Shutting her eyes and rubbing them didn't help much. And the feel of her hand against her face was strange, sort of but not quite like the disconnected numbness of when a limb fell asleep. Her whole body *felt weird.* It wasn't merely the headachy nausea of the hangover; it wasn't simply the aches and pains riddling her body, the weary throbbing in her mouth. Her whole body felt *off*.

She hugged herself, ran her hands down her torso, but before they reached her waist she froze in chilled horror. Her whole body was swollen; her boobs were fleshier, and her middle was far thicker than ever before. And the flesh had a spongy, repellent give to it.

She was really sick. Something dramatic and strange. She looked fearfully at the strangers ignoring her as they hurried past—she wanted help, but she was also ashamed of whatever was wrong with her and wanted not to be seen.

Running her hands over her body had led her to notice her clothes, and she frowned down at them. They were nasty—a filthy, holey green sweatshirt coming undone at the seams, stained and ancient shapeless blue jeans stiff in patches with the residue of mysterious substances. Inside her sneakers her hot feet itched, and she had a feeling she'd been wearing these shoes and socks a long time. But that was impossible, because she'd never seen them before in her life.

Although the more she stared down at herself, the more the clothes seemed familiar. Like she *had* seen them before.

There was something wrong with her hands. They were bony, they had cuts. Her manicure was gone, her nails were broken and there was dirt down at the quicks. Had she sleep-walked and tried to dig something up with her hands? Dug hard enough to scrape all the polish off her fingers? Her hands were the last straw, they trumped whatever embarrassment she felt at stopping someone for help. She managed to stand up and then nearly toppled over, partly because she was still dizzy with her hangover, but there was more to it than that—her balance was fundamentally off, and she couldn't just automatically *move* anymore without thinking about it. Brain damage, she figured. A stroke?

There was a pretty redhead running up the sidewalk, heading Farrah's way. In fact, she was running to Farrah, specifically; the redhead was staring at her, her mouth wide like she was going to call out, but instead her jaw just hung open.

As the girl drew closer, Farrah realized that she looked very familiar. When she recognized her, her own mouth fell open and she dropped painfully to her knees, too shocked to scream. Yet.

Somehow she didn't plummet all the way onto her side, somehow she was still up on her knees when the girl reached her—*when she herself reached herself*—and gripped her by the shoulders, saying, "Don't worry, sweetie, I didn't even really mean to do it, I just was drunk, I'll change it back just as soon as I handle some things...."

Farrah recoiled. The face was her own, but alien in this context; the voice was not the one she heard when she talked, but she recognized it from recordings. Something was in her stomach, she realized, right before she lurched over and vomited up a fizzing red mess. When had she eaten anything like that? Her messy rotten tongue was coated in an acidic red winey taste. *This was not her body.*

Her double managed to hop out of the vomit's way, talking all the while: "I'll give it back, I swear. Just give me a day— or two. But Farrah, listen, in the meantime you'll have to be careful." The familiar stranger took her by the shoulders and shook her, to make sure she was paying attention. "You've got to find Kris. Okay? Find my friend Kris. In my ... in *your* pocket there's a brochure for the hotel she's staying at. And she told me she gave your Uncle Tim her card."

Farrah was crying. It came out as a wheeze that fell oddly on her ears. Tears and snot ran down her face. Although it wasn't like she'd never cried before, there was something weird about the sensation now: the tears flowed in a subtly different pattern down her cheeks, they were at a subtly different temperature; something like that, some variation impossible to pinpoint.

"Don't cry," her double was saying, in distress herself. Awkwardly she patted Farrah's back. "It'll all be over soon. But, listen, you have to go to Kris, because some bad people are going to be looking for you. Until I can handle them."

Farrah couldn't answer. Mild convulsions shook her. She rolled her head away from her double.

Her double sounded more and more urgent. "Farrah, do you understand me? About how you should find my friend Kris and get her to help you?"

The double stepped around Farrah. Farrah cringed, before realizing that the double was going for a battered notebook lying nearby on the concrete. Farrah hadn't noticed it. As the double picked it up, she said, "Remember. My friend Kris. Either find her at the hotel, or else contact her through your Uncle Tim."

The double stepped in close. Farrah's breath hitched and she recoiled. The double moved slowly, trying not to spook her. Trying to calm Farrah with her eyes, the double placed her fingers on her cheek as carefully as if Farrah had been a shying horse. "I'm so sorry, sweetie. But it's only for a little while."

One final cold shock drenched Farrah. *"Mom?!"*

A proud grin blossomed and broke through the worry on the double's face. "You always were so smart," she said.

This was her fucking mother, Farrah realized. All those buried or foresworn childhood memories came back, of floating toys and other magic tricks around the house, of the lessons she'd rebelled against until her mother had given up on them. If all that were true, then this would start to make sense.

Her mom was spouting some sort of soothing babble. Farrah shut it out, determined not to be fooled, trying to figure out for herself what was happening. She looked down at her strange self again, at the dirty tattered sweatshirt.

Later she would decide that her mom had been wrong— she wasn't very smart. Because it was only at this moment that she understood whose body she must be in, if her mom had stolen hers.

With a wordless croak she lunged at her mother, bringing her filthy nails up to scrape her face. Her mom jumped easily out of the way, though at least she lost that stupid smile; she seemed to have more control over the body she'd stolen than Farrah did over her new one.

Farrah looked at the battered old notebook her mother was clutching to her chest. All the mother-daughter stuff about how she should take care of herself and contact what's-her-face was bullshit; she'd come back for that notebook. It looked like garbage, but it meant something to Mom.

Farrah grabbed at it. Her mom twisted out of range before Farrah could do more than slide her fingers against the cover. It felt good to see the fear spread through her mother's face.

"Don't touch that," her mom said. "I need it."

Farrah threw herself at her mother, clawing and grabbing. Between the sickness and the disorientation, she was clumsy enough that her mom easily sidestepped her, but she did finally attract the attention of some of those passersby. "Miss, are you okay?" she heard a guy saying. She was about to reply that no, she wasn't, when she realized he was talking to her mom.

She blinked as hard as she could, several times in succession. Her vision remained blurrier than she was used to, but she could see that people were stopping to watch the commotion and a few were stepping closer, closing in on her in a ring. Three already had their smartphones out and were videoing her. They were on her mom's side, she realized.

"Be cool," urged her mom. She had the gall to sound like she was losing patience. "It's just for a couple days. I give you my word."

Farrah hollered and lunged again, but her mounting rage left her even clumsier than before. Hands were grabbing her, holding her back.

"Stop her!" shrieked Farrah. "Thief!"

Nobody believed her. Nobody even paid attention. Her mother scowled as if she were the one being betrayed, then turned and ran. Strangers held Farrah back, as her mother got away.

Nine

Beth hesitated. But in the end she went ahead and used her daughter's credit card.

She had no choice—for her plan to work, she needed new, sexy clothes, some makeup, some perfume. (She hadn't thought to grab any of that stuff from Farrah's, when she'd come out of the trance to find herself on her daughter's couch in her daughter's body, suddenly no longer drunk—too many things had been spinning through her mind.) And she also needed a place to prepare, so once she left the Abercrombie and Fitch store in midtown she stopped at the first hotel she came upon and got a room. It was staggeringly expensive. She blanched as she handed the card over to the desk clerk. It seemed unimaginable that her little girl could possibly have a credit limit high enough to pay so much. Yet the card went through, and the clerk handed Beth a magnetic key card. She wondered suspiciously why the guy was being so nice, before she realized that it was because she had her daughter's unspoiled face, and was wearing her daughter's clean clothes. (True, they had been slept in, but by Beth's standards they were pristine.)

She took a long, delicious shower. This was the first chance she'd gotten to really spend time with this body. It was beautiful. Beth spent an hour under the shower-spray, looking at the body, washing it, feeling its clean nerves transmitting to her mind the feel of the water. The pleasure was almost frightening.

After the shower she went to the window instead of getting dressed right away. The window ran from the floor all the way up to the ceiling. Beth put her palms on the pane and leaned her new naked body slowly forward, looking down. The vertiginous view made her tremble. It was two blocks to the next building that was as tall as this one. Someone could probably see her from there. But not only did she not care, she realized that she wanted them to see her.

For the first time in ages she wasn't in pain, her back didn't ache, her hips, neck, knees; her head was clearer, even. The synapses were crisper. Still had that new-brain smell.

That shower lingered in her mind. To feel the water trickling down this pure unruined flesh: she hadn't known pleasure like that existed. Beth knew that it had been wrong to forcefully switch bodies with her daughter, that it really had been a monstrous crime. But it wouldn't be exactly true to say she was sorry.

Better to say she regretted the necessity of fucking over her daughter. Only briefly—she'd give the body back, just as soon as she'd fixed Mannis. Nobody could blame her for fighting to keep herself alive. Meanwhile, what would it hurt for her to enjoy these brief fringe benefits? What good would it do anyone for her to mope, to berate herself, to wallow in guilt?

And besides, she told herself as her lip curled, the whole thing might do Farrah some good. Maybe in the long run she'd be lucky someone had brought her down a peg. A little tough love. It wouldn't hurt her to learn how lucky she was, to find out how people treated you when you were a stinking homeless lady missing a few teeth. Why should Farrah be the only one to ever get to use this beautiful body that, after all, Beth had given her? Why should she be the one with this amazing credit card and miraculous access to this palatial hotel room, with its shower and its view?

All this time her kid had had the power to grant Beth a shower and a room like this, and some decent clothes. And had she ever been moved to do so? No. And yet didn't a mother have the right to some occasional kindness from her own daughter? Well, sometimes, when nobody stepped up and offered you the things you had a right to, you had to take them.

Still, what she had done was horrible. As soon as she was safe again, she would reverse it. And try to make it up to Farrah.

70

The grimoire was on the bed, a deep battered blue against the pale blue of the crisp sheets. Bringing it around Mannis would be a risk. But even if she hadn't needed it for her plan, and even if there had been a safe hiding place, she craved having it with her too much to leave it behind. Power resided in it, power she knew how to use.

Before getting dressed, she sat on the bed and cast a linking spell on the grimoire. (It was delicious to be able to sit up straight on the bed without worrying about a back that wanted to stoop.) It was a complicated spell, but anyone who knew the words could do it, if they had the training and the skill. She used the grimoire's own charge to cast the spell; the charge contained in the grimoire removed the need for one's own bio-thaumaturgical wells.

Now, if Mannis took it by force, the spell would befoul the grimoire. All its lore, wisdom, and secrets would be scrambled, rendered unreadable. Beth wondered how that would manifest; would the lines of text, handwritten in ballpoint pen, twist around each other, characters swapping places, chunks of text dispersing themselves randomly throughout the pages? She couldn't quite picture it. But the point was the grimoire would be transformed into useless trash. Of course, this wasn't an especially spectacular grimoire, particularly now that she had nearly depleted the extra power Kris had endowed it with—just enough remained to kill Mannis, and even for that she'd have to be careful. But every grimoire, no matter how modest, had its own special wisdom, its own character, its own irreducible, singular quality. Although not exactly alive, they were like people that way.

Having the grimoire's power bound to her almost made her feel like she had her own power back, almost made her feel human.

She left the window and went to lie on the bed, on top of the covers and still nude. It had occurred to her that Farrah might trace her credit card purchase online, and thereby find her here at the hotel. But she had a hunch Farrah would be too hung over and freaked out to think of that. Anyway, she'd just have to take the risk. She needed a quiet, private place, till the time came to go see Mannis.

So she drove those worries from her mind as she lay on the bed, and went into a trance.

If her crazy plan was going to work (it really *would* have been smarter to strike down Mannis from a distance with the grimoire's full, pre-switch charge, but she'd been too drunk to think of that), then she would have to rehearse it mentally. Walk through the spell step by scrupulous step, in order to make sure she didn't waste a drop of the grimoire's remaining charge.

Meanwhile, she was becoming more and more aware of this body. And not merely of its physical qualities.

Farrah had never abused her body with any chemicals harder than marijuana, tobacco, and alcohol, and there was still untapped bio-thaumaturgy within her, channels which had yet to be formed but which, once they were there, would be clean and smooth. It would be impossible to explain just how Beth sensed this—it was not sensory data that could be translated into the terms of any other senses, and if she tried to look at it directly it slipped away. With time, if she hadn't been determined to return this body, she *could* have looked at it steadily. She could discipline this body to be as powerful as she herself had once been, if only she didn't have to give it back. She'd always been convinced that Farrah must have inherited her gifts. Well, she was vindicated now—Farrah had a huge source of power here, and she was squandering it.

She stopped thinking about it for now. It wouldn't do her any good tonight; it wasn't like she'd manage to open the channels in time for that bio-thaumaturgy to do her any good against Mannis. Even if it had been possible, she couldn't have done that—if Farrah got put back into a body with open channels, without being trained in how to use them, then she'd be really fucked.

For hours she rehearsed the spell, until five o'clock.

Time to go; for that she had to dress. Spaghetti-strap blue top, flattering tan slacks, nice-looking flats. Sad as she was to hide this beautiful body from herself, she was compensated by the excitement of taking it back out into the world, and by the terrifying thrill of what she was going to do.

An hour later she was a few blocks southeast of Port Authority, near the fabric store on Thirty-Seventh Street. The store was only a few minutes' walk from the hotel, but she spent a long time wandering around in circles, working up her nerve.

It was a couple hours before she was supposed to give herself up to the straw party.

Alone in that hotel room, the fact that she was wearing this hot young body had given her a high. Once she was back out in the streets, though, she discovered that she hadn't quite processed her new situation. Oddities leaped out at her from her own most intimate corporeal self, little micro-adjustments or clumsinesses. People were looking at her more than she was used to, sometimes even turning their heads as she passed by to let their stares linger. Beth tried to tell herself she was being paranoid, but she couldn't shake the idea that they all knew she didn't belong in this body. She must be doing something wrong, some sort of clumsy graceless thing that the person naturally born into this flesh would never be guilty of. After she finally worked up the courage to be near the fabric store, she leaned against a wall half a block down and across the street from it, with her hands in her pockets and her gaze down, trying to make herself quiet and small.

Dolan came out of the store. Beth's breath hitched and then quickened as she tried to burrow her head further down her neck, while twisting her eyes under her brows to track him as he passed. From this distance he was small, yet he towered over her in her mind.

Through the brick wall she leaned against she could feel his foot pinning her between the shoulder blades—she could feel the ghosts of all sorts of petty torments, and remembered promises he'd given of more to come. Dolan was smart, and he knew about magic. Surely he would be able to look at her and

73

see there was something off about her, be able to recognize the same old pathetic hag within.

Her palms were sweating bad enough that she could feel the moisture through the lining of her pockets and against the skin of her thighs. Without letting herself think about it any more, she pushed off from the wall and walked after him. It was a cloudless day and the sunshine shot down strong and clear onto the street. Despite her terror, Beth's head was coaxed back upright by the colors of the day and its crisp details: she hadn't seen this clearly since the last time she'd owned a pair of eyeglasses. The beauty comforted her and lent her strength. It was best to set aside a part of herself that wouldn't get too overwhelmed by terror to appreciate things. After all, she wouldn't have such sights very much longer, whether it was because Dolan killed her or because she gave back the body.

She reminded herself that she was obligated not to get killed, since otherwise her daughter would be cheated out of a body.

When they turned onto Eighth Avenue, it was more crowded, but Dolan still stood out. At first Beth thought that was because he was taller than the bland pedestrians around him, but then she realized that there were others who were as tall, there were others of the same skin tone. There were others who were dressed hip-hop style (although it seemed to her that Dolan wore an old-fashioned version of it: a light-green tracksuit, instead of, say, baggy low-hanging jeans and a jersey). He just popped more vibrantly to her eyes. She wound her way through the crowd, keeping an eye on him. She was sure he would turn and glare at her, or double back and taunt and hurt her. He simply had to have seen and recognized her.

But he showed no sign of that. Beth reminded herself that her fears were all in her head. *She* knew she was still the same old piece of shit, but to the outside world she had a whole new face.

Dolan stepped into a dollar-pizza place, a crowded open-air nook with some aluminum stand-up tables out front. Beth lingered a block away. Mannis must give Dolan good money, it was funny that he still ate dollar pizza.

When Dolan stepped out to lean on a stand-up table and chomp down his pizza, Beth sidled over to him.

Now he noticed her, and from afar. As she closed the distance he kept his eyes on her, aggressively appraising her body, suspicious. He was no dummy. He wolfed the pizza down fast, and by the time she reached him he was wiping the last of the grease from his mouth and giving her a mocking, challenging, curious look.

Beth smiled at him. "Hey," she said, trying to make it sort of a saucy smile.

Dolan's eyes cooled. His face became a smooth mask. "Yeah?"

Beth had the strange urge to apologize, but she set it aside so forcefully that she was no longer even aware of it herself. "What's the matter?" she demanded. "You don't want to talk to me?"

"Why would I want to talk to you?"

"You don't like pretty girls?"

"I can get plenty of bitches on my own."

"Sure. But everybody's different, right? We're all special snowflakes. Right?"

"You're the snowflake, honky."

"For example, *you're* different from other guys." She was only playing a role, Beth told herself. No one would see through her if she could balls her way through. "Tall. Dark. Handsome. Works for Mannis."

Was that a flicker of interest? Or alarm? Or only her imagination? "Who's Mannis?"

"The guy I want to see."

"Well, then, you must've got it twisted, because you're talking to me and I don't know no Mannis and don't know where he is."

"Oh, my mistake, then. I guess in that case you won't have to worry about what he'll do when he finds out you fucked up his chance to get this thing he would want."

"What thing?"

"This valuable magic thing I have."

"'Magic'? What are you, a little kid or something?"

"Bye," she said, and turned her back on him and started to walk away.

He called after her: "Hey, white girl!" She stopped and turned back around. He beckoned her with his fingers; she came, but only halfway.

Dolan wiped his mouth again, even though there wasn't any more grease on it. "What you got?" he said.

Beth patted her bag. "A grimoire," she said.

Dolan glanced around, checking the other diners standing around their own pizzas. Some were listening to their iPods; there were two twenty-somethings going over the lines of a script; one Latino guy who just chewed pizza and stared into space, close enough to hear Beth and Dolan but apparently not listening.

Dolan turned back to Beth. "Obviously you're crazy. First, because there ain't no such thing as magic, so there's no such thing as grimoires. Second, if there were such things, what's to stop me from just taking it off you?"

"A linking spell. I guess you could probably take the grimoire away from me, before I managed to turn you into a toad. But without me there, it's just a wirebound notebook."

"Guy like Mannis might know some people who could break that spell. Assuming there is such a guy as Mannis, which, far as I know, there isn't."

"He probably does know guys like that. But their services are awful expensive. Probably be a lot less trouble and money to buy it off me, and hire me to unlink it myself."

"I guess. Except what would a nice little normal white girl like you be doing, running around selling grimoires and casting spells? And how would you have heard of Mannis? Aside from him being your imaginary friend, I mean."

"We have a mutual acquaintance. You know her too, in fact. Beth."

Beth had expected Dolan's face to explode in immediate recognition. God knew that Dolan and Mannis loomed so large in her own mind that no one could utter their names without

76

it hitting her like a physical blow. But Dolan only stared at her a long moment, totally blank. Then he began to blink his way through the mist. "That drugged-out bitch?"

Beth laughed.

"How you know *her*?" he demanded scornfully.

"She's my mom."

The disbelief with which he looked at her was both frightening and exhilarating. How far had she come from her old self? How far could she go?

"Seriously?!" he said, and when she smiled and nodded he threw back his head and laughed. Again he gave her that appraising look, this time with a grin. "Man, the apple sure fell a long way from the tree of that dried-up crazy cow, didn't it?"

Beth laughed again too. "I'll take that as a compliment."

"Actually, you know, I can kind of see it," he teased. "You kind of look alike. No offense."

"Yeah, I'm what she would have looked like if she hadn't been a drugged-out slut who got knocked up and then spent the next twenty-odd years morphing into a crazy bag lady."

Again Dolan laughed. Beth grinned along with him. She was doing a good job of being Farrah, she felt like.

His laughter faded into a chuckle; his eyes were still appraising her, but at least he was enjoying himself now. Of course, Beth knew from experience that didn't necessarily make her any safer.

He said, "Okay. So why are you talking to me about it?"

"Duh. You're my date tonight. How else am I going to get into the party and meet Mannis?"

"What party tonight?"

"The party you're my date to."

"How come you have to talk to him at some party?"

"Because I'm a party girl."

"Listen to how you talk. What do you think you are, in some movie?" He was studying her, like he was growing more and more interested, albeit still not particularly concerned. Like he thought she'd prove pretty pliable. "Either way, I can't just trot you over to Mannis without giving him some heads-up first."

"Oh, sure, call him. Call him and tell him that Beth's kid is here and she's got the grimoire of one of Old Sullivan's apprentices." *And I hope he shits himself when he realizes that his old chew-toy Beth knows people who know people like Old Sullivan.*

Dolan shrugged. "Yeah, all right, maybe I'll tell him." He took his phone out of his pocket and made as if he were going to walk away, to go make the call out of earshot.

"Wait!" said Beth.

He stopped and looked at her.

"Buy me a slice first," she said.

"Why would I buy you a slice?" he demanded, but his tone was playful.

"Because you like me."

He smirked. "The fuck makes you think I like you?"

"Fine. Because you think I'm fun, then."

His smile came back. It was a very cold one now; one of the fun things he liked to do was hurt people. But she could tell that he thought she was pretty, and after having hated herself so long, that was almost enough.

"Buy you a slice, huh," he said. "You think you worth a dollar?"

"You tell me."

He nodded. "Yeah, all right."

Ten

Farrah watched her mother get away in her body while a couple of guys held her back. Cops showed up. Someone slipped in her vomit and fell with a curse—it felt like a big churning melée with her at its center. She tried to keep shouting at them to go after her mother who was stealing her body, but what with her rage, panic, sickness, and disorientation all that came out was a ragged gargly spittle-dripping roar.

She was berserk, so the cops forced her down onto her knees and then her belly and cuffed her hands behind her. Her chest was on top of the warm vomit, she could feel it soaking through the soiled sweatshirt and moistening her strange, swollen, floppy breasts.

The cops were telling her to calm down. And she must have calmed at least a little because she was able to form words again, shouting, "Uncle Tits! Uncle Tits, and Aunt Ass!"

That didn't garner her much more credibility than the inarticulate, formless screaming had done. She remembered that those were just their joke names, and really they were Uncle Tim and Aunt Ann; and soon after that she was able to give the cops their full names.

Ann left work and drove Tim to the police station to fetch her—Tim hadn't driven for years, but Ann was from the Midwest and couldn't imagine life without a car. The police released Farrah to them. Farrah had wised up enough to quit insisting to the cops that her mom had stolen her body and she was really Beth's daughter, Farrah. She'd noticed that the claim did not make the police more inclined to release her.

Once they were in the car, however, she leaned forward from the backseat and said, "Uncle Tim, you have to listen and not freak out. It's me, Farrah."

"What?" said Tim. "What do you mean, Beth?"

"I'm not Beth. I'm Farrah. My mom switched bodies with me. She stole *my* body and left me in this one."

She saw Ann give Tim a cautious, worried look—less worried about her, than about Tim, and how her madness would affect him.

Indeed, when Tim spoke again, she could hear his heavy sadness: "Okay, Beth. Why don't we wait and talk about all that at the apartment, after we get you cleaned up."

Farrah had almost gotten used to her new smell, but it came crowding back up her nose now. There was still beer-and-wine-and-liquor vomit caked to her green sweatshirt. Ann and Tim both had their windows down.

"I'm not supposed to smell this way," she complained. "This is *Mom's* smell." Again, Aunt Ann snuck a surreptitious look over at Uncle Tim, who only looked down at his lap.

It sounds like I'm crazy, Farrah realized.

All the way back to their apartment Farrah tried in fits and starts to explain what had happened to her, always giving up and falling back into silence; all the way back Tim and Ann withheld any comment. Inside the apartment, Ann said, "Beth, maybe you could—"

"Stop calling me Beth!"

"Okay, *Farrah.*" One could hear the frayed quality of Ann's nerves. "Maybe you could hop in the shower. We don't have any clothes here in your size, but I'll run out and get some sweats and T-shirts and meanwhile you can wrap yourself in a towel."

"No." Farrah shook her head stubbornly. Taking a shower would mean having to actually look at this fat ugly blobby body, having to run her hands over it.

Apparently her aunt and uncle had a lot invested in this shower, though. "Beth, please..." her uncle started to mournfully say. Aunt Ann cut him off: "Beth, or Farrah, or whatever you want me to call you, I'm trying to be nice but you *smell* bad. Those clothes already stank when you were here yesterday and now they're soaked in booze and vomit! I'm sorry, but you can't ask me to just let you contaminate my apartment. You're welcome to stay, but only if you let me burn those clothes."

This sounded non-negotiable. "I wasn't here yesterday," Farrah muttered, as she made her way to the bathroom. She averted her eyes from the mirror; cuts and bruises marked and mottled her face. When her mom had come knocking the day before, Farrah had refused to give her the satisfaction of noticing them. Now she was stuck with them, herself.

Once she was in the shower with the curtain drawn and the water on, she heard the door open. With a whimper she raised her arms to cover herself. "I'm just getting your clothes," Aunt Ann called. It took a while, probably because she was handling them gingerly—Farrah heard the rustling of a plastic garbage bag. Soon the door shut and she was once again alone.

The shower was strange. In a way she supposed it did feel good, but she had a hard time accepting how good it felt. Never had she been so aware of the qualitative mutability of sensation. One could grant this body the most intense physical pleasure conceivable; she would still experience that pleasure as a violation, something forced upon her, a fleshly affront to her spirit.

Dutifully she lathered and rinsed, lathered and rinsed. Washed her hair. Forced herself to look at the invader body, to make sure there were no missed spots. Why the fuck should *she* be the one who had to clean this fucking hulk of meat? It was her mom's responsibility—her mom was the one who'd let herself go.... Also, it *was* her mom, and she didn't want to touch her fucking mother.

She turned off the water and started drying herself with the fluffy pink towel Ann had left her, big enough to wrap herself in. Every glance at this body body inspired hatred. Hard to believe how ashamed she'd always been of her old one; she longed now to have it back.

Standing on the bathmat with the towel wrapped around the body to protect herself from the sight of it, the texture of the bathmat obscured behind the unfamiliar callouses and fungal itchings of the body's feet, she felt a sort of dark, bubbling pressure needling low in her innards, and wondered with meek fear what new bad thing was about to happen. As it dawned on her what the feeling signified, she felt a new breed of horror.

No, she thought, *no, I won't.* She started to weep again, biting her arm so as to do it quietly and keep Tim from hearing her shame. *Fuck her, she can take this stinking thing back and do that herself.*

But it was no use. Suddenly she had to drop her towel right away, and plant herself onto the toilet just in time for the angry burning blast to come shooting out of her. It hurt, and stank like ammonia, death, wine, and whisky.

Farrah's weeping must have been audible, because now Tim was on the other side of the door: "Beth, are you all right?"

"Go away, please!" she yelled, too desperate to get rid of him to bother telling him not to call her Beth. She heard him slowly move away.

How he could bear to be anywhere near this bathroom, she couldn't comprehend. They say your own shit doesn't stink—but this shit did not belong to Farrah, and even holding her nose she could feel the sickness of it coating her mouth as she breathed. That was not meant to be her violated asshole down there, it had been palmed off on her.

With her fist she wiped tears and snot off her face, and gritted her teeth. *I'll kill her for this. I'll stick her back in this filthy fat body, and then I'll kill her.*

After taking the shit, she showered again, forcing herself to stay closed up in the bathroom with that catastrophic stench. During this second shower, she thought about that woman her mom had told her to contact, and she decided not to do it. All she knew about the person was that apparently she was in cahoots with Beth, and that made her someone to avoid.

She'd hoped that by the time she finished showering again Ann would have returned, and slipped some clothes into the bathroom—preferably baggy shapeless sweatclothes. It was still only the towel, though. Just as well—Ann might not have been able to stand the smell. It might have given her unborn baby a birth defect.

Farrah emerged from the bathroom, feeling stupid in that pink towel. Against her moist skin the air was fresh and cool—for a millisecond she was almost taken in by its pleasantness, then remembered the feeling was coming to her through foreign nerves and immediately experienced it as stinging needles of air drilling into her pores. Although Farrah shied away from her uncle's eyes, her state of undress seemed the least of his worries—as far as he was concerned, it was his sister he was looking at, not his young niece. Besides, he'd probably seen Beth in all sorts of undignified situations.

"I've called your friend Kris," he announced. "She's in a cab on her way here."

Deciding not to call that woman had been the one small act of resistance Farrah had been sure she could manage. *"Why?"* she moaned. "And stop talking to me like I'm my mom! That woman's not *my* friend!"

"All right, then, your *mother's* friend, Farrah! As for why, well, I don't know, I guess I was hoping she could maybe shed some light on things. I mean, don't you think it's a crazy coincidence that this happens to you right when this Kris person comes to town?"

"Yeah," said Farrah, staring off darkly. "I do."

Tim kept giving her that worried look. "Beth, why are you talking funny? Are you having trouble pronouncing your words?"

Yes. She was. Because she could not bring herself to fully use her tongue. She could not bear the thought of letting it fill her mouth; without thinking, she kept trying to scrunch it up in on itself, so that its edges would not continuously brush against those shocking wet soft gaps in the back sides of her mouth, where molars should have been.

"My teeth hurt," she muttered, ashamed. It was true, they did hurt. Till now, her mouth pain had been subsumed into the morass of her hangover, her body's aches, her nausea, her weary itchy feet. The mouth pain wasn't just shadow pain in the holes where teeth ought to be—there was a light constant throb in her upper left bicuspid, mostly dull but with a sharp lace. Was it going to suddenly disintegrate at some point?

"I see you're not wearing your dentures." Farrah could hear in Tim's voice how he was trying to be gentle. "Do you know where your dentures are?"

Farrah shook her shaggy head. "No," she said, as humiliated as if it really had been her who'd lost them.

"You and Kris didn't take some new drugs, did you, Beth? Did she maybe turn you on to something new, something you hadn't tried before?"

Farrah began to sob. She waved Tim away when he came to hug her. "Uncle Tim," she managed to say through the tears, "I swear, if you do not stop talking to me like I'm my mom...."

"Okay, okay. Farrah. I'll try to remember." He sounded tired.

Farrah was still sniffing and wiping at tears with the back of her wrist when they heard footsteps on the hall stairs. "That's probably Ann," said Uncle Tim, relieved that he would have someone else around to help handle her.

"Doesn't it sound like more than one person?" said Farrah.

Indeed, when Ann opened the door a brunette woman stepped in with her. Must be Kris. The taxi had dropped her off in front of the building just as Ann was returning with bags of clothes—cheap workout clothes, but she'd bought a lot, as if she didn't expect this to be the last time they would have to dress Tim's sister.

When Kris looked into Farrah's face, at first it was with an automatic happiness, as if this were a face she was always happy to see; then there was a hitch in the flow of her expression. She blinked twice, taking it in.

"Wow," she said, appreciatively.

Farrah glared at her. "You're one of them, aren't you? You're like my mom. One of those witches."

"Never as good a one."

"One of those *bitches*, more like."

Farrah had hoped Kris would get angry. Instead Kris only met her eyes with stony indifference.

"I don't get it," said Ann. "Beth, don't you two know each other?"

"I keep telling you that I'M NOT BETH!"

"All right, all right!" Ann held out a plastic bag heavy with purchases. "Here, I got you these clothes. Why don't you go into the bathroom and change, and we'll all have a seat and wait for you."

Kris took the invitation, walking over to the sofa and planting herself on one end of it, elbows on her parted knees and hands clasped before her as she leaned forward, looking a little too ready to leap into action for anyone to call her relaxed, but not looking remotely nervous. Uncle Tim, on the other end of the sofa, did look nervous, eyeing Kris and Farrah both. Aunt Ann sat in the wooden armchair by the window, apart from them all, exasperated.

Farrah just stood there in her towel, holding her bags and making no move to go get dressed. Kris regarded her steadily.

"Tell them," said Farrah. "Tell them I'm not Beth."

"Oh, you're not." Kris turned to Tim and Ann. "Sorry, didn't realize that was in dispute. I forget how strongly most people disbelieve in magic."

"Magic?" repeated Ann.

Tim, though, studied Kris thoughtfully. She returned his gaze, and said, "Except maybe you have an idea what I'm talking about. Don't you?"

His eyes flickered up to Farrah. His mouth opened to speak, then froze; she could practically see the wheels turn in his head as he tried to gauge what to call her. Finally he said, "Beth used to talk about her mom. About this weird sort of, uh, cult they were both in."

"It's not a *cult*," scoffed Kris.

Ann was watching Tim with a worried eye. He must have told Ann about all that stuff, Farrah realized; about the witchcraft thing, that her mom and the grandmother she'd never met believed in.

"Were you part of all that, back when you guys were kids?" asked Tim.

"Yes," said Kris. "Beth's mother took me in, after my own parents.... Well. They died. I grew up with Beth and her mom. Her mom was my mentor, my teacher, practically *my* mom. Until her cancer. And Beth was my sister. I owe them everything."

"I didn't know any of this," said Ann. Neither had Farrah, and she wondered if it was all bullshit.

But Tim was giving Kris a strange look. "I remember Beth talking about her foster sister. During one of the times we saw each other, growing up. And I remember her telling me about all the things she and her foster sister and mother would do. But then she stopped when I told her my mom and dad said that was all fibs. That she didn't even have a foster sister."

"Except it wasn't fibs, was it?" demanded Farrah. Rage still choked her, but piercing through that was the memory of how her mother used to float blocks.

"No," said Kris.

"Ex*cuse* me," said Ann. "I'm sorry, but what are we doing? Tim, why are we playing along with this?"

"Let's just hear Kris out, honey. I know it's loony, but … well, *something's* going on. And I've told you before, some pretty weird stuff used to happen around Beth, when we'd visit each other as kids."

"And we've also talked about dozens of rational explanations for that weird stuff. And there are probably hundreds more we didn't bother coming up with."

"Well, *something's* going on," said Farrah. "Something's happened to me."

"Yes," said Aunt Ann. "Yes, I know something has, Beth. *Beth.* You're having some kind of episode. I'm not a psychiatrist, but it's pretty plain that the stress of whatever brought you here yesterday has … well, the truth is that you haven't been psychologically ship-shape for a while now and frankly I think you must have started using drugs again." She turned on Tim and Kris. "And I don't see how it does her any good to humor her this way!"

"We're not humoring her," said Kris. "Beth used the power stored in my grimoire to charge a spell, and switch bodies with her daughter. I figured she would use its power for a more straightforward way out of the jam she's in. Make an ATM spit out all its cash, something like that. But, well, we were both pretty drunk. I guess she came up with a different plan. Something she needed your body for. Whatever that plan is, I guarantee you she'll switch the bodies back once she's done." She looked at Farrah as if she were sizing up a particularly boss convertible. "I gotta say, I'm impressed. That's a pretty complicated spell for someone who's drunk, and it requires a lot of energy. Beth must have really had to shepherd the small amount of power the grimoire holds. It's the kind of thing she could have done asleep back in her heyday, but she's been out of the game a while."

"I can't wait to give her a fucking blue ribbon," spat Farrah.

"Why am I the only one not crazy?" said Ann. "And what is a 'grimoire'?"

Tim said, "It's a book with, like, spells written in it, that has magic powers. It's a prop in lots of horror stories. Bound with glue made from squished demons' eyeballs. Written in blood on tanned baby skin. Stuff like that."

"Um, it's written with ballpoint pens, on the paper pages of a wire notebook." Kris curled her lip at Tim. "'Tanned baby skin'? What is wrong with you?"

"Well, I just meant for example, like in Lovecraft stories...."

"Lovecraft is fiction, this is real life. 'Bound in the glue of demon eyeballs'? Only mass-produced books are bound with glue, you can't mass-produce grimoires. Also, you can't make glue that way...."

"*My point is*," said Ann, "I don't understand why we're indulging in this fantasy, instead of trying to get Beth the kind of serious help she needs."

"It's not a fantasy," said Farrah.

Tim stared into the distance, frowning, looking almost frightened. At last he said, "You know, I do have all these memories of Beth *doing* things, back when we were really little. I always thought I'd imagined them, but maybe...."

Ann stared at her husband like he was a stranger who'd invited himself in and started talking to her. "We're enabling Beth with this kind of talk. This won't help her get better."

"Open your mind to the possibility," suggested Kris. "At least in a theoretical sense."

"No," said Ann. "It's going to take a lot more than people telling me about their hallucinations to get me to believe in magic."

Kris shrugged. Farrah stepped close enough that she loomed right over her. It made Tim and Ann nervous, but Kris looked up calmly.

"You could prove it to her, though," said Farrah. "Couldn't you? You have the same sorts of powers as my mom."

"Never as good," repeated Kris.

"Prove it to me," challenged Ann. "Really prove it to me, and I mean in the next two minutes, please. Otherwise we're dropping all the mumbo-jumbo and calling a doctor."

Again Kris shrugged, and Farrah caught her making a lazy but quick gesture with her fingers. It was so slight Farrah might have imagined it.

Aunt Ann was looking at her, embarrassed. "I'm sorry, Beth," she was saying, "I know we don't always get along but I'm really not trying to be a bitch. I just...."

Ann was cut short by a shocked intake of breath from Tim. Her head whipped over to him: "Tim, what's the matter?" Her features twisting, she said, "How are you moving like that?"

It was she who was moving, though. Floating up. Tim and Farrah, who were gaping up at her, figured it out before she did; she seemed to assume there was some problem with her vision, until she felt her legs unfold and dangle as she rose from her seat and into the air. "Hey!" she exclaimed, and curled her legs back up against her belly. "Hey, put me down!"

As far as Farrah could tell, Kris maneuvered Ann into the empty space above the middle of the room with nothing but her eyes, and there began gently spinning the levitating woman. "Let's wait till you're convinced," she said mildly. "Check there are no strings."

"Stop! Put her down!" cried Tim. "Put her down, she's pregnant!"

After that, Tim was convinced, and Ann was close enough as made no difference. Tim claimed that deep down he'd known even before his wife had levitated; he said he'd just somehow felt that it wasn't his sister Beth looking back at him out of those eyes. Seeing as Uncle Tim and her mom had never been super-close siblings, Farrah wasn't sure she bought that, but as long as he believed she didn't really care when or how that belief had started.

Besides, she had more pressing business. "You're responsible for this," she insisted to Kris. "You gave my mother that grimwald and look what she did with it."

"What's a grimwald? I gave her a grimoire. And what she did with it is *her* responsibility, not mine. I didn't even realize she was capable of this."

"It was your responsibility to figure out what she was and wasn't capable of before you gave the thing to some crazy bag-lady junkie." The ripple that passed across Kris's face scared Farrah, but at the same time it felt good to get a rise out of the woman. "Now, you have to help me put things back the way they were."

"I don't think I can do that."

Farrah punched the wall, hard enough to hurt her hand. Good—it was *Mom's* hand. "You mean you *won't* do it!"

Farrah's wall-punch had made Tim and Ann jump; not Kris, though.

"Right," she said. "I guess that's what I mean."

Eleven

Dolan left Beth while he went and asked Mannis for permission to bring her in. Like she'd expected, the mention of Old Sullivan was all it took to win an invitation.

She waited at the pizza place. When Dolan came back it was in a car; he pulled over to the curb, she got in, and as he pulled out again he handed her a clean do-rag. "Blindfold yourself with this," he said. "And don't cheat and leave it so you can peek out, or I'll know." He didn't infuse those words with any particular menace, but that was because he didn't have to.

Tying the blindfold was hard because of her trembling fingers. It was a flashback to helpless times, when she'd been blindfolded prior to being led in to beg Mannis for succor, to be tormented and laughed at. For a moment she thought that Dolan and Mannis had seen through her.

No. I'm Farrah. Making her wear a blindfold didn't mean they knew she was Beth—blindfolds weren't something these guys subjected Beth to, they were something *everyone* got subjected to. *I'm Farrah, I'm Farrah, I'm Farrah.*

But then she thought, *No, I'm not.* She thought, *I'm Beth who looks like Farrah. There's a big difference.* Her fingers stopped trembling, and she tied the cloth with ease.

Neither Dolan nor Mannis had any idea who she was. They thought she was some hot little goose who'd nabbed a grimoire from her wreck of a mom and had only a vague idea how to use it. Instead she had all the knowledge of a first-class witch.

She sat still, feeling the car move.

After a while the car stopped. From the echoes of Dolan's door slamming she could tell they were inside some cavernous space. Presumably some other entrance to the lair under the fabric store. Beth waited for Dolan to come around to her side, to open the door for her. He took her by the arm as she got out. There was the familiar rigmarole of him leading her down winding steps.

He gripped her arm above the elbow, and now and then let the backs of his fingers glide against the side of her breast. Such tricks hadn't been unheard-of when it had been Beth's body he'd led downstairs, but it felt different now that it was Farrah's. Less mockery, more desire; though the mockery was still there, too.

Her plan was to somehow lure Mannis into the room where the straw party was going on. Mannis would have to weaken his warding and binding spells in order to enter the space; otherwise, those wards would smother the evil magic that kept the straw party going, and the games would end. With his warding and binding spells weakened, Beth reckoned she could kill him and end the party, disrupting its magic field with a quick sharp burst of thaumaturgical static. Once that field was disrupted, she could use the grimoire's last ounce of juice to kill the lights and cast a tracking spell to lead her back up and out of the lair in the dark—in the sudden magical chaos of the disrupted field, she should be able to get away, as the surviving mages regained their bearings. All this would require absolute precision in shepherding the grimoire's remaining charge—doing so much with so little would be the work of a real master witch. But the very craziness of the plan excited her. She'd show them.

Depending on where and how they were being held, the designated victims of the straw-suck would even have the chance to escape in the confusion. Beth didn't have enough power to rescue them, exactly—but she could at least give them a shot at rescuing themselves.

Mannis would be off-guard, because he would expect her to be ignorant. Even if she did know what a grimoire was, there was no reason for him to assume she knew what a straw party was, or that being in the same room as one would make a mage more susceptible to attack. Anyone could look up the word "grimoire" in a dictionary, but straw parties were something one only learned about after some time in the life; Mannis knew that Beth and her daughter were long since estranged, and that Beth had never given her any real training. And besides, straw parties were not material for mother-daughter bedtime stories.

As long as she was alone with Dolan, she felt a certain calm; he was a known quality. That confidence dissipated when Dolan removed the blindfold and she saw her new surroundings.

Her plan, already crazy, only covered killing Mannis. She assumed he'd meet her one-on-one, or with nobody around but Dolan. It had never occurred to her she'd have to face him, as well as all the big mages he'd apparently invited to the straw party.

Crammed into the bunker-like room with Mannis were fourteen men and women, all of them around Mannis's age, nearing sixty, teetering on the verge of elderly yet with plenty of strength left in them; weaklings couldn't run in these circles. The men wore dark suits, the women dark pantsuits, as if they were all dressed for a funeral. Everyone was standing. Glancing around she saw that Dolan had already disappeared.

The room itself wasn't remarkable, merely the sort of cramped cool concrete-walled dungeon one would expect to find so deep underground. Above them the long fluorescent tubes hummed on the edge of audibility.

From within her floppy purse she could feel heat radiating from the grimoire, a heat she knew was intended solely for her. It somehow directed her eyes to a thin puckered face whose eyes, she realized, were glass, and yet who seemed able to see. Looking at him, she knew somehow that this was Lefebre, the Frenchman who'd tangled with Old Sullivan.

Even as she shivered, she was impressed that the grimoire not only could have discovered such a thing, but that it had been able to tell she would want to know and then had communicated the knowledge to her.

Mannis was watching her, with an ironic and speculative gaze. "So. This is the little girl of our friend Beth. Hard to believe."

"Why, because there's no resemblance?" said Beth. "Glad to hear it."

He tilted his head; caressed the brass head of his cane with a thumb. "No," he said. "I wouldn't quite say that...."

"Your mother was to join us tonight," said blind yet somehow-seeing Lefebre. The French accent was barely perceptible in his clipped words. "She was to give us such sweet dreams, for nothing spurs nightmares as does the loss of great power. I wonder if her debt ought not descend unto you?"

"Now, now, *mon ami*," gently scolded Mannis. "I'm sure the contents of that notebook in her handbag should more than make up for the contents of her mother's skull. Besides, visiting the sins of the parents upon subsequent generations is Biblical policy, and I don't think any of us have truck with that."

He gave Beth a faux-charming smile. The others in the room betrayed little with their stony faces. Beth looked blankly at Mannis, trying to hide her panic. What the fuck was she going to do? Killing Mannis, that middle-manager of hell, would be one thing. But the grimoire was no match for a guy like Lefebre, a man whose name had been entered in the Black Book, much less him and thirteen of his peers. Only the might of a true warrior would have a chance of taking these folks on.

"All right, then," said one of the women, matter-of-factly. They all seemed matter-of-fact, except for Mannis and Lefebre. "She has a grimoire. And?"

"That depends on you guys," said Beth. "On how much you want it."

"Young lady," said Mannis, "even a modest grimoire is a worthwhile investment, and as long as your terms are reasonable, I see no reason why we should exert ourselves with trying to take it by force. And those terms are?..."

"Release my mom from her debt."

"As I already said, the contents of that grimoire are undoubtedly worth a great deal more than your mother. Even if it should prove only a very ordinary sort of grimoire. Anything else?"

"I don't know. A bunch of money, I guess?"

"Someone here ought to be able to rustle that up. And now, my dear, if that's all settled, why don't you join us for our little soirée?"

Beth blanched. She leaned back, away from Mannis; it was hard to keep herself from taking a step back. She hadn't even had time to start maneuvering him into making the offer, and here it was already. "Me?"

"Of course you, dear. We're having a party. It would be rude not to invite you, now that you're here."

"That's very nice of you, but cut the shit please." Once they left this room and entered the area set aside for straw-sucking, all these guys would be vulnerable to magicks. They had to be—if there were global protection spells in place, that would inhibit the straw-sucking. They had to know the grimoire gave her power she might try to use against them. So why were they pretending to want her with them in that other room?

Beth had intended her brassy remark as a way of letting them know they couldn't intimidate her so easily. But she saw a few of the mages bristle, and not in a good way. Not in a hey-we-underestimated-this-girl way. While it might amuse the big shots to watch small-fry Mannis play the movie villain, they were much less interested in seeing her play the movie hero. She didn't rate that indulgence.

"There's no 'shit' for me to cut, dear," said Mannis. "I'm politely inviting you to our little party. Anyway, you claim to have come to talk with us, and that's where we'll be." As he put an avuncular hand on her shoulder, she tried not to cringe. She found herself filing out along with them.

After all, things were going according to plan. Technically. Except she hadn't banked on all these other mages, all more powerful than Mannis.

Lefebre sidled up to her. The lack of sight organs continued to make no difference to him. He inclined his mouth toward her ear and pretended to whisper, even though he hissed loud enough to be audible to everyone: "Maybe we haven't taken the grimoire yet because we're still 'sizing you up,' as Americans say."

Beth made herself smirk in response and leave her eyes pointed straight ahead. A couple of the mages glanced over at her and Lefebre, but they betrayed little reaction to his taunt. Except for Mannis, who half-turned and mildly waved his hand at Lefebre, as if to say, *Calm down, dear.* Or as if to say, *Not yet.*

They're trying to psyche me out, said Beth to herself. Then: *They* are *psyching me out.*

They were moving along a fluorescently-lit raw-concrete hallway, walking slowly in a clump between the narrow walls.

The sounds of a hubbub began to build. The noise appeared so suddenly that it must have been thaumaturgically dampened in the proximity of the little conference cell they'd had her in. It came from beyond a pair of plain-looking steel fire-doors coming up on their right. The party was beyond those doors. Beth began amping herself up, rallying herself from the scare Mannis and his posse had given her. Nothing had changed. She would kill Mannis. She would kill the lights. She'd zap the party's field, setting loose a miniature magic storm that would hopefully obscure her from view long enough for her to escape. Shit would be more dangerous, since she'd be in such close proximity to these big-shot mages. But shit was always going to be dangerous. As long as their attention was elsewhere at the critical moment (and it would probably be on the straw party), she'd have a chance.

Lefebre was beside her again. In a low, soothing tone, he said, "I wonder why we didn't simply come aboveground to treat with you? That way you would have known nothing of our little gathering. Unless we mean to have our way with you in the end, anyhow."

He glided away as her steps faltered. Good point; she felt stupid and blind. She'd been so fixated on how she was going to have to come here for the straw party, that instead of telling herself she no longer needed to come at all, she'd started planning how she could come yet still defeat her enemies. Why hadn't she followed through to the logical conclusion, and just skipped town? They would never have found her, in this body....

No, she remembered now—she couldn't do that because she had to return this body to Farrah. And she had to take care of these guys because if she just slipped away, they'd come looking for Farrah. For *her*, that was, but they would mistake Farrah for her.

Plus she could at least give the other victims of the straw-party a chance to escape, by disrupting the thaumaturgical field. That would prove for once that she could be the hero, too. Like her mom, like Kris, like Kris's parents who'd fallen in battle.

Mannis pushed the fire doors open with a *whump* and led the entourage through. Within was a big room, though not as big as it seemed; there was a raucous crowd, but at second glance it wasn't as big as it seemed, either. Her fear gave it an outsized place in her mind.

A group of men and women huddled around a central point, illuminated by a single harsh overhead lamp. Outside the bounds of that spotlight glare was near-black gloom. Beth could guess which of the mages gathered around the table were the most junior, based on the abandon with which they cheered and howled.

She couldn't see through the thick press of people. But she could guess what they were gathered around.

As she approached with her grim escort, a naked boy so pale he was almost pure white was tossed out of the clumped spectators. Beth flinched involuntarily, then made herself keep walking, hoping no one had noticed her weakness, knowing they had. The boy was maybe sixteen. His bright red hair and pubic hair was shocking against his snowy skin. He drooled, and Beth could imagine the low formless moaning noise he was making, if only the crowd would stop cheering and shouting long enough for anyone to hear it.

The mages exchanged chits, comments and jokes, those who had engaged in the straw-suck's obscure and complex gambling either gleeful or angry, depending on their fortunes. Soon enough they had a new distraction: the next naked screaming victim, being dragged over now. As soon as his shrieks were audible Beth's eyes snapped over to him, but most everyone else in the room preferred to wrap up their conversations or transactions before checking him out.

This one was older than Beth. His pate was bald and on the sides and back of his head grew a wild shoulder-length spray of gray hair. A potbelly rocked over his large, flopping penis. Though his arms and legs were almost spindly, he struggled and thrashed with all his might, the tendons standing out on his neck and what little muscle he had taut as thin rope. Since he was bigger and taller than the slight, waifish boys who pulled him along by the arms, it might have struck the unschooled eye as odd that he was unable to break away.

Beth tried to hang back on the outskirts of the crowd and not get so close to the central spectacle. But Mannis again put a gentle hand on her shoulder and pulled her forward, saying, "This way, dear. What's the point in coming all the way down here if you don't watch our little show?"

"So far it's been only men and boys, I understand," Lefebre remarked. "Hopefully we'll add a female to the mix before dawn."

At the center of the crowd there was a table, a low metal slab like some industrial altar. It had no need of physical restraints. As the waifs flung the weeping, screaming, hopelessly fighting middle-aged man onto his back in the center of the horde, Beth tried to repress a shudder.

Once the mages got their straws out, their thaumaturgical field would mask anything Beth might do, magic-wise. Mannis and the others probably didn't realize the grimoire carried an auxiliary charge—they wanted it for the knowledge it contained, and didn't know that Kris had packed it full of extra power to make up for her lack of access to her own bio-thaumaturgy. They wouldn't be prepared for an attack originating from that quarter.

On top of all that, she reminded herself as the naked slob on the table screamed, blinded by terror and the light, there was the fact that she ought to help this guy. Strange incense could not cover the smell as he shat himself with fear.

She took half a second to close her eyes and clench her jaw. *I am not going to fuck up.* She had a plan and it would work. She would kill Mannis and the lights, disrupt the magical field, cast a guiding spell to find her way out. And she would even grab this bald guy as she went, and save him.

The racers, two shock-haired blonds with weathered faces, were pointing their long straws of polished rock crystal, the smooth ends in their mouths and the spoon-shaped beckon-ends toward the victim's head. Power thrummed silently and invisibly as the racers prepared themselves. This was the moment, now while she had the cloak of their thaumaturgy but before the victim had been damaged. *It's now or never,* she told herself. *Now or never.*

Now or never.

… Well, she said to herself, with a silent bitter laugh, looked like it would be never. She couldn't even get her own breathing under control, much less do the complicated mental and spiritual acrobatics that would be required to kill Mannis and end this party.

The racers pulled at their crystal tubes, cheeks puckering as the bald man jabbered and shook and grew paler and paler, as if all the blood were being slowly teleported out of him. Only moments remained for Beth to do something—permanent damage had been done, but there was still a human soul there that could be salvaged. Only if she moved quickly, though, only if she acted right now....

It was like a heavy piece of concrete blocked her escape from some flooding room, and she had to strain with all her might to lift it so she could get out in time. And it was like her strength suddenly gave out; like something broke inside, like the root of her willpower snapped. All she could do after that was slump against the immovable block and feel the chilly water rise, with fear but also with a certain relief that nothing more would be required of her.

"You're sweating, my girl," murmured Mannis, slipping his low voice into her ear underneath the surrounding cacophony.

"No I'm not," she insisted, even though she was.

There was a lull in the commotion as the racers finished, slurping up the last dregs of the brain-suckee. To those who knew how to watch, it was clear which of the two had cleaned out the biggest portion of the guy, and the audience burst into either cheers or curses, depending on their bets. The victim had turned, not the gray of a corpse, but the same shade of snow on a cloudy day as his predecessor. Nothing but a zombie now, he put up zero resistance as the same handlers who'd brought him out grabbed his wrists and yanked him off the table and onto the floor. A scrawnier, more frightened-looking servant darted through the crowd to wipe away the bald man's excrement and urine. What was left of the man himself was dragged off.

Beth could feel Mannis's eyes on her. She refused to look directly at him. She had the feeling he'd known all along the sort of thing she'd been planning, and hadn't minded giving her the opportunity because he'd been so confident she would fail.

And he seemed to confirm that by saying, "You know, you really are so much like your mother." Beth hated herself then, even more than she ever had before, far more than she hated Mannis. *I'm sorry, Farrah. I guess I really fucked up. I guess you'll never get your body back after all—I guess when I don't get in touch, you'll figure I just ran off with it.*

While the mid-level mages were still shouting and cheering and swearing, Mannis put his gentle hand on her and led her out of the crowd. The rest of the VIP mages also seemed to know it was time to leave. Beth could feel Lefebre behind her, watching her.

Panic and incredulous self-loathing sloshed around in her abdomen, then started bubbling up till it reached the inside of her throat and choked her. How could she have frozen like that? Now she'd missed her shot, and they were going to kill her, if she was lucky. More likely she'd wind up even worse off, on that table herself, shitting and whitening.

No, that wouldn't be worse; she didn't want to die, she'd rather anything else. On top of all the rest of her failures, she was a coward.

As if she were merely an observer in her own brain, it came to her that she really was going to sell the grimoire. What had been only a ruse to get her inside had turned into her one hope of getting out. Maybe the mind games had just been to soften her up, so that she'd do a worse job of bargaining. Kris would understand—even if it fucked her over, Kris would prefer that she sell the grimoire, rather than getting killed or brain-sucked. Right?

Kris, am I really going to do that to you? Am I really going to betray you like that? Help me, Kris. Please don't let me sink that low.

But Kris couldn't hear her or help her now. Kris had given Beth all the help she could.

Mannis and the others led her back to the little room where they'd started. There were a few upholstered black armchairs against the walls. Some of the mages sat in them, keeping their calm, distantly cruel eyes on her. Lefebre and Mannis were among those who remained standing. The mages surrounded her in a loose clump, not crowding her but nevertheless cutting her off from the exit. Beth almost missed having Dolan there—at least he was familiar, and the dangers he posed were mundane and comprehensible.

"So," said Mannis. "What now?"

At least she managed not to physically tremble. "We do a deal, I guess," she said. "Assuming you want the grimoire."

"Oh, I think we do want it." Mannis turned to the Frenchman. "Lefebre most of all, I believe. So perhaps we should let him set the price."

"Perhaps we should let *me* set it," snapped Beth. "My mom's debt and her life, as a baseline. Over and above that everything's negotiable, as long as it's a lot." She didn't really care about getting anything more than her own safety, and Farrah's for as long as she wore Beth's body. But if Lefebre and Mannis figured that out, they would read it as weakness.

Not that they seemed bowled over by her strength. Mannis allowed the cruelty lurking behind the skin of his face to drift out to his mouth. "As I said, I'll let my good friend here handle our side of the negotiation. Lefebre? What do you say? Does the grimoire strike you as valuable? Perhaps the girl will allow us to handle it, just to be sure."

101

"No hands," said Beth. If they physically handled the grimoire it might give them a powerful enough influence that they would be able to slip a wedge into her linking spell and bust it loose. "Even through the linking and warding spells, you guys should be able to sense its aura well enough to know it is what I said."

"No fear of that," said Lefebre. Contempt oiled his words. "The stink of that cow Old Sullivan is on it, yes. It was a great disappointment that he died before I could kill him. Despoiling him in death may bring some consolation."

Beth shuddered. Greed was a mundane motive, and no matter how dangerous these guys were it was a motive she felt she could manipulate, with predictable results. But for Lefebre the grimoire was wrapped up with some sort of vendetta. That sort of motivation was simultaneously wilder and more disciplined than greed, harder to control.

Most Black-Bookers must have that sort of intensity, she supposed. After all, they'd been willing to pay an eternity of hell for the ecstasy of committing some crime. (Not that Beth really necessarily believed being entered in the Black Book condemned you to the Black Ice forever, not *really*.) Beth had never dealt with any Black-Booker, though, the way Kris had.

She said, "I guess despoiling him must be worth a lot of money to you."

Lefebre sniffed. "Money itself is worth very little, girl. The fact that your imagination stretches toward no more ambitious goal speaks to your weakness. If for some reason I ever need money, with my power it is the easiest thing in the world merely to take it. By the same token, there is little reason for me to take money when I could simply take the things I would have it buy. Now, girl, I'll have a look at that grimoire."

"I told you, no hands. You can feel what it is, you don't need...."

She broke off and stared down at her bag, into which her hand had suddenly disappeared and where it was gripping the notebook, drawing it out. She pushed the command to open down into her fingers and wrenched her empty hand back out of the bag.

Sweat beaded on her forehead, from the exertion of fighting off Lefebre and also from fear. "I told you guys before," she spat at him, "cut the shit."

"Yes, you told us," he agreed. "And when you did, I thought to myself: This one, she doesn't know. She doesn't understand who it is that gets to *talk*, and who it is who has to *listen*. Does she really think her schoolgirl spells can keep away the likes of myself? Though I do admit, I am surprised you were able to resist my commands. Even if only for a moment."

"It'll be for a hell of a lot longer than that, asshole. I'm not some pathetic old hag like my mother."

"Really, dear," scolded Mannis, "you ought to be more polite. I do understand that you're trying to bluff your way into an appearance of strength, because you think that will discourage us from killing you. But as a civilized person speaking to your betters, you should stay within certain limits. Oh, and by the way, I wouldn't so cavalierly throw around such nasty words about your mother. True, she's nothing much now. But there were some glorious forks in her path, which she sadly declined to take. Why, in her day she might have given us all a run for our money. Who knows, she might have had a chance to succeed in this stupid gambit that's going to leave you a shitting white husk. Don't worry, we'll put you to good use—I have a little pack of the most adorable chihuahuas, and they do so love fresh meat."

"This one's mother, you say?" Lefebre's unblinking glass eyes bored into her. "I find it hard to believe this one spawned from anything worthy of notice."

"Well, as I said, her best days are behind her. And presumably she's the one who sent her own untrained, weakling daughter down here into the lion's den, which bespeaks a certain idiotic, ruthless desperation."

Beth was trying to open her mouth. Trying to muster the strength to tell them she wasn't quite so stupid and weak as that, that she wasn't beaten yet—more, she tried to muster the strength to do something, anything, quick, now, before it was too late. Instead she found herself unable even to take a full breath, as if her ribs had ceased giving way for her lungs. They were going to do something horrific to her, and they weren't particularly worried about her fighting back. Some of the gathered mages were still watching the confrontation between her and Lefebre and Mannis, but none with much interest, and others had pulled out their smartphones and started fiddling with them, to pass the time till it was all over.

A sudden pins-and-needles feeling sprouted all over her right arm. She tried to look down at it, but couldn't. She could tell that it was dipping back into her handbag, though.

At least it was dipping into it slowly, though that cost her some more sweat. She gasped for air and stared into Lefebre's mute eyes, unable to keep the begging out of her own. When he spoke he sounded only somewhat less than completely bored: "Yes, fight, please. As the years pile up, I find my amusements evaporate so quickly. Of course you realize that I am leaning upon you only with the strength of my mere little finger. I crush people so often, it grows tiresome if I don't add variety. Though I will confess, you are doing better than I expected. From what Mannis told us of that pathetic hag you mentioned earlier, I assumed you had been raised entirely without training. Yet I can feel vast wells of untapped power within you. A shame those wells shall be spilled tonight, and you'll disappear without ever having been any use to anyone."

She felt Lefebre crush her linking spell—the grimoire would be perfectly legible when she handed it over. It hadn't been a very strong spell, it had only been intended to make stealing the grimoire more trouble than it was worth to *Mannis*, who was much weaker than Lefebre.

Beth's hand inched closer, closer, past the edge of her bag. It moved with such excruciating slowness that if someone had glanced over in passing they might not have seen any movement at all. For an instant she was able to halt its motion, even yank it back up a millimeter or so; but right away Lefebre's will was there to push it back on its course again, and she felt the crushing invisible dark weight of the power that he held in abeyance, so that his conquest of her might take longer and so prolong his pleasure.

From far away, she felt her fingers close on the notebook. "Please," she gasped.

"Ah," he breathed. "Very nice. Somehow, I never get tired of the begging."

Tears were on Beth's face now. The strength of her resistance faltered—and at the same time, so did the pressure Lefebre applied, so that he would not have to see his pleasure come to a premature end.

"Feeble cow," he crooned. "What a boon you've brought me. Were you wise enough to comprehend the magnitude of the destruction it allows me to wreak, I might be tempted to keep you alive long enough to see it. You say this grimoire once belonged to Old Sullivan; and before and after him, I'd wager it belonged to those with whom he was close. I shall use the book to trace my way back to its true owners. Within hours I shall have melted away all the book's protection spells. And from there I will use its secrets to find and desecrate the remains of Old Sullivan, and to kill his minions, great and small."

Kris was one of those minions.

Beth felt like she would throw up. Theoretically, she realized, what Lefebre proposed was possible—a powerful and subtle enough mage *could* use the mystical links a grimoire would automatically form with its true owner to track that owner down, piercing her camouflage, her shrouding spells, all her protections. Such a feat was beyond her ken, and sure as hell beyond Mannis's. But she hadn't banked on running into mages of Lefebre's caliber.

Beth's hand trembled. Her teeth clamped together hard enough to hurt her jaw. Lefebre raised an eyebrow. "One last effort, child?"

Dicking Kris over was bad enough. It was one thing to steal the grimoire. Even worse to lose it to Lefebre and probably get her best friend kicked out of that coven. But only now did Beth realize that she might wind up getting Kris's skin slowly peeled off in a dungeon somewhere.

Her hand trembled harder. That vast dark will pressing down on hers paused, relaxed slightly for a moment and looked at her speculatively. "You *do* have unsounded depths," remarked Lefebre. "I begin to ask myself if it might be worth foregoing the pleasure of destroying you, and instead send you somewhere to be trained in exchange for your allegiance. It would take time to teach you. But I have time. Surrender and kneel, and I shall consider it."

Her hand trembled harder yet. The force of his will came down upon it hard, to still it, but she pushed back even harder. Her eyes stung and she realized from a distance that sweat was pouring out of her. On the periphery of her awareness she noticed that some of the mages were looking up at the struggle with rather more interest than before.

She glared into Lefebre's glass eyes and choked out, "Fuck you, motherfucker."

"I beg your pardon?" he said, with dry, dangerous amusement.

She continued to push back against his pressure, but underneath that, deeper within, there were other stirrings. It happened too fast for Beth to follow or understand; it was like the light suddenly broke upon a New World within her, one that had always been there, one far vaster than the Old, one whose discovery quadrupled, quintupled the area of her inner map. In that new region vast waves of force and strength retreated, contracting like the sea just before a tidal wave. "I said you're a MOTHERFUCKER!" she screamed, and the last words came out funny, as if the sound waves in the room were suddenly acting up. Warding spells were blasted away like dandelion fluff before an inferno; amid the warbling shrieks of old men and women Beth raised her exultant face to watch the ceiling come crashing down to meet it.

Twelve

Farrah had railed at that bitch Kris, demanding and begging that she help her get her body back. The bitch had not budged. She'd had the gall to look Farrah right in the eyes and say, "If Beth did this it was because she felt she had to. She's not a thief. She'll return your body once she doesn't need it anymore."

Her mom demonstrably *was* a thief, since she'd stolen Farrah's body. Another thing that drove her crazy was how her Uncle Tim and Aunt Ann rolled over for everything this stranger said, as if she were the expert. It wasn't like she had presented her credentials or anything.

Fuck them. Farrah still remembered the location of that party her mom had said she had to meet those gangsters or whatever at.

So she'd stormed out of her uncle's and aunt's apartment without telling them where she was going. On the sidewalk she'd realized she had no money or subway card, so she'd had to head back upstairs, thereby diminishing the power of her grand exit. "At least give me some walking-around money, if you won't help me get back any of the shit my mom stole from me!" Her uncle had hastily pressed some bills into her hand. She'd left again and headed up to midtown Manhattan, powering through her headache and nausea. Worst hangover of her life, and she hadn't even gotten to have the fun of earning it. Did her mother feel like this all the time? What a disgusting lifestyle she must have.

That fucking address where the gangster party supposedly was going to be really was nothing but a goddam fabric store. Chump that she was, Farrah actually went inside and poked around, as if there might be some sort of conclave in between the bolts of fabric.

Darting back outside, she looked up at the façade of the building. It was two stories. The second floor looked derelict. That was weird, right? Wasn't it? Considering property values in Manhattan? Maybe it was kept disused for a reason. Maybe it wasn't actually disused at all, maybe warlock godfathers used it for their quiet soirées—quiet, since no noise of any party leaked out into the street or downstairs to the store. Maybe it hadn't started yet. It was only around eight.

Farrah went back into the fabric store and walked up to the Asian proprietor. "I'm sorry, is there a party going on here?" she asked.

The proprietor gave her a strange, wide-eyed look.

"Is there?" she pressed. She tried to smile. "Like, a get-together or something? Maybe in a different room?"

The guy only kept on staring at her like she was nuts. She couldn't blame him. Obviously nothing remotely of the sort was going on here—chalk it up to more stupidity from her addled mother.

Farrah was about to give up and leave when a black guy walked in and spotted her. He laughed and said, "Well, well, well."

Jesus, thought Farrah, believing he was about to hit on her, *I don't have time for this.* She started to walk by him.

His arm shot out and grabbed hers. "Where you going, bitch?"

She gaped at him, affronted, then tried to jerk her arm away. His grip was like iron. "Let go of me!" she said, and stared at the proprietor. Unbelievably, he acted like he didn't notice anything.

Wait, thought Farrah. *He's not flirting with me, no one's going to flirt with me, I look like Mom.*

He shook her by the arm, the way one would do with a misbehaving kid, and with a kind of disdainful curiosity said, "Exactly where do you think you're going? You already done showed up for your appointment. Now be a good girl and come take your medicine."

Only now did Farrah get it. "Wait," she said, trying to dig her heels into the linoleum as the guy dragged her toward the back of the store, pulling her by the arm he still had hold of and pushing her with a hand in the small of her back. "Wait, who do you think I am? Because I'm not Beth, if that's what you're thinking, I'm her daughter."

"Whatever, Beth, tell it to the man."

"No, come on, let me go, I'm not Beth, let go of me!" She twisted in his grip, tried to catch the proprietor's eye, and cried, *"Help! Someone help!..."*

The black guy's hand left her arm long enough to slap her in the mouth, hard, then gripped her again before she could try to escape. For a moment Farrah, stunned, merely let herself be dragged along, tasting her blood and feeling the sting rippling through her head—no one had ever hit her in the face before. Her legs went noodly underneath her.

As they neared the back of the store Farrah began to thrash around and tried to cry out. The black guy swung his hand around to clap it over her mouth, and with his other hand he grabbed her wrist and twisted it around behind her back. She squealed her agony uselessly into his palm. He said, "If you keep playing I promise I will choke you out and carry you down these stairs. Or just kick you down them ahead of me, if you get too heavy."

Through the tears welling from the pain Farrah saw that they were approaching some big red rug or piece of fabric hanging against the back wall. The guy started to herd her behind it like it was one of those curtains people were always hiding behind in old-fashioned plays. She renewed her struggle one last time, and he wrenched her arm up so high she was certain he'd damaged it, and even through his hand a strangled cry escaped.

"Quit *playing!*" he said, really exasperated now, though not taking any of it seriously enough to get truly angry. "You know the drill!"

There was a trap door hidden behind the fabric, and they went through it. Right away they were walking down a winding stairwell illuminated only by tiny yellow light bulbs set in the curving walls; her captor hurried down behind her, and she, weak as she was, forced her legs to move in time with his. If she fell down these stairs, and he didn't let go of her arm, then it would break.

What had she done? She was doomed. "Just one last trip downstairs," the black guy was telling her. "Just one last, and your debt's paid. Now, won't that feel good? Not to have it on your conscience? Not to have nothing on your mind?"

All she'd been able to think about was tracking down her mother and bringing her to justice. Even though she'd known her mom was in deep shit with these people, it still somehow hadn't sunk in that they were going to confuse the two of them. *You stupid, ugly fucking retard,* she said to herself.

Maybe she could explain to the guy about the grimoire, she was thinking—when suddenly the air in the dark stairwell grew thin, and the sounds of their feet scuffing along the stairs grew dimmer; and then there was a *foomp* sound and the stairs disintegrated underneath them. Farrah cried out as they fell through a crumbling wall.

Who knew how far the drop was—she guessed twelve feet or so. They must be in a room that had been behind the curving walls of the stairway. A big room. Crude naked bulbs were set into the walls, their glow hazy in the concrete dust.

The walls of this subterranean chamber had fallen in, just like those of the stairway that had run down through it like a tube. The floor here must have been sturdier—it seemed solid enough underneath Farah, anyway. She was pinned under a chunk of concrete that had fallen over her waist. She didn't bear its weight—it was propped up against something jutting from the side walls, which bore it up just high enough that it didn't crush her—but it lay across her waist at precisely the right level and angle to trap her big fat hips underneath it. Her leg had gotten banged up in the fall.

I hope I broke her fucking leg, she thought savagely, before reminding herself that *she* was the one stuck with this leg, now.

The black guy was unhurt; he scrambled to his feet and ran off, shouting, *"Mannis!"*

"Hey, don't go!" said Farrah, then clamped her mouth shut. What, did she think this guy was going to rescue her? Better to wait for the cops. Even if she wound up being gnawed by rats, she doubted this guy had anything nicer in store for her.

For a long time she strained to drag herself out from under the rubble. She didn't manage to budge, but there was nothing to do but keep trying. She didn't think her leg was badly injured, at least.

From deeper in the cavern, she heard what could be the scuffling of footsteps, and froze, telling herself it was probably nothing but debris shifting, chunks of cement and foundation slipping loose and clattering down.

But no, that was definitely the sound of someone approaching. And although it was impossible to be sure because of the echoes, she thought it was coming from further down below, meaning it probably wasn't the police or firemen. More likely that black guy. Farrah held herself as still as she could, like a bunny closing its eyes so no one will see it.

She tried to hold her breath, to be even quieter as she blinked the building's dust out of her eyes. About ten yards away, a female figure stepped around the corner and into the hazy glow, picking her way through the rubble. She was not outwardly menacing, but she made Farrah's breath stop. Again there was that strange disconnect, the sense that the person was irredeemably alien, yet simultaneously the most familiar face in the world. The contradiction was less overwhelming this second time around, though, as Farrah watched her mom pick her way toward her in her stolen body.

Farrah couldn't decide whether she should call out to her mother for help, or try to stay quiet and unnoticed till she passed. This was her enemy, after all. But it wasn't like she could go hide somewhere. All she could do was lie there, stuck, as Beth approached. Soon enough her mom saw her, with that same shock of affronted horror and recognition spasming her face that Farrah knew must have marked her own.

The shock was instinctive, and could never be completely counteracted by mere intellectual comprehension of what

111

was going on. But Farrah saw Beth shake it off as she hurried over. Despite how desperately she needed help, Farrah was in some ways even more scared of her mother than she had been of that black guy. Beth was disheveled, dusty, although Farrah noticed that she was also dressed up. She clutched that beat-up wirebound notebook.

"Farrah!" she said, crouching beside her among the sharp and uneven debris. "Are you hurt?"

"Just stuck."

"Sweetie, you shouldn't have come—I was able to handle these guys."

Dumbfounded, Farrah realized that her mom thought Farrah was here to *help* her. The gall! Did she not realize that what she'd done was so horrible that Farrah was bound to hate her forever? Her mother had such an exultant, a *happy* air, that Farrah had trouble even looking at her.

Beth was worrying over the concrete chunk. Farrah had her eyes on the notebook. "Is that that grimoire thing?"

"Yes," said Beth. "I had it in my handbag but then my handbag got torn on some exposed broken pipes while I was leaving the conference room. So I just grabbed the grimoire out of it." She paused, frowned. "Wait. How do you know about the grimoire?"

"Your friend. Kris."

"Oh. Yeah. So you found her, like I told you to? She explained things?"

"Can you use your magic powers to get this block off me?" *Or switch bodies again—it should be* you *stuck under here with these fat hips.*

Beth rocked back on her heels, looking over the concrete chunk, taking in its size and shape. "Maybe," she said. Then, excitedly, "I bet I can do it using my own bio-thaumaturgy, too, without even tapping the grimoire's charge. I mean, *your* own bio-thaumaturgy. Sweetie, I was able to find your body's wells of power, and then to sort of force open a channel—usually it takes months of exercise, but I guess all the stress sort of jumpstarted things.... I only have enough for one more spurt, but with some practice we could really open those channels up.... Oh, honey, wait till you get back in here and start using your own body's magic, you just can't imagine what it's like, how amazing it is. I'd almost forgotten...."

Farrah glared. Not only was her mom happy, she expected Farrah to rejoice with her! Her own mom had violated her body in the most intimate way possible, had basically raped her, and now was acting like it was some Mother-Daughter Day event!

Beth caught her daughter's look. She quieted her enthusiasm. "I think I can get the block off," she said.

But then she couldn't keep the excitement from her voice as she added, "And I do think I can do it with that last spurt of bio-thaumaturgy, without having to use the grimoire's charge."

She got up from her squat, and stepped back carefully across the treacherous floor. After sizing up the block one last time, she closed her eyes and extended her hands toward it.

Farrah watched. Her reflex was to say, *Are you for real?*, to make fun of Mom and of the way she was playing Gandalf. On the other hand, this magic stuff obviously worked. A thought occurred to her: "Are you the one who caused the whole building to cave in?"

Beth's eyes snapped open, her concentration broken. "Yeah," she said. "You have *so much power* inside, Farrah. I was able to throw a warding bubble up around myself, knock out all those other motherfuckers' protection spells, and bring the roof down. Nothing touched me, and they're all dead." Noticing Farrah's expression, she cut short her jubilation. "I didn't know *you* were here! I would have taken some sort of precautions if I'd known that!"

"Whatever. Just, can you get me loose, please?"

Again, Beth closed her eyes, and held her hands out toward the concrete block, palms down. Farrah waited, trying to control her rapid frightened breath. Sirens were seeping down through the wreckage—how long had that been going on? Suddenly Farrah hoped the fire department or cops would hurry up and rescue her first, so that she wouldn't have to owe her goddam body-thief mother anything.

Sweat was popping on her mother's forehead (on *her* forehead). Farrah remembered what her mom had said about not using the power stored in the grimoire, but only the remnants of whatever she'd conjured up from her own body. She said, "Maybe you should use whatever juice is left in the notebook, instead of trying to prove something to somebody."

"Quiet," her mom muttered, without opening her eyes. She was sweating hard now. "Don't distract me."

Farrah shut up and let her mother work.

For what felt like a long time, nothing happened, and Farrah was afraid she was going to be stuck down here; by now the ground level ought to be crawling with emergency response people, and yet the sirens still were only a thin, muffled whine. Presumably her own cries would be equally muffled by the layers of debris, and possibly inaudible until they'd already dug down a ways. Even if they heard her, how long would it take to dig her out?

The block started to tremble.

It vibrated harder and harder—she could feel it buzzing against her side. For an instant it rose a couple centimeters but then collapsed back into place. "Hey," said Farrah, "you're not going to make it worse, are you?"

Beth didn't bother to open her tightly-squeezed eyes; she was slick with sweat now, and her outstretched hands were shaking. "Almost ... tapped out," she gasped. "From when I brought ... the ceiling down." Puffs of cement dust swirled up out of the wreckage, stirred for no clear reason.

Farrah didn't see why her mom didn't use the grimoire. But she kept her mouth shut. She decided to wait until it became indisputably clear that her mom was going to fail, before bullying her into using the notebook.

But her breathing came in quicker and shorter gasps as she realized that, no, that was not a trick of the eyes, the block genuinely was levitating, rising off of her hip. It was floating over her now. Farrah lay there prone, staring at the block, practically hyperventilating, afraid to budge lest she distract her mother, praying her mother would be able to move the thing away before her strength gave out and she dropped it.

Her mom looked like that might happen any second. Sweat dripped from her crimson face, and shivers wracked her body. With her eyes still squeezed shut, she gasped, "Wriggle out! Wriggle out, while I've still got hold of it!"

Jesus, Farrah said to herself, she was so fucking stupid. Why the hell was she lying here waiting for her mom to do everything, especially when the woman looked about ready to faint? Like a clumsy worm she wriggled her way out from under the block.

With great effort she got to her feet, hauling herself up by handholds of jutting debris. Beth still had her eyes squeezed shut; "Are you free?" she cried.

"Yeah," said Farrah.

Beth snapped her eyes open. The block collapsed back into place—it hadn't risen very high, so the bang of its fall was anticlimactic. When Beth let go of the block it was like she let go of herself too—she collapsed back onto her backside.

In a different mood Farrah might have thought about how that must have hurt, and would have asked if her mom was okay. Right now, she only noticed that Beth had put down the grimoire. It rested on a broken block, blurry in the dusty light.

Beth blinked her eyes open, looked around till she found Farrah. With a weak, wavering smile she said, "Good, good, you're all right…. I'm wiped out, but it'll all be rejuvenated soon…. I'm telling you, Farrah, there's amazing potential in this body. You've really never sensed it before?… When this is all over, once we've switched back, you've got to let me help you learn about it…."

She seemed so harmless and trusting; but when Farrah darted for the grimoire, Beth moved so fast to head her off it was almost like Farrah's attempt hadn't even surprised her. Actually, that wasn't true—she went for it a split-second after Farrah did, it was simply that she was in a younger, stronger body, despite all the strain she'd just put on it.

They each held one end of the grimoire.

"Let go," snarled Farrah.

"No," said Beth. "Why? What can you do with it? You haven't had any training! You can't even read the languages these spells are written in, and you wouldn't know what to do with them if you could!"

"So I'll take it to your friend Kris. Maybe she can figure out how to use it to undo what you did."

"Kris doesn't need the grimoire for that!" exclaimed Beth scornfully. She tugged on the notebook, but Farrah wouldn't release it. "Kris knows the spell, and she has her own power, she doesn't need the grimoire's charge. Making the change in the first place would be hard, but switching us *back* wouldn't even require enough power for her to have to break her oath. If she wouldn't change us back, it's because she trusted me to do it, when the time is right! Which is soon, very soon. Now, just let me have the notebook back...."

"No way. I don't trust you to use it to switch me back."

"But I just told you I would. And anyway, it isn't like *you* can do anything with it!"

"Then I just don't want *you* to have it anymore, after what you've done!"

"But this is all I needed your body for! I already explained to you that I...."

Farrah gave the grimoire a great wrench. Beth pulled, too—they both lost their balance and went flying backwards. Farrah made one more snatch at the notebook as it flew out of her hands, but only managed to rip a page from it as her mother fell, still gripping the grimoire. Somehow it slipped through Beth's fingers upon impact and tumbled through the air behind her.

Both women struggled upright, raced over to where it seemed the grimoire ought to have landed. Once there they could only gape at first, without comprehension. Where they had expected to find the grimoire, the black crevasse that had been the stairway opened upon inky depths.

"I think it must have fallen down that hole," said Farrah.

"No!" cried Beth. She couldn't believe it. The thing was gone.

Beth's eyes snapped to the piece of paper in Farrah's hands: all that was left of the grimoire. She lunged for it. But she was exhausted from the strain of levitating the concrete block, and Farrah leaped out of the way and shoved her mother, sending her face-down onto the broken concrete. She felt a resentful, sympathetic shudder, since by rights that was *her* body slapping the floor. But she didn't let that her slow her down as she rushed away, folding up the ripped-out page and shoving it in her pocket without even trying to read its foreign gobbledy-gook.

The remnants of the staircase only descended about four feet down from the ceiling into this chamber—below that point, it had disintegrated. The bottom remaining step was on a level with Farrah's chest. Unsure whether it would support her, Farrah hoisted herself up onto the remnants of the cracked staircase. It would have been pretty hard even in her own body, and was torture in this one. There were worrisome creaks and groans from the broken stairs. Beth started to try to follow her, but over their heads a flashlight beam suddenly cut across the haze, and they heard a strangely thin voice call, "Hello? Anyone down there? Hello!"

There was something weird softening the voice of the cop or fireman or rescue worker or whatever he was. Some sort of magical shit, for all Farrah knew. She had given up labeling things impossible or unnatural.

Hauling herself up onto the broken staircase had nearly taken out of her everything she had left, and she turned to see if her mother was giving chase. But Beth hung back, staring up at her uncertainly, almost fearfully. Maybe partly she wasn't following because moving the block had left her wiped out. But Farrah bet the fear was a visceral reaction to the cops' approach, to the prospect of being found out. What she'd done simply had to be a crime, after all. Perhaps not a crime anyone could ever prosecute or would ever believe in, but all the shame of a terrible crime must still come with it. She didn't want Farrah telling people about it, certainly not right in front of her. And who knew, maybe in her current state of exhaustion and fucked-uppedness, she believed that forcible body-switching was the sort of thing they might take her to jail for.

Farrah turned back to the searching flashlight beam overhead: "Down here! Help, please! Please!"

Below and behind her, her mother hissed. She loped away into the shadows, stepping quickly but gingerly through the broken stones, pipes, and concrete, glaring back at Farrah before turning her eyes forward to pick her way through faster. Farrah bared her teeth, tempted to leap back down, to go after her mother and beat the shit out of her.

But she still felt sick, and her headache was worse than ever. And besides, the grimoire was gone; without that, her mother wasn't shit. So she pointed her face back upward and began clambering up the unstable steps toward the flashlight beam.

Thirteen

Stumbling through the rubble, Beth paused to wonder if maybe she wouldn't be better off going back up into the light and being rescued along with Farrah. She'd been glad to climb up and away from all those crushed corpses, even if she hadn't been able to see them under the blocks and in the gloom—she'd still known they were there. Now she was diving back into them.

But she wanted nothing to do with the rescuers up top. Not that any of them could have connected her with the building's collapse—only another witch or mage would have figured that out, and Beth figured they would have owed her credit for managing to only destroy the one building, killing no one but the assembled mages and the Asian couple working in the fabric store. That couple had worked for Mannis knowingly, so fuck them. Beth had done nothing wrong.

Nothing.

Still, she couldn't go up to the rescuers. Even if no one was going to arrest her, they'd hold her a while, there with Farrah. They'd think Farrah was Beth, so they'd call Tim, and Kris might be with him, and it was hard to guess what she'd do.

Which page had Farrah managed to rip out of the notebook? Goddam that little bitch! What did she need with a piece of the grimoire? She couldn't do anything with it—she'd never paid attention as a kid when Beth had struggled to teach her the basics of magic, she'd just griped and whined and called Beth crazy and now it was too late. All Beth had wanted, now that Mannis was gone, was just another hour or so with the body. Maybe one night. Now that her fear was gone, now that she didn't have the straw party looming over her, all she'd wanted was a little bit of time to relax: to soak in the bubble bath of pain-free youth. And maybe to use the grimoire to cast a couple spells for old times' sake. Out of spite, Farrah had robbed her of that.

Unless of course Beth used the body's own bio-thaumaturgy, which was only accessible at all thanks to her. But now she was tapped out—who knew how long it would take the wells to rejuvenate? With use the time needed would shrink, but right now everything was new and raw.

Anyway, there was definitely an argument to be made that she had a right to keep the body until she could coax enough power out of it for just one joyride, since Farrah had robbed her of the fun night she'd planned on having with the grimoire.

The noise of her own raggedy breathing nearly distracted her from the dry sound of pebbles sliding down a rough concrete surface. What with the echoes, and without any access to magic, she had no idea what direction the sound had come from. Down here there was less light than when she'd found Farrah—the bulbs closest to the origin of her fury had been pulverized.

She told herself it was almost certainly just more of the same constant background noise, sounds of the building settling.

Someone grabbed her from behind and clapped his hand over her mouth. Dolan.

"You ain't gonna scream for those cops if I let you go, are you?" he hissed in her ear.

She shook her head, as much as his tight grip would allow. Once he released her mouth, she tried to turn and face him; he didn't give her enough freedom of movement, though, so she merely whispered into the near-darkness, "You see I'm running *away* from them, don't you?"

"Yeah. I do see that." Now he spun her around, still gripping her tight by the upper arms. "Why, exactly? You got something to hide from them? Like maybe that you was the one to kill Mannis and all the rest?"

Beth looked at Dolan's face. In the dimness it took her a second to be sure, but his eyes were red and wet. For Mannis?

You'd almost think the guy had been his friend, or uncle, or dad, and not an effeminate, white quasi-gangster warlock employer that Dolan could not have had much in common with. "How do you figure I did that?" demanded Beth. "Do I look strong enough to tear the whole building down?"

Dolan twisted the flesh of her arms in a way that had made her whimper plenty of times in the past—she wasn't going to do that in this body, though. "Don't you play fucking *stupid*. You think I forgot you were bringing him a grimoire? This is all magic shit, and you were walking around with magic shit and bringing magic shit to him, right where he got killed."

"Why would I kill him if I wanted him to buy the fucking thing?…"

He did that thing to her arms again. She still didn't cry out, but it was harder this time. "Quit *playing*! Someone killed my boss, and you are looking mighty fucking suspicious to me right now. You walk in with that grimoire. While you're down there your dumb-ass mom shows up, just like we *ain't* gonna fuck her up the next time we see her. And in the middle of all that the building falls apart thanks to some kind of magical terrorist attack. Now, you better give me a name for the person who did this, otherwise I'm gonna pick the one that's right in front of me."

So he knew that Farrah had been here. That eliminated any need to hide the fact. Maybe it served her right to have Dolan after her, the ungrateful bitch. She laughed, and squirmed her body against his.

"What the fuck're you doing?" he demanded. When she continued to writhe, he added, "You really think that's going to help you?"

"I don't care," she said, grinning. "Look in my eyes and see for yourself."

He did look into her eyes. And maybe she really didn't care, because she could tell that whatever he saw in there made him believe her.

"You don't care, huh," he said. "You ought to care."

He didn't stop her from slowly grinding her hips against his. She felt him getting hard—fucking animal. "Why should I? It sounds like I'm going to die soon. That makes me horny."

"Why would that make you horny?"

"Because I haven't been fucked in a long, long while, and I swore to myself I'd get laid at least one last time before I die. So if you're about to kill me, this must be it."

He looked at her with lust. It didn't stop him from wrapping one arm around her to hold her in place while he raised his free hand to her throat. "Tell me something or I'll kill you," he said.

"It was Beth," she said. "It was my mom."

"Beth?"

"You guys were going to kill her, right? So it was y'all or her. She must have rigged up a snare spell in the grimoire. Something that would blow after it came into contact with Mannis." The hand on her throat started to tighten. *"I didn't know,"* she said. "I wasn't part of the plan. If I had been I wouldn't have been standing next to them when it went off."

"Then how come it didn't kill you along with them?"

"I have no idea yet. But Beth could have worked something into the grimoire where no magic it produced would hurt her, or her flesh and blood." It was impossible to work any such thing into a grimoire's charge; she waited to see if Dolan knew that.

He didn't seem to. But he stayed suspicious: "How come she showed up, then? If she knew a bomb was going to go off?"

Beth laughed. "For me, silly! You know how moms are! She came because she figured out I had the grimoire and that I'd brought it here, and she came running to stop me before I hurt myself." She laughed again, a little manically.

Dolan stared at her, trying to work it out. "She didn't know you were bringing it."

"Of course she didn't know, I fucking stole it from her."

"Why?"

"To come and sell it to Mannis! Just like I said!"

"Hey, keep it down, the cops...."

"I stole the thing from her, but that fat cow had to come running after me so she could rescue her sweet little baby. She knows better, she knows I could give a shit about her, but with mothers, you know, it's a compulsion. They scrounge at love like an addict begging a pimp to give her a fix out of the goodness of his heart. They're fucking pathetic but at least you can do anything you want with them."

He shook her. "Okay, okay, you don't have to be a fucking poet about it." He scrutinized her face. "I can't tell if you're full of shit or not."

"Make up your mind and then either kill me or help me get out of here."

"I don't know. Why should I keep you around?"

"That's not my problem, man, don't ask me. Just make up your own mind like a grown-up."

He shook his head, and said, "All right. I don't know why, though. I'd be safer killing you."

"You'd've been safer working at McDonald's like a good boy."

With Dolan in the lead, they picked their way through the ruins. It wasn't like they could just go back upstairs to the rescuers. The authorities were going to figure out pretty quick that this building went much deeper underground than it was supposed to, and they were going to be thoroughly questioning anyone who came up from its depths. Especially if they found that wealth of corpses from the party.

This underground lair was bigger than Beth had ever dreamed. She doubted Mannis himself had been responsible for building it—he must have inherited it from one of his betters. At the end of the day Mannis had never been much more than a flunky, and it was a little sad how badly he'd terrified her. She knew there would be no point asking Dolan about the history of this structure. If Mannis was small, Dolan was nothing, the flunky of a flunky. Not bad to look at, though, as she followed him through the silvery haze of the emergency bulbs.

I own him now, she gloated. *I know more, and I have more power; or I will in a few days, once the wells in this body are primed. And he won't get rid of me before then. Because I'm so beautiful now.*

The sounds of their would-be rescuers grew louder and more distinct: the echoes of their footfalls, their urgent pleas for any survivors to cry out. Dolan thought that was because they were getting closer, but Beth explained that it was because the warding and dissimulation spells were dissipating. None of the mages had bothered to invest enough energy in their wards for them to long outlast the spellcasters' deaths.

They went through a door hidden in the wall, then another, then another. Then they were walking through a corridor with pipes running overhead and dingy gray walls, that Beth was willing to bet did appear on some blueprint on file somewhere, did have some official existence. The hall led to an ordinary, battered door leading to an ordinary filthy staircase; they took it up one flight to ground level and exited into the blue-gray gloomy lobby of some anonymous building housing offices and rehearsal spaces and whatnot. Slumped behind a plastic-and-metal desk near the windowed front door was a fat, tired security guard, staring into space and oblivious to all.

Dolan said, "All right, see you," and started for the front door.

Beth grabbed him, pulled him back and pushed him against the wall, pressed herself against him. The security guard looked over with a flicker of interest.

Dolan laughed. She wasn't strong enough to push him against the wall if he hadn't wanted to let her, but she still felt like the stronger one because she had known that he would indeed want to let her. "I don't think you want to get rid of me that fast," she murmured.

He put his hands on her hips. "Yeah? And why's that?"

"Because with me you get all the things you want. You get back in the game. And if you want revenge for your boss, I can help you get that too."

She watched his eyes as she said that last bit; shit, he *did* want to avenge Mannis. Whoda thunk it?

But he only pressed his hands tighter into her hips. Almost tight enough to hurt, but she didn't mind. "There's something else I want to get in, first," he said.

"Unh-uh," she scolded. "Not yet. And only ever on one condition."

"What's the condition?" he asked.

She told him, moving in close and putting her mouth to his ear so no one else could hear.

After she'd spoken and moved her head back, he sized her up all over again.

"Whoa," he said, not unappreciatively.

Fourteen

Before the knock came on her door, Kris already knew to expect the witch. Not because she'd predicted it with her magic powers; just out of common sense.

She was fully dressed except for her socks and shoes and was lying in bed, head propped up on pillows as she played video games on her iPhone. "It's open," she called. Meaning there was no locking spell, of course, since the door's physical lock locked automatically when one closed it. But for people like her visitor, mere mundane locks were no barrier.

The witch stepped in, closing the door behind her. Kris rolled out of bed and stood up, showing the respect due to an equal. And possibly more than an equal. The witch didn't look like much; five years or so older than Kris, a frumpy short chubby woman with a pug nose, graying frizzy hair, and a baggy dress. But Kris knew she was from the compound she'd sensed from the Greyhound, the compound which drew power from the Stone of Pellerian. That compound didn't let just anyone in.

"Kris Bouts," the woman said.

"Yeah. That's me."

The visitor's eyes marked out the iPhone still in Kris's hand. "Did your coven send you all the way to Brooklyn from Hungary so you could play video games?"

"I'm sorry, remind me of your name again?" Kris tossed the phone onto the mattress. "There's a lot going on and I was trying to take my mind off stuff. Shall we sit down?"

"Whatever you prefer."

There was a rock-hard loveseat in front of the window, and scrunched into the corner next to it was a particle-board desk that for some reason had been painted blue, and a chair. Kris gave her visitor the loveseat, and turned the desk chair around to face her. The visitor watched impassively.

Kris sat in the chair, her bare left foot up on the seat and her arms wrapped around her left knee. Once more she took stock of the upstate witch. Her skin looked like a dirty peach snow cone, sprinkled with droplets of cherry. Kris knew the frumpy, baggy dress was probably less a fashion choice than a requirement of her Order not to wear constrictive clothing; up at the compound they probably wore robes. If there were men in her Order they probably had to wear kilts or something when they came to town.

"So," Kris said, once it was clear that her guest didn't plan to kick things off. "I suppose I can guess why you're here."

"You've created quite a mess, here in our backyard."

Briefly Kris was tempted to weasel out of the blame. But the only person she could have foisted it off on would be Beth. "I know. I'm sorry."

"Killing Mannis and his unsavory masters isn't worth many tears. But you nearly brought down a city block in midtown Manhattan...."

"*I* didn't," Kris began involuntarily, then bared her teeth as she realized she'd lapsed into blaming Beth after all.

"Your friend did," said the visitor.

"And what did she stop, by bringing it down? Unless I'm mistaken, there was a straw party going on." And Lefebre had been at that party. (She'd learned this via the mysterious, mystical tendrils that carry such news automatically through the Silent Society.) That *really* burned her up. If she'd known Black-Book villains were going to be present, her Oath of Constraint wouldn't have mattered—she'd have been *obligated* to go knock his soul out of the Tapestry and into the Black Ice. And she would have damn well enjoyed it, too.

"Like I said, nobody is shedding tears for Mannis. If someone had wanted to launch a rational attack against him, no reasonable witch, mage, or warlock who serves the Light would have objected. But the public destruction of the building is a concern. The authorities cannot possibly rest until they find a reason why that building collapsed. They'll excavate, and when they do they'll find dozens of corpses. Many of those corpses will be unidentifiable, because no official record was ever made of their birth; others will be foreigners whose entry into the country left no paper trail. Most baffling of all will be that warren of subterranean chambers, for whose construction no official history exists. Questions will be raised that will not go away for decades."

The prospect of this conversation was what had driven Kris to distract herself with mindless video games. "Everything you say is true. Mistakes were made, the worst by me. But with all due respect, this kind of thing has happened before."

"It has. And sometimes it's happened with grievous consequences. But leave that aside for now—it's probably true that we can trust in the modern world's disbelief to allow us to remain hidden in plain sight. Any evidence they find of the truth, they will automatically discount. But a potent grimoire is loose."

"No it isn't," said Kris, with a grimace. "It's gone." Kris had gotten the story from Farrah, over the phone. Freshly released by the rescue workers and back at her uncle's apartment, she'd managed to explain what had happened, just barely. And oh, how she'd railed and shouted when Kris had still declined to switch the bodies back.

They'd all bought Kris's impassivity: Tim, Ann, Farrah. That's what had pissed Farrah off so bad, was that apparently Kris felt what Beth had done was just a matter of course. It wasn't, though. Kris had simply done a good job of hiding her shock.

What the fuck were you thinking, Beth? she thought again, now. And, again: *Oh, well—shit'll all shake out according to the Warp and Weft of Destiny.*

The look her visitor was giving her grew even less pleasant. "So. The grimoire is out of your possession. Could it possibly still carry any charge?"

"I can't imagine it does—Beth must have squeezed every last ounce from it. Anyway, it fell down a deep hole in the ground. By the time anyone finds it the charge should have dissipated. And the odds of it being found by anyone who knows how to use it are pretty low."

"It must have had a hell of a charge to begin with, for Ms. Weaver to have been able to take mages of that caliber by surprise."

"Not really—only about two thousand vrools." Kris bit the insides of her mouth to keep it from twisting into a proud smirk at the Westchester witch's flurry of blinks. Yes, Beth had fucked up, no doubt about it. But at least she had fucked up like a true bad-ass.

Frumpy, though, seemed to think the feat passed beyond the impressive and into the realms of the impossible. "With two thousand vrools, there's no way she could have done this."

"She must have used the mages' black magic against them. In some sort of judo-move; something like the pahn'gull, for example. They wouldn't have expected that, they thought they were dealing with a novice." Kris couldn't help but add, "Still, it must have taken an unbelievable level of skill."

But Frumpy shook her head, still not buying it. "Such a use of dark magic ought to have left a very specific sort of trace, and we've sensed nothing like that. Are you sure that body has no access to any of its bio-thaumaturgy?"

"Absolutely certain. I've met the daughter. She's not an initiate."

Frumpy sighed and shook her head. She changed the subject, giving Kris a funny, careful look: "And what about you? Does your Oath of Constraint allow you enough use of your own bio-thaumaturgy that you could use it to restore each player's body to her rightful self, without breaking your word?"

"Yeah. I could, if I'm careful and economical." Switching them back would require far less power than the initial trick had—it was easier to restore the natural order than to wrench it out of whack. And even if Farrah's body turned out to have its own bio-thaumaturgical wells, they couldn't have had time to open yet, meaning Beth wouldn't be able to resist her. Kris cleared her throat, lowered her left foot to the floor and brought her right one up, wrapped her arms around that knee instead. Here came the hard part. "I'm not actually willing to do that yet, though," she said. "I trust that Beth will get in touch with me when the time comes. If she hasn't yet, that's because she still needs the body. For what I trust are reasons of life or death."

Her visitor regarded Kris speculatively. "I see," she finally said. "And yet Mannis, the man who directly threatened her, is dead."

"I assume so. Maybe she's still got to take care of some of his cronies."

"We had a report that she seems fairly cozy with one of those cronies. Someone named Dolan."

Kris didn't respond to that. It seemed weird; she would need to hear from Beth before deciding what she thought of it.

Her guest waited. When Kris didn't volunteer anything she went on: "When you say that Beth needs the body a bit longer, do you mean that she needs it in order to avoid being killed by someone? Or do you mean that she needs it for some psychological reason, and that it's a matter of life and death because you're afraid she may become suicidal?"

Kris smirked, as if that were a ridiculous notion. She didn't answer, though.

"You feel very loyal to your friend. Don't you?"

"More so than to anyone else. I owe her everything."

"I understood it was your friend's mother who raised you. Isn't she the one you owe?"

"I guess I don't really see the difference."

"Mm. Yes, I can understand that," the witch said. "We can't always choose our obligations."

Anger Kris had thought she'd stifled came steaming out. "Yeah, well, except sometimes we do, right? The cleansers at that Ithaca coven failed, but I bet you guys at the compound have plenty of power to fix the damage to Beth, and restore her. But you can't be bothered to take charity cases."

The other witch raised an eyebrow. "Do you really think it would be so easy for us to throw aside our other duties and become a Betty Ford clinic? And if we did, do you really think your friend would be so easy to patch up? Beth's powers are cut off from her forever. The channels that give access to her stores of bio-thaumaturgy are hopelessly scarred over. And that damage was self-inflicted...."

"All right." Kris knew perfectly well that the compound existed for reasons of vast cosmic import, that its residents' outward lives of meditation and repose were overshadowed by their immense tasks of caretaking on the mystical plane. Kris had not been initiated into the specifics of their mysteries—she could not have said which foes they fought, or exactly which manifestations of entropy they strove to arrest and reverse—but, again, she could taste the flavor of their power, and she knew to what sorts of uses it was put, the uses to which its very nature dictated it be put. Suggesting that they were all sitting around up there on their cushy asses, or that their time would be better spent chasing around minor mystical gangsters, was ignoble and false. Yet she couldn't shed her belligerence completely, not with Beth's life at stake. "So she's not perfect, big deal. Am I? Are you?"

Her guest shook her head. "This is exactly what we feared," she said. "You're taking this very personally, Ms. Bouts. Because you love Beth, and because you're loyal, which is to your credit. But your judgment is clouded."

"I don't think it is. But I guess the catch is that I wouldn't know, would I?"

"How well do you know her anymore? Weren't you separated and taken abroad at fifteen?"

"Not by my choice," snapped Kris.

"Your friend is an emotionally damaged woman, Ms. Bouts."

"Who wouldn't be a little damaged after all she's been through?"

"I'm not trying to pass moral judgment on her. What concerns me is that you let an emotionally unstable, frail, desperate woman steal a powerful grimoire—or else you simply gave it to her—and now that she's wreaking havoc you plan to do nothing. Even though it seems you could put her back in her own body, without breaking your oath. What are you planning on? Are you going to wait and give her time to open the channels of her host body? That could take weeks—what will her poor daughter do in the meantime? What will your friend be capable of after she has access to that power? And why would she ever willingly switch the bodies back, after she does? If she does, how will the daughter adjust to her sudden access to power?"

The insinuation that Beth would keep the body forever made Kris so angry that she didn't trust herself to reply.

Frumpy's eyes were not cruel, but they were pitiless. "You came out here to rescue your friend. Over the last few years, you've had the growing sense that something had gone wrong with her. But you were busy—you were a soldier. Now there's a fragile peace and you finally have the influence and the elbow room to do her some good. But you misjudged her. You wanted to restore her dignity. Fine. You figured helping her rediscover a sense of agency would do the trick. Fine. But your method of restoring that agency was to hand a great deal of power over to a desperate woman, who'd been corrupted by fear, suffering, and shame."

Kris's mouth muscles bunched up in resentment. She looked down at her foot, and finally said, "I know what it looks like," in a slow, self-consciously calm voice. "I know that any sane outside observer would see things your way. All I can offer against that is my personal knowledge of and faith in my friend."

"Knowledge proves false every day, and so do friends. Meanwhile, we at the compound mustn't be called upon to interfere. Violent action would disrupt our channels of flow and interfere with the work we do, and that work is very important."

"Just tell me what it is you're asking."

"If it doesn't turn out like you think it will—if your friend won't come to heel, won't return the body, continues to create chaos—then we need your word that you'll take care of it. No matter what."

"Well, you're in luck. That's a promise I don't mind making, because I know you'll never get a chance to call it in."

"Good. Believe me, we want nothing more than for you to be right.... We've heard a lot about you, you know. Under different circumstances we would have enjoyed getting acquainted with you better."

Silly as it was, that bit of praise cheered Kris.

"You know," continued the other witch, "it's a serious concern that your friend might be opening the bio-thaumaturgical wells in that body. If the daughter returns to a body with open wells, that she herself has not opened through a process of training, she'll have no control over them. If she's even mildly powerful, that'll make her dangerous."

"It won't come to that." Kris was sure that Beth merely wanted some time to enjoy living in young flesh again. A day or two. After all, Beth certainly knew the unsavory things that some might think it necessary to do to Farrah, if she were suddenly plopped into a powerful witch's body. But such a process would take weeks.

Her guest nodded. "Let's hope not," she said. "But just know—we've taken an interest."

The woman abruptly stood to leave. Kris accompanied her to the door and closed it behind her.

In the privacy of her isolation, she admitted that Beth really had put her in a jam.

Once more she lay on her back on top of the bedcovers. This time she wasn't playing video games; the phone rested beside her, forgotten, as she let today's problems percolate through her mind, waiting to see if any good ideas would present themselves. The phone rang. She reached for it—could be Tim or Ann, reporting some new development. "Hello?"

"Hey, Kris," said Beth. Even through Farrah's throat, Kris could distinguish Beth's cadence, her spirit.

Kris felt her insides flash-freeze. For an instant she couldn't even breathe. For decades she had longed to hear Beth's voice, but had refrained because to use a telephone to remotely have an important conversation with an important person was an impious act. That was why she'd had to come all the way here from Hungary. What did it mean that Beth would casually ring her up? Was she not important to Beth in the same way Beth was to her?

But a quick call to set up a meeting was different, she reminded herself. Lots of good people thought so, anyway. "Hey Beth," she said. Regardless of whose fault this situation was, Kris resolved to continue being there for Beth.

"You mad at me?" said Beth. She didn't seem to realize the reason for the tightness of Kris's voice was the impiety of this call.

"Worried, mainly."

"I'd like to talk," said Beth. "But just you. No other witches or mages. Not my brother." Her voice got harder as she said, "Not Farrah."

Kris could think of few things she wanted less than to host Beth's and Farrah's reunion. She agreed to the conditions and asked where they should meet.

Fifteen

Kris sat in a booth at the Kellogg Diner in Williamsburg, waiting. The decor inside and out was a self-consciously retro, garish jumble, glittery red barstools against blue walls, a gleaming but non-functioning jukebox, and so on. Kris gazed out the window at the passing hipsters.

Ideally, Beth would approach without Kris noticing—she would just turn her head, and there her friend would be. Kris wouldn't have to watch her approach, all the while wondering what expression to put on, whether she ought to force a smile that she didn't quite feel, or force a disapproval that she couldn't quite muster; whether she ought to get up and embrace her, or whether she should be cool.

Only after she'd already sat down had it occurred to her to wonder what she'd do if Beth wasn't willing to turn over the body—she assumed discussing that was the whole point of this meeting. Now that the grimoire was gone, Beth would need help to make the switch. She would wait and let Beth bring it up, though. She'd leave her that much dignity.

She did see Beth's approach, as it turned out. Saw her climb the steps out of the subway and head directly for the diner. Kris noted the way guys followed Beth with their eyes as she crossed the street—it seemed like Beth didn't even notice, and Kris would have liked to point it out to her.

But the action of Beth's own eyes were nothing to be proud of; Kris felt ashamed of the way her heart sank at Beth's suspicious glances as she scurried across the street. Like a guilty criminal. It came back to her, the way Beth had talked at their one dinner: *Was I some kind of soldier?*, she'd asked. No, she sure wasn't.

Beth entered the diner, looked around, and spotted Kris. Kris felt the urge to grin, but she restrained it because of the gravity of the situation. She couldn't help but stand, though. They hugged each other a long moment, then slid into the booth. They ordered waters and coffees, more to get rid of the waitress than because they really wanted anything.

Kris could see plain as day that it was Beth in that body.

"You have a pretty daughter, I see."

"She came out all right, considering what a craggy old hag she sprang from."

"Don't say that. Stop talking like that."

"Okay."

That exchange pulled them out of the emotion of seeing each other again. Beth said, "Are you pissed off at me?"

"For what?" asked Kris, reflexively. Only after the words had left her mouth did she remember that by most reckonings she had lots of reasons to be mad.

"For stealing your grimoire," said Beth, a little disbelievingly.

"Not to downplay your thieving skills, but we both know I let you have the grimoire."

"Yeah," grinned Beth. "I was just trying to give you some deniability."

Kris smiled too, but tightly. Now Beth seemed to be taking too much for granted. "Of course, I didn't know that you were going to use it to switch bodies with your daughter. When you nabbed the grimoire, there was enough of a charge in it that you could have killed Mannis from a distance. From across the street, certainly; maybe from further. Once you'd done the switch, though, it was so depleted that you had to actually get in close. Pretty dangerous, Beth."

"It worked out, though."

At each flippant word from Beth a chasm opened wider in Kris's heart, and she knew if she dared peer down into it she would see despair. "It worked out in the bare sense that you're alive and Mannis is dead," she said. "But there are a lot of people pissed off, Beth. Not to mention the risk you took. Not only for yourself. What would your daughter have done, if this body had gotten killed?"

At the mention of her daughter, Beth's face closed like a drawbridge. Kris reached across the table and took Beth's hand; Beth allowed it, but grudgingly. "I'm just saying, Beth. You know you're still the only person in all this that I really care about."

"No, no, you're right. What human being should have to be stuck in a creaking oozing hulk like mine?"

Kris made herself give the hand a squeeze. "What are you planning, Beth?"

The closed doors of Beth's face cracked open, but only to show the uncertainty within. "I'm going to give it back," she started by reassuring Kris.

Of course you are, sweetie, thought Kris. *Does that seriously need to be said?*

But Beth continued: "I'm going to give it back, but I just need it for another day or so. Just long enough to be a hundred percent sure of Mannis."

"I thought Mannis was already dead," said Kris, startled. If it had been anyone but Beth, she would have suspected bullshit.

"Maybe he is. But he could have managed to get away during the explosion. And you wouldn't necessarily be able to feel his presence, even if you were looking. There *are* such things as muffling spells and hiding charms, you know."

"Yeah. I know. This is me, remember? But even the upstaters seem to think he's dead. The Pellerian Compound folks. And they have some powerful mojo working for them."

"Well, so maybe they're right. Hopefully they are. All I'm saying is that I want to take the time to be sure, really sure."

Kris watched her. "What are you planning?" she asked. "Even if Mannis *is* still out there, there's nothing you can do about it."

"I can handle him."

That was insane. With the grimoire gone, Beth would have no means of fighting a mage, unless she could somehow manage to take him by surprise with a gunshot, or a bonk on the head.

"If Mannis is still out there then it sounds like maybe you *can't* handle him."

"There were lots of other guys there. It was complicated."

Kris was shocked to realize that Beth was offended. Two days ago she'd been panhandling, her powers permanently lost—now she was getting prickly because Kris had called her sorcerous abilities into question. "I know it was complicated," she said. "That's kind of my point. What you did should have been impossible. That you did it at all is amazing. It's no surprise that you used up the full charge of the grimoire, during the attack." She dropped her eyes to the tabletop. "And now you don't even have the grimoire anymore, Beth. So what are you going to do?"

Beth's face was stricken. "You know about me losing the grimoire." Her mouth worked anxiously. She was afraid Kris would be mad at her, Kris realized. "It was when my kid and I were fighting over it," she confessed.

Kris didn't give a shit about the grimoire. Most of the knowledge it contained would be recoverable once she got back to Hungary, albeit with some trouble. She looked out the window and watched the street traffic. The grimoire still might have contained a little power, possibly enough for Beth to switch back bodies with her daughter, without assistance from Kris. But with it gone....

Kris turned sharply back to Beth. "*Are* the bio-thaumaturgical wells in that body already opening up? Are you managing to do that? Is that how you were able to take out all those mages? It wasn't just a matter of shepherding the grimoire's charge, or even using some spiritual judo—you had your own bio-thaumaturgy to draw on."

Beth looked away.

The possibility dazzled Kris. She drew her hand away, falling back against her bench in shock. Such a process generally took months of training. Of course, dropping an already-trained mind into a high-potential body would speed things up … but for it to be sped up to this degree, you would need an extraordinarily great potential, and an unheard-of skill level.

Well, why shouldn't one expect Beth's child to have extraordinary bio-thaumaturgical potential? And as for the skill level—it was true, Beth could have been one of the greats.

"Answer me, Beth."

Beth shrugged, and assumed a defiant air.

Kris fumbled for words. "What about Farrah?" she said. "What will she do? She'll come back to a body streaming with power, with no idea how to handle it."

"The channels won't be *fully* opened by the time I give it back...."

"If it's enough power to take out someone like Mannis, not to mention whoever else was there, it's more than a girl like Farrah will be able to handle. *Way* more."

"But I'll be here!" Now it was Beth who reached across the table, to take Kris's hands. "I'll be here, to train her. To show her the way."

Kris remembered all she'd heard Beth and Farrah say, the way they talked about each other. Almost unwillingly, she said, "But will your daughter listen to you, Beth? I don't want to seem … I mean, it just seems like the two of you...."

"Yeah, I know. But that's my point, don't you see? She'll … she'll need me now, and this time I'll take care of her, and it'll be a new beginning for us."

Tears stung at Kris's eyes, and she had a sick feeling. "That seems like a bad way to win your daughter back, Beth."

"It's not my *plan*. But if it just works out that way … well, you know?..."

Kris tried not to squeeze Beth's fingers too hard, but she couldn't help it. She looked down at the young-girl's fingers: so different from what she'd expected. Yet not so different from the ones she *remembered*, from so long ago.

"Listen," said Kris. "There can't be much power available yet. Your wells—your daughter's wells haven't had time to open. If you use what power you have to effect the switch back, then the body will be so thaumaturgically drained when Farrah re-enters it that someone will be able to safely take her in hand. Cast a binding spell on her, till she's trained. But if you wait till the channels are completely open, then there won't be any way to avoid dropping her into a fully-functioning witch's body, with no training. She'll be a threat, Beth, and people will feel they have to neutralize her."

"I'm not going to let that happen. Seriously, Kris—I'm not gonna let it go that long. Just a day or two. Just give me a little bit of space for that long."

"You know, a lot of people would say that what I should do is just force the switch back now, while I've got you in my sight." The muscles in Beth's face went crisp, and Kris felt her own heart crackle in sympathy. "But I won't do that to you. I can't."

Kris looked away from Beth. Set her eyes on the tabletop. A stone swelled in her throat. "It would mean you couldn't go with me to Hungary," she said.

Beth's face melted a bit—but, though Kris told herself it was only her imagination, she thought she saw behind Beth's expression a certain triumph. As if she knew now that she had Kris where she needed her.

"Maybe not right now," said Beth. "But someday soon, if you still want me. After I finish helping Farrah."

"I mean you could *never* go." The truth was that the coven wouldn't want her around, on account of what she'd done *already*. Uncertainty and dread churned within Kris. "Seriously, Beth. If you do this to the body, and then drop Farrah into it unprepared, she could be really fucked."

Now it was Beth who squeezed her hand. "Of course I'm not going to leave Farrah in the lurch that way. She's my daughter, right? Aren't I her mother? I know I fucked up. But give me just a little credit."

Kris gave Beth a careful look, and finally returned the pressure on her hand. She couldn't imagine any mother doing anything that horrible to her own daughter, not *really*.

Sixteen

Farrah was out hunting—alone, since no one would go with her. When she left Tim's and Ann's apartment it was almost midnight, hours after Kris and Beth met at the diner. While Kris had been meeting with the witch and then with her mother, she'd been asleep, zonked out, finally succumbing to the strain of recent events.

Even though she knew it was a stupid wild-goose chase for her to be out hunting her mother, even though she had no leads or resources or clues or anything, she couldn't help it. Even yesterday, before she'd passed out, she'd been gung-ho to go looking for her.

After the cops had released her, shortly after dawn, she'd taken a taxi back to Tim's and Ann's (Tim had come outside to pay the fare). Upstairs Farrah had told Ann and Tim roughly what had happened. But she left out the fact that she'd torn a page from the grimoire and had it folded up in her pocket. It probably wouldn't matter, but maybe it would, and she no longer trusted anyone enough to share secrets with them.

Tim felt the only responsible thing to do would be to call the police and tell them that Beth was still in the wreckage—they could call her Farrah, if they wanted to. Farrah tried to persuade him otherwise. After quietly listening to their back-and-forth, Ann finally interrupted to say, "Maybe you should call that Kris person and ask her advice."

Farrah and Tim both stared at her. "I thought you didn't believe in that magic stuff?" said Farrah.

"The woman did levitate me. Either way, I'm interested in what she would have to say."

When they called Kris, the conversation drove Farrah into a frenzy. "What do you mean you don't think we should try to stop her?!" she shouted into the phone.

"Now, Farrah, let's try to be a little calmer," said Tim. He was happy because Kris had agreed with Farrah that Beth had probably found some alternate route out of the wreckage.

Farrah had kept shouting. Once she realized that no one was going to help her find her mother and force her to undo her crime, Farrah's focus narrowed down to saying something that would make Kris angry. But the other woman wouldn't give her the satisfaction, calmly responding whenever Farrah asked a direct question and otherwise saying nothing, till at last Tim pried the phone from her fingers, told Kris he'd be in touch later, and hung up.

When Farrah recounted what had happened, she didn't mention any of the crazy shit her mom had said about her bio-thaumaturgy or whatever. Nor did she tell Kris how her mom had levitated the concrete block. She was concentrating too hard on demanding Kris take action to bother with excess details; and maybe she also didn't like to admit to having needed help from her bitch of a mother. Besides, her little trickle of information was the only thing she had control of, and she didn't like to give it up. If Kris had known about that stuff, her conversation with Beth at the diner a few hours later might have gone differently.

Farrah had wanted to leave the apartment, but Tim and Ann blocked the door, begging her to stay and rest. When her legs gave out and she collapsed onto her knees, it became a moot point; she'd had an eventful, stressful day of trying to maneuver around in an unfamiliar body while suffering the worst hangover of her life as she was taken prisoner and a building fell on her. She needed sleep. Tim and Ann carried her to their bed, and she passed out before they finished tucking her in.

She slept through the whole day and much of the evening. When she woke up, over the protests of Tim and Ann, she'd left the apartment. If no one would help her find Beth then she would just do it herself.

And now she was wandering around Brooklyn.

Clouds that looked like gray rippled tin ridged the sky. People were out, people her own rightful age, celebrating the night as if it were their duty. They all seemed gripped by a frantic fatigue, their smiles painful twists they'd pinched into their faces to keep themselves awake. For her first hour outside Farrah had shied away from the eyes of passersby; now, though, she felt like grabbing one and shaking him. She would walk toward an oncoming group so that they would have to duck out of the way, and the glances they tossed at her as they did so, of distaste and annoyance, were gratifying. Always she had hated it when guys looked at her—even when it had been a guy she'd thought was cute and that she'd wanted to attract, she couldn't help but assume he was judging her fat thighs and flat chest, her chunky arms, her limp hair, her clumsy makeup, her ugly shirt, her bloated ass.

But that discomfort was nothing compared to this torment of not being looked at, at all. Farrah had walked out of Uncle Tim's and Aunt Ann's apartment keenly aware of how *wrong* this body was, and she'd expected people to gawk at her accordingly. But they didn't notice her. She was edited out of their gaze. It was like she was the fucking Ghost of Christmas Never, and she felt she might do something drastic, just to attract some interest, to feel like she was at least permanent and solid enough for light to bounce off of.

Had it been like this yesterday, on the way to midtown, and then after the building had fallen in on itself? On the way to that crazy fabric store she'd been too freaked out to pay any attention to how people looked at her, too busy avoiding their eyes. And to the firemen who helped her out and the police who listened to her bullshit account of the building's collapse (telling the truth would have only wasted time), she'd been a source of information, ergo worthy of notice.

But to these people out here on the street she had zero sexual or utilitarian value. Attention was a resource, and giving her some would not have been cost-effective.

145

Whatever. She'd get her body back, and never call it ugly again.

Farrah had been out walking for hours, and her feet and legs hurt. You would think her mother's body would be used to endlessly roaming the streets, but any extra walking endurance it had developed must have been counteracted by its generally shitty condition.

Her knees had developed a sharp new pain, a tickling twinge that warned of worse things to come every time she took a step. Although it bothered her more and more the longer she walked, Farrah reminded herself that once she got her mom stuffed back into this body, it would be *her* pain.

She was wandering aimlessly through the Williamsburg area where she'd woken up in this body, countering the obvious futility of her hunt with the compulsion to do *something*, and the hope that maybe this was a regular haunt of her mother's. This neighborhood was where she'd cast the body-switching spell, at least, since the body had still been here when Farrah woke up in it. Then again, this was *Farrah's* neighborhood, and she never saw Beth around here.

This body's vision was so blurry that even if she did happen upon Mom, she might not recognize her if she were, say, twenty yards away. Deflated, exhausted, she sat on the sidewalk, her back against the wall of a shuttered comic book store. She was in this homeless body now, may as well sit around on the streets the way homeless people did. Farrah leaned forward, her hand over her eyes. *If Mom's eyes are bad, why the hell hasn't she ever gotten glasses?*

A car honked. Farrah ignored it. Then she heard someone shout, "Yo, Beth!" and she looked around quickly to see if her mother was the Beth they were talking to. Wait, no, duh, it would be her they were talking to, whoever they were. Her eyes lit upon the car idling at the curb, a black Lexus; its driver was leaning all the way across the front seat, grinning at her out his passenger's-side window. A black guy in a red tracksuit. The same black guy who'd grabbed her in the fabric store and herded her down the stairs, before the building had collapsed.

She didn't rush over to say hello. He honked again. "You gonna sit there staring at me all day or you gonna come over and give me a kiss?"

"I'm not going to kiss you," she called across the sidewalk. There were people walking by; surely this weird verbal exchange would arouse someone's curiosity. They kept going their oblivious way, though.

The guy laughed. "Man, get in the car, Beth," he said. "Your daughter wants to talk to you."

"That's not my daughter," snapped Farrah.

"So what? I don't care. You know who I'm talking about, don't you?" Instead of answering Farrah only continued to glare at him. "Whatever," he went on. "She told me to drive around looking for you and if I found you to say come with me if you want to see her."

"'Drive around looking for me'? What, you mean all over New York?"

"Nah. Just around this neighborhood. She said you'd probably be out looking for her, hoping you'd bump into her somewhere near 'where you woke up.' I don't know what the fuck that means, but it's what she said."

Farrah was livid. The very thing that she'd been trying to do, that Uncle Tits and Aunt Ass had thought was so stupid and that she herself had had to admit was stupid, was how her mom had found her! She didn't know shit about how to find her mom, yet Beth could see through her like water!

"You getting in the car or not?" the guy demanded. He popped the second half of a candy bar into his mouth and seemed to swallow it without chewing.

"Why should I trust you?" Passersby kept walking between them, ignoring the dialogue.

"Bitch, I don't care if you trust me or not. Your kid said you'd probably be out here looking for her. Here you are. You want to find her, hop in. You don't, fine, I don't give a fuck."

It would be stupid to get in the car, possibly suicidal. But she felt compelled to face her mother, and she had no way to

147

find her. Her only idea for tracking her down was to aimlessly wander around this random neighborhood. And the fact that her mother had used the exact same retarded strategy on her, with perfect success, was a slap in the face but also a challenge that Farrah would have felt like a chickenshit for ignoring.

She got to her feet and walked to the car. The guy smirked, as if he'd known she would relent yet still couldn't believe it. He rolled a toothpick from one corner of his mouth to the other. It glinted, like metal.

"If I get in this car with you, you'll really take me to … to my daughter?" She tried to infuse the demand with menace, as if there would be consequences for dicking her over.

"Cross my heart," he said. "Hope to die."

Farrah got in. Before she'd even shut the door, the guy had peeled out from the curb and was weaving through traffic in a way she wouldn't have thought possible on this narrow avenue. He nearly ran over a couple of people. Horns blared. Farrah had decided not to buckle her seatbelt, because she was grasping for anything that might make her look like a hard-ass. After he blew through a red light she scrambled to get it on.

This seemed like an even worse idea than she'd thought. But now the guy slowed down, as if the point of his earlier recklessness had only been to scare her.

They cruised along wordlessly, till Farrah said, "So where is my mom? I mean, uh, my daughter?"

Not even that blunder provoked a flicker in his expression. Either he already knew what was up, or else he truly did not give a fuck what she said.

"Do you know?" she asked. "About our situation?"

Still nothing. Fine. Farrah turned to face forward. She tried not to think about how she had shut herself up in a car alone with a guy who the other day had held her in a chokehold.

They went a long way. Farrah had never been on a car trip this far through the city streets; whenever she'd been on a cab ride that covered this much distance, the cabbie would switch to the expressway, instead of stopping and starting at every traffic

148

light or stop sign. She watched as the area grew less and less residential, less fit for humans, as it transformed into a patchily-illuminated post-industrial moonscape of scattered warehouses that, as far as she could tell, were mostly deserted.

The silence got to be too much for her. "What's your name?"

"If I told you that, then I'd have to kill you," he said. "It's Dolan, by the way."

He was only fucking with her, she told herself.

He pulled the car into one of the vast deserted parking lots. Put it in park.

Farrah tried to press her body against her door, to make herself small. She lowered her head and looked sideways up at him: "You're not going to hurt me, are you?"

He laughed and his arms shot out and yanked her in so fast that she only had time for a brief squeal. Then he had her turned around, her back pressing into him and his forearm around her neck, squeezing off the air. She tried to get her feet up, to kick against the door. Not that she was likely to break it open, and meanwhile the seatbelt constrained her as well.

A little bit of air was still getting in and out of her lungs, enough to produce a feeble wheeze. "What's that?" said Dolan cheerfully, his mouth right beside her ear. "What's that you said? You trying to beg?" He eased the pressure on her windpipe just slightly.

"Please," she rasped, "please...."

"Please *what*?" he demanded, and shook her, like a dog with a rat in his jaws.

The pain shot dull spikes up her neck and down her back. "My mom ... take me to her ... please...."

"Beth, I don't know what the fuck you smoke nowadays, but I don't think you mean your *mom*, you mean your *daughter*. Anyway, who do you think asked me to kill you? Promised me some good pussy for doing it, too."

Tears flooded Farrah's eyes. *"No...."*

"Yes. You must've been a shitty mom, Beth. Now you're about to get the payback for it." And he started squeezing again, cutting off all air, all hope.

Her clawing hands were not going to budge Dolan's arm, nor scratch through his tracksuit. She gave up and sent them thrashing through the interior of the car, hunting for anything like a weapon.

She knocked something off the dashboard, a container the size of a matchbox—it popped open in midair, and things spilled out—Farrah managed to snatch one of them off the seat where it landed. It was sharp, like a needle. She had no clue what it was, but drove it behind her, pointy end first, right into the guy's face.

He howled, and his grip loosened enough for her to break free. She scratched his face and then scrambled upright, clawing through the blur of her tears for the door handle—she popped it open and expelled one bleating half-formed scream—then Dolan's hands were pulling her back. She managed to get her own hands up over her face just in time to block his arm, before it could reclaim its killing grip.

"Quit playing, bitch," he growled. "Quit playing with me, because I'm through playing with you. I'm about to snap your fat neck."

It seemed beyond comprehension that anyone would genuinely be trying to break her neck. Yet she could hear how serious he was; his arm was descending toward her throat despite all the strength of both of hers, and if he could succeed in working his other arm out from where it was wedged under her—which he would do any moment—then he would be able to pluck hers away, and she'd be dead a minute after that. *No, God!* Even if it had to be in this body, she wanted to live. She wet herself, and couldn't even gather the breath for another whimper....

A flurry. Farrah couldn't tell exactly what was happening, but the door was open and there were other people in the car with them; there were fists, someone flopping on top of her and driving the breath out. "What's going on, son?!" someone was yelling. "What's going on, son?!"

Whoever they were, they were unbuckling her seatbelt and dragging her out of the car ... she was being rescued.

Dolan was fighting them—she could tell that from the cries, the jostling as the various bodies grabbing at her were shaken by blows—she was too close, too frightened and confused, to follow what was going on. Her tormentor was outnumbered, though. Unless he had a gun or supernatural ninja powers (neither of which she would rule out), he was bound to lose this fight.

Suddenly her knees and then her arms were on the asphalt, and she was being dragged across it. She blinked, trying to get a better view of her saviors—they were all young black guys dressed in low baggy jeans and hoodies, the type of group she would have normally given a wide berth. Some had bloodied faces: noses bloody, lips busted. One of them had his iPhone out and was videoing the whole thing.

She blinked back the way she'd come, back at the car she'd stupidly gotten into. Dolan was literally kicking out the last assailant. Once again, he peeled out before he'd even managed to close the passenger door.

Farrah didn't have a chance to feel relief at seeing him go before he was turning the car back around. For a bowel-rattling moment she thought he was going to run them all down, and as he screeched to a stop she wondered why he didn't—then she caught him glaring at the kid with the iPhone. For all Dolan knew, the kid was uploading the video onto the cloud in real time, or was on FaceTime with someone. Not a good idea to commit murder on live-stream. He spat out his window and said, "I should've just killed you in Williamsburg—there wouldn't've been none of these meddlesome niggers around to help you, there."

He fishtailed back onto the road, and disappeared.

Seventeen

For Farrah's sake, the boys who'd rescued her thought maybe they should call the police, but she didn't want to and they didn't argue. They helped Farrah find a taxi: a herculean labor, in this neighborhood, at this hour.

It felt like it ought to take the taxi hours to drive her back to Uncle Tim's and Aunt Ann's, like she'd traversed worlds since leaving in a huff that evening. But the ride didn't take long at all, though Farah realized it was almost dawn when she saw the pinkening sky through the cab's window. Tim and Ann had given her a key—she let herself in, went to their bedroom, and shook them awake. They called Kris when Farrah demanded they do so, a frantic edge to her voice.

Kris agreed to pop over. She arrived so quickly that Farrah, Tim and Ann all privately wondered if she might have used magic, but actually she had just gotten lucky with her cab.

Only after Kris was in the apartment did Farrah tell her story. Tim and Ann listened with horror and disbelief; Kris looked pretty grim.

When she had finished, there was a brief silence. Tim was the first to break it: "Farrah, that's awful. I am so sorry that something like that could happen to you, to anyone. But you've got to believe that your mother had nothing to do with it."

Farrah stared at him. "'Nothing to do with it'? Do you think I would ever have seen this guy if he didn't have some connection to my mother?"

"Well, okay, technically she may have had something to *do* with it, but my point is that there is no way she put that guy up to, to *killing* you! That is absolutely insane!"

Ann didn't participate in the debate, yet; only watched with a light and thoughtful frown.

Farrah said, "If I'm gone, she keeps my body. Why wouldn't she want me dead?"

"Because she's not a monster," snapped Kris. Once again, something in her tone and eyes frightened Farrah. "Yes, she's fucked up badly. What she did to you was bad, but she was drunk and terrified and not thinking straight. And I'm the one who got her drunk—that's on me—I could see she was in a fragile state of mind and didn't know what she was doing, I should have known better."

"She knew exactly what she was doing—she managed to cast that complicated spell, didn't she? The reason I'm stuck like this isn't that you got my mom drunk, it's that you gave her that stupid notebook."

"*Regardless*. I don't know yet why one of Mannis's old henchmen would be gunning for you, but it is not because Beth ordered him to. No mother could ever do that to her child."

Ann spoke up: "That's not necessarily true." Meeting their gazes, she shrugged and said, "I'm just saying. You can call it unnatural if you want, but just go online and google 'mother kills daughter,' and see how many cases pop up."

"But this is *Beth*," said Tim.

Ann gave him a kind, but firm look. "I know you love your sister, Tim. But she isn't stable."

Kris turned back to Farrah, her mouth savage and tight. "Okay," she growled. "Convince me."

"Um. What?"

"Fucking convince me that your mother would want to kill you. I knew your mother. I loved her, and I still do. Your mom and grandma are the only family I ever had. And now you ask me to believe that things between the two of you are so foul that she would do this heinous thing? Does not compute. So if you want me to believe, you'll have to convince me."

"Well, she's a big druggie, for starters."

154

"Nuh-uh. Fuck you, if that's the best you've got." Maybe it was her imagination, but it looked to Farrah like the air around Kris was shimmering, and she felt her hairs beginning to stand up. Never had she seen a face so angry. "Tell me something that happened between you that could have made her hate you that much."

It dawned on Farrah what Kris was asking. "What, you mean a confession?"

"Sure. Call it that."

"Well, I never did anything to deserve getting killed over, if that's what you're asking!"

"Fine. Then if you never did anything to deserve getting your ass kicked, I can't see my friend kicking it. If she never, say, suffered a betrayal so awful that it twisted and perverted her heart and soul, then I have to believe she's still my same old friend, who was like a sister to me. And there would never be any need for me to protect my friend's own daughter from her."

Kris stalked to the sofa. She sat down, pulling her phone out of her pocket and glaring at it as she started playing Angry Birds.

Farrah gaped at her. On the one hand she was relieved the woman had walked away, instead of punching her in the face or turning her into a lizard; on the other, she still needed help. She turned to Tim and Ann, but they only gave her funny, unclassifiable looks.

"I don't even know what you're asking," she said to Kris. "Are you asking if both of us did things that hurt the other? Of course we did! But she was the mother, you know, and I was just the kid. So why should I be the one responsible for whatever happened?"

Nobody answered. Tim and Ann weren't looking directly at her anymore. The only sounds were the soft bleeps and bloops of Kris's video game.

"What, you want a horror story?" said Farrah. "You want me to tell some horrible thing I did to your oh-so-innocent buddy, who used to come and go whenever she pleased when I was a kid? Who would pop in to play mommy every once in a while, till she decided it was time to go back to real life and suck some pimp's dick? Sure, I guess every once in a while I felt like getting back at her for that shit."

Now Tim and Ann definitely were not looking at her. Kris kept her glare affixed to the Angry Birds on her screen.

"Fine," said Farrah. "Fine." And she told them the story of how she'd slipped cat turds into her mother's purse when Beth was on her way to that interview she was so excited about. As she spoke her words fumbled here and there, but she got it all out.

After she finished she realized that she'd dropped her eyes during the course of her story. She raised them now, to find Tim and Ann staring at her, aghast. Kris was still playing her video game, with the volume on but soft. Almost like she hadn't been listening at all.

Except that then her phone fell silent, and she lowered it to her lap. She gazed up and looked straight ahead of her, and said, "Yeah, okay. I guess that's shitty enough that someone might decide you deserved to die."

Farrah took a slow breath. Her lungs had to really tug to get the air into them; the air was still clear and invisible but it suddenly had the consistency of snot, cutting her off from the sounds of the world. A web of nausea nested low in her groin and sent its tendrils out to all her limbs. The idea that her mom had tried to kill her wasn't exactly news—after all, she was the one who'd been insisting on it. But Kris's acknowledgment dissipated her outrage, and now she found herself all alone with the notion.

Kris stood and walked to the kitchen. She went to the cupboards, got out a saucer, got a fork out of the drawer.

Farrah watched uneasily. "So … you'll help me?"

"Right now I don't give a fuck about you," said Kris. "Whatever I do is for my friend. Say for the sake of argument that she is trying to kill you—I don't believe that, but say it's true. I don't believe any mother could live with herself if she killed her own child, and so I can't allow that to happen. And that's my only concern, when it comes to you." She set the saucer on the counter of the kitchen nook, and stood with the fork. "Come here."

Farrah made herself step forward. At the counter Kris took Farrah's right hand and yanked it toward her. She moved the tines of the fork toward Farrah's fingertips.

Farrah tried to snatch her hand back, but Kris had an iron grip. "Don't worry," she said, "I'm not going to hurt you. My friend's got to go back in this body, remember? I'm not going to damage it."

Farrah controlled her fear enough that her fingers didn't tremble too badly as Kris eased a fork tine under each of her nails in turn. She scraped a bit of gunk out from under each nail, and used her own fingers to rub the gunk off the fork and onto the saucer, before moving on to the next finger.

Farrah waited till she was sure her voice would be relatively steady, then asked, "Why are you cleaning under my nails?"

"You said you scratched the guy. So any of his skin you gathered, I can use to find him."

"What about finding my mom, though?"

"Later. This Dolan is the guy who's actually trying to kill you at the moment, right? Regardless of who asked him to do it, he's the one we should be most immediately worried about."

Farrah looked at the waxy, dirty pellets Kris had collected. Thinking of how they were in part made of shreds of Dolan's skin, she found them especially repulsive. "So, uh, you, like, do a spell to find him?..."

Kris took the saucer and carried it to a corner of the living room, one that to the three uninitiated she seemed to select at random, and sat down cross-legged, setting the saucer before her. "Yes," she said. She hovered her right hand over the saucer, letting it form quick, subtle gestures and mudras that the three onlookers would have been hard-pressed to replicate. "I take the skin cells onto my tongue—I also have to put all that other crap from under your nails onto my tongue, too, so thanks. As it dissolves, and as my body absorbs his flesh, I do a locator spell. For that I'll need quiet, if you guys don't mind."

"Sure," said Ann, and "Absolutely," said Tim.

Farrah said, "Is that how you found my mom, when you came to town? Did you have some old skin cells or a lock of her hair, that you ate?"

Kris was using her right index fingertip to mash all the pellets into a paste that adhered to her finger. "No," she said, "I didn't need to—your mother's always been a part of me." She put the finger in her mouth, wiped its contents on her tongue, and sat ramrod-straight, her eyes closed and her palms on her knees.

Farrah knew she was supposed to keep her mouth shut during this part. But she had to ask, "Then why don't you just vibe out where she is, now?"

Kris didn't open her eyes. "Because she doesn't want to be found," she replied. "Now be quiet, please."

Eighteen

Dolan still had the keys to a few apartments scattered throughout the five boroughs, safe-houses maintained by Mannis; but there was no telling whether someone would be stepping in to fill Mannis's place and take over his assets, and they didn't want any nasty surprises or unexpected visitors. So they'd peeled some bills from Dolan's wad of cash and gotten a hotel room in Brooklyn.

Dolan's nerves jangled from lack of sleep, but he'd pulled multiple all-nighters before and could handle it. Beth, though (or "Farrah," as he thought of her), didn't seem remotely tired. As if she were drawing energy from somewhere. Dolan was privately impressed by her stamina.

He was on the bed with Beth, sniffing at her and running his hands along her body toward its crevices. He needed sleep, but he'd like a little pussy first. She waved him off. He moved off the bed and into a side chair, gingerly and sullenly touching the scratches on his face and the puffy puncture wound on his cheek as if confirming that he had indeed earned the right to fuck her.

It was like she could read his mind: "My mom's still alive, isn't she?"

Dolan laughed. "You really are a cold-ass bitch, you know that?" He reached into a bag of chips that was open on the bed, and crunched a handful into his mouth.

Those words cut her more deeply than Dolan could have guessed. Within her rose a howl: *Are you going to kill your own daughter to steal her body?!* Beth clamped a quick seal back over that abyss. Time enough to deal with the grief and guilt of the crime, after she'd irrevocably secured its benefits.

Besides, maybe she wouldn't do it at all. Maybe she'd kill Dolan, instead. She hadn't one hundred percent decided yet.

Eyes half-focussed, she said, "I'm concentrating."

"Concentrating on *what?*"

"It's witch stuff," she said. "Now leave me alone, please."

By squinting her third eye she could see the mystic spaces within her more and more clearly, and the wells of power they contained. While with one part of her mind she trained herself to see them, with another she gently squeezed and pulsed the nascent mystical muscles that eventually would give her access to that power and allow her to wield it. Soon she would be able to do the kinds of things she once had ... and more, she was beginning to realize. Way more. The bio-thaumaturgic capacities of this body were vast, even greater than her own body's had been back in its top condition. She felt disgust and anger at the way Farrah would have squandered it. Even without any training, how could she have been so blind to her own potential? Especially when Beth had told her as a little girl that she herself was a witch. If Farrah had chosen not to believe her mother, that certainly wasn't Beth's fault.

The thought brought her back down into the hotel room, as if her personal gravity had been turned back on. Who the hell was she kidding, it wasn't her fault? She laughed.

Dolan scowled at her. "What're you laughing at?"

Beth looked at him and smiled. She didn't think it was gallantry that kept him from trying to rape her. No—Dolan had been around power enough to know the smell of it. He was a little scared of her, she thought.

Awesome.

Of course, he didn't want to *seem* like he was afraid of her. Dolan continued to poke compulsively at his wounded face. "Well, next time *you* can go hunting after your crazy mom." His idly probing fingers hit an especially tender spot and provoked a hiss. "On second thought, why don't you go ahead and save her for me."

"Hush," said Beth.

Dolan opened his mouth, ready to explain that he didn't take kindly to being told to *hush*, especially not by women who were lucky enough not to have already been killed by him. But then he just let his mouth hang open, and didn't push any words out. Maybe he really did intuit some formidable power emanating from her as she lay with her eyes unfocussing into the middle distance.

When he did speak, it was almost humbly: "Is there somebody close?"

It was Beth's grim, almost fearful expression that put Dolan on alert. "Yeah," she said. "Someone's coming."

Dolan's eyes flickered through the room, checking for weapons. But then his gaze landed on Beth. Whatever the threat was, he had an inkling it was best left to her. Beth didn't look at him. Although she stayed reclined on her back, there was something unrelaxed in her manner, something ready.

Finally there came a knock on the door. Beth laughed again. She knew it was Kris out there, and Kris could have blown that door off the hinges without ever using enough energy to break her Oath of Constraint. "Come in," Beth called.

Dolan gave her a look and said, "It's locked," even as the bolt clicked and the door swung open to reveal Kris standing a foot away from it, hands nowhere near the knob. She stepped through the doorway, giving Beth a neutral look but Dolan one dripping with disdain.

He said, "Yo, maybe you can turn me into a fucking eye of newt or whatever, but that doesn't mean I'm gonna sit here while you look at me like that."

"If I get in the right mood, you'll sit there for hours while I materialize millipedes all through your digestive track." Now *that*, Beth knew, would be impossible without breaking her oath and going over her power cap. As Kris turned back her way, Beth forced herself not to flinch. "Nice friend you got here," Kris said.

"He has his points."

Kris stepped further into the room. "I wouldn't let myself believe I might find you with this scumbag. I even repressed my sensitivity, so I wouldn't know where you were. That's how seriously I take your asking me to give you your space. Do you know what this guy did, Beth?"

"I know a lot of things he did."

Dolan looked at Beth. "'Beth'?"

Beth kept her eyes on Kris, forcing her face to stay blank. Kris looked like she might cry—but not with sadness. It was more like the face of a kid on a playground, so worked up with rage and injustice that the tears are about to explode. "You told him to do it?" spat Kris.

Beth didn't answer. Because her face was blank, it probably looked like she just didn't give a shit. The truth was that she didn't reply because there was no way she could have forced any appropriate words out.

Her silence egged Kris on. "I asked you, did you tell him to do it? Because what I'm wondering about is the precise manner in which you bullshitted me at the diner. Did you believe it yourself when you told me you were going to give back the body, and then decide to break your word? Or did you all the time know you were going to kill your own fucking daughter, and meanwhile you looked me in the eyes and lied to my face?"

"I lied to your face. I'm sorry. It wasn't like I could tell you what I was up to and ask for your help."

"It sure as shit wasn't." Kris took another step forward. A weird electricity thrummed in the air. Beth knew that if Kris felt like she really wasn't going to be able to stop herself from crying, she might get so angry that she did something violent, possibly violent enough to screw her with the new coven. "How could you do that, Beth? We were like sisters. Your mom, she was like my mom, too."

Beth felt a pang at the use of the past tense. "I didn't want to do anything to you," she said. "That's why I lied to you, was to try to keep you from getting involved."

Kris threw back her head and laughed—a wild, frightening laugh.

"From getting any *more* involved, I mean," said Beth. "I didn't want to expose you to being complicit in anything...."

"You have the gall to think I would ever be complicit in something like this?"

"If I'd told you, you would've had to stop me. You might have felt you had to do something that would endanger your standing with that new coven."

"Gotcha. Thanks for saving me from yourself." The thaumaturgic potentialities were building to dangerous levels. There was nothing specific to notice, because nothing had actually yet manifested, but it was like a high-pitched whistle was being blown in the room, at a frequency too high to hear but that frazzled the nerves. "And why exactly do you think that I'm not about to do something *now*, to stop you?"

"Because now *I* can stop *you*." Beth moved her fingers too fast for even Kris to see, and spoke a word whose sounds could not be borne by earthly vibrations, and a white blare of charm light filled the room.

It was a pure white blinding light that seemed to explode from every single point. Kris cried out in pain, and so did Dolan. Even if he'd been warned in time to shut his eyes it wouldn't have done much good; spurts of light also materialized behind the eyelids, and all three of the room's occupants rolled, groaned, and gasped. Luckily no maid or other guest walked by the room's open door.

Everyone's physical eyes were hurt, but that damage faded fast, into blobby tearful red afterimages. More important were their mystical eyes. Dolan didn't have one to speak of, and Beth had known to shut hers; but Kris writhed on the ground, hands covering her face, and she stayed that way as Beth and Dolan blinked their way back to sight. The charm light's spectral aspect had pushed through Kris's mystical eye and into her thaumaturgical channels so roughly that it broke through into her mundane neural net, temporarily disabling the connection between her brain and eyes.

Dolan's sight recovered first, and he staggered over to Beth and hauled her upright. As they were rushing out of the room they nearly tripped over Kris where she lay curled on her side with her hands over her eyes; Dolan gave her a kick in the ribs.

"No!" cried Beth, shoving him away from her prone friend.

He stared at her like she was crazy. Naturally it never occurred to him that one of the reasons she'd disabled Kris was, not to kill her, but to prevent her from doing something that would get her expelled from her coven.

Beth raced from the room with her henchman in tow, slamming the door behind them.

For a while Kris rolled on the floor, gasping in fury and panic. *Blind!*, she howled inside, and *Beth blinded me!* That was the cruelest part, was that it had been Beth. The pain of having been kicked paled in comparison to the betrayal.

Blind. But she knew what charm light was, what it did, and for about how long it did it. There was nothing physically wrong with her eyes; this blindness was the effect of her mystical eye having been flooded. That was why the locator spell she'd cast in regard to Dolan was suddenly transmitting fuck-all. She'd been blinded inside and out, to both the everyday world and the real one.

But only for a bit, she reminded herself. *A day at most, or maybe two.* And once she recovered there would still be time to stop Beth from doing anything too hideous, too unforgivable.

There would have to be.

The first thing she had to do was calm down. She stopped writhing, forced herself to lie still. Her breath still came in shallow gasps, but it was more even now.

Beth's daughter. Beth was going to kill her daughter, if Kris didn't buck up and make herself useful. And once Beth did that, there would be no turning back.

Kris used a breathing exercise. Soon she was no longer a stricken victim, but only a calm blind person lying on the floor, with bruised ribs.

With her mystical and her mundane senses compromised, she was going to need help. She considered shouting until a hotel worker or guest came to investigate, but that might involve lots of explanations, and possibly the police. Instead, she reached into the hip pocket of her jeans and edged out her cell phone.

Running her thumb over the smooth touch-screen of her iPhone, she thought of how useful real buttons would be. She sat up, folding her legs, and held the phone before her. Clearing her mind of all distractions, she pictured the black frame of the screen. She rested her thumb on the power button, ran her fingers along the edges of the device to gauge its exact dimensions. In her mind she divided the screen into quadrants.

Soon she had a clear picture of the black screen in her mind's eye. Then a picture of how it ought to look when she hit the power button. She pictured the keypad that was appearing on the screen, pictured the layout of the numbers. Methodically, she tapped her fingers upon the exact spots she reckoned were where the numbers of her security code should appear. She visualized the screen that should appear after that, the distribution of icons—she made herself see where each icon should go. She tried to be methodical, but she couldn't go too slowly because she had to tap the icon before the screen faded and the security lock activated.

She tapped her finger where the "Contacts" icon should be. Then she tapped her finger where the "Search" icon should be, on the new screen. The "Search" icon ought to lead to an alphanumeric keypad—if her fingers had landed in the right spot every step of the way, that would be what was on the screen before her now. She placed her finger where the "T" should be—she needed local help, and while there were witches and mages in the tristate area who owed her favors, for discretion's sake she preferred to keep the players limited to those already involved. Of all those, Tim seemed the one most likely to pick up his phone.

Laboriously, she typed out his entire name. At least, she hoped she had. At the end, she tapped what she hoped was the "Call" button, and held the phone to her ear.

Nothing. No ring tone, no nothing. Dead silence. She reconsidered screaming for help. As concentration games went, this was pretty impossible.

But fuck impossible. Once again she sat up straight, held the phone in front of her, and pictured it in her mind's eye. Hit the power button again, and made herself see the screen as it must be appearing before her.

Methodically she went through the whole process again, and then again and again. At last she put the phone to her ear and experienced the incomparable thrill of a dial tone, only to find she'd accidentally called a pizza place in Tucson; she must have placed an order there years ago, during her adventures in the Southwest, and she was annoyed to find their number still cluttering her list of contacts. Still, she must have done a lot of things right to achieve the final mistake of that wrong number, and she tried again. This time she must have hit the iTunes icon instead of the Contacts, because all of a sudden Patsy Cline was singing to her. She let herself listen a moment before groping around to shut off the music and start over again.

There was a ring tone, then Tim saying, "Hello?" It was plain from his voice that he was expecting bad news.

Good, figured Kris. That attitude gave him a head start.

Nineteen

While Beth and Dolan were finding a car that they could take upstate, Ann drove to pick up Kris. She'd taken the week off from work, citing "family stuff," so she was available. Kris insisted someone should stay with Farrah, because she wouldn't be safe alone—Ann thought that sounded like they ought to call the police, but Tim refused to call the cops on his sister. Ann chose not to argue, if only because a police investigation would kick up the subject of magic.

Tim wanted her to take a taxi rather than drive out there herself, but she said there was no point in owning a damn car if she was never going to drive it. Besides, while she didn't understand what had happened to Kris, it sort of sounded like she was injured, and a cab driver would just be one more person to whom they would have to explain why they weren't taking her to a doctor. Since Ann was having trouble understanding that herself, she didn't want to have to explain it to another person.

She found it even harder to understand after she'd located the hotel, made her way up to knock on the door of the room, and found Kris. "Are you *blind*?" asked Ann. "If you've gone blind in the last hour, I strongly feel that we should take you to a doctor."

"Can't," said Kris, grimly and firmly, her head turned in the direction Ann's voice was coming from, her eyes floating aimlessly. "Help me downstairs and to your car, please. I need to get to Farrah."

"How are you going to help Farrah?" Consciously, Ann was still trying to take this whole body-transfer thing with a grain of salt—but, almost without even noticing it, she'd started thinking of the person back at her apartment wearing Beth's body as "Farrah." "You can't even see."

"I *will* be able to see. And right now I'm the only player interested in keeping both Farrah *and* your sister-in-law alive—anyone I could call on for help would have an ethical obligation to make sure justice was done to Beth." Her hand waved around blindly, searching for Ann's arm. "Come on. Lead me out. I get it that you don't understand what's going on, but I need you to know that I have a job to do, and it's one I'm very competent at."

Kris had hit upon just the right way to appeal to Ann. Without further argument, Ann held out her hand and led Kris downstairs to the car.

Rush hour had begun, but Ann knew how to choose a route through less-traveled streets, and soon they were home. "We're near my apartment," Ann informed Kris as they were undoing their seatbelts. "Got pretty lucky, parking-wise."

Ann came around to the passenger side to open Kris's door and offer her arm. Kris waited patiently till Ann said there were no cars coming, then they slowly crossed the street. Kris's hearing was acute enough that she would have known when it was safe even without Ann, but she was still grateful to have her there. Even though they'd exchanged few words over the last couple days, and despite Ann's almost aggressive skepticism (which she seemed to forget more and more often), the mere fact of Ann assisting Kris in this way forged a bond between them.

Upstairs, Farrah and Tim both cried out when they saw that Kris was blind, and wanted to know what had happened—Kris kept the explanation succinct, since her blindness was the least of their problems.

"But I don't understand," Tim kept saying. "'Charm light'? What the heck is 'charm light'?"

"Stop worrying about that," said Kris. "The more time we spend worrying over stuff you've never heard of, the less time we have to worry over the fact that Beth is going to kill Farrah."

Tim refused to believe that his sister would ever do such a thing, but his very vehemence seemed to camouflage some doubts. "Believe it," said Kris. "And our concerns go bigger than that. Because once a woman kills her daughter, there's no telling where her fall will stop. There are a lot of bad things that might not seem like such a big deal, once you have a sin like that under your belt."

"Okay, well, so we have to stop her," said Farrah. "Obviously. You talked before about how you'd sworn some vow against doing any really big magic except with the power stored in that grimoire. But now it sounds like you think my mom is getting prepped to do some pretty bad shit. So maybe it's time for some promise-breaking."

"Agreed." The word was loaded with anger but also, smothering that, a load of grief and disappointment. The others sensed that breaking that vow would have heavy consequences for Kris, even if they didn't comprehend what they were. Kris began groping around, and by the time anyone figured out she was looking for the sofa, she'd already found it and sat down.

"Agreed," she said again, sounding wearier this time. "But there are complications. I guess I should have gone ahead and done the spell when you asked me to. You were right, but I just ... well, anyway. The point is that now, with what Beth did to my mystical eye, I'm not going to be much good for anything for about a day. Even if we had the grimoire, I wouldn't be able to direct the magicks stored in it, much less use my personal bio-thaumaturgy." Her sightless eyes gazed out with especial bitterness. "Such a simple thing she did to me. I should've been ready, but I just never thought."

Wringing her hands, Farrah said, "But, so, we just wait, then? Until you get back your eyesight, and ... your other stuff?"

"We can't do that, no. Beth's getting stronger by the hour— that's an amazingly powerful body you've got, Farrah. Your powers are going to be even more potent than your mother's. Far more. She's probably already too strong for me to forcefully undo the switch, without her cooperation. It's amazing that she was already able to launch that kind of attack on me. The period needed for her to rejuvenate is going to get shorter and shorter, and her powers are going to be getting stronger too. And if she's planning on hanging onto that body, she's going to be looking for ways to accelerate that process even more, because she knows she's going to have to fight for it. She's already been noticed by some local players, and they are not going to want a destructive rogue witch in their territory, free to wreak whatever havoc she sees fit. Beth must know they're going to try to put her down. She'll be trying to beef up her strength before that."

"'Put her down'?" said Tim. "What does that...."

Ann cut him off. "Beef up her strength, how?"

"There's a power stone, the Stone of Pellerian, about an hour north. It's buried out in the woods, in the middle of a large perimeter fashioned according to the laws of sacred geometry. It'll take Beth some time and some concentration to cross the mystical barriers, but if she does, and if she reaches the Stone, she'll be unstoppable."

"Unstoppable?" said Ann. "What do you mean, 'unstoppable'?"

"I mean that I personally will be unable to stop her from doing anything she wants, to anyone she likes. The Sisterhood attached to the Stone of Pellerian would probably have the raw power to handle her, but there are procedural reasons why they may not be free to do so. Which would mean some big guns would have to be called in. Whoever that was would probably not be happy about having to make the long trip, and so not inclined to be merciful once they got here. Not to mention, they wouldn't come at all unless Beth had already done significant damage."

"What kind of significant damage?" said Ann.

"I don't know, man. With the Stone of Pellerian, she could theoretically conjure a herd of T. Rexes and send them to chow down at Times Square."

"Beth would never do anything like that!" protested Tim. "Even if it were possible."

Kris shrugged. With an unhappy twist to her mouth, she said, "Before, my heart would have told me to agree. But like I said—if Beth's willing to murder her own daughter, I give up guessing about what is and isn't likely."

170

Farrah didn't say anything. Kris's grief at the fact that her mother wanted her dead made her feel ashamed, as if she had long been taking for granted something she ought to have been trying to fix.

Ann said, "So, you can't tell for sure where Beth's going because you've lost your magic powers, but the Stone is your best guess. And I guess we can't exactly call the police about it … unless this Stone of Pellerian is on private property, and she'd be trespassing?…"

"Nah. It's federal park land."

"So what do you want to do?"

"I've got to get up to the Sisterhood, see if they can help, either directly against Beth or else by helping me recover. And I'd like to get Farrah up there to them—if anybody in-state can keep her safe, they're the ones."

"Okay." Ann had picked her purse back up, and was rummaging through it to make sure her keys were still inside. "Sounds like there isn't a lot of time, so we'd better get going before I remember I don't believe in fairy tales.…"

Farrah was startled to see Aunt Ann so gung-ho. Even Kris raised her eyebrows in appreciative surprise. Tim put a hand on her arm; "Wait a second," he said. "Why would *you* go up there?"

"Because you haven't driven for years," she told him. "And if they've got to go to some park upstate, a car will be faster than the train. Besides, I don't imagine it would be easy for Kris to navigate the train, while she's blind.…"

"So we'll call a car service for her!"

Ann squeezed his hand as she worked free of its grip. "That would cost a fortune, honey." She went to the sofa to help Kris to her feet.

Tim followed her, eyes wide. "But you're *pregnant!*" he said. "I don't want you putting yourself in danger while you've got our baby inside you!"

Ann carefully kept her eyes off Tim as she led Kris to the door. Farrah tagged along uncertainly, and Tim trailed all three

171

women. Ann said, "That's part of the point, honey. I don't want my baby born in a city where there's someone who can do the kinds of things Kris is talking about."

"But Beth would *never do that*! Even if she could! I mean, siccing T. Rexes on tourists?!"

"Maybe not. But I also don't want my baby to have a mother who stood by and did nothing while another mother stole her daughter's body and killed her."

"Beth is *not* going to *kill* Farrah. And as for stealing her body … well, Beth *made* that body, didn't she? And anyway, who the heck are we to judge her? Has it been exactly easy for Beth? Didn't we all sit here and listen to Farrah talk about how she intentionally ruined Beth's life?"

Now Ann did stop. She turned and fixed upon Tim a wordless, reproachful look.

He faltered under it. "I just don't want us to fight my sister, Ann."

She said, "I know, sweetheart. But it's the right thing to do." And she turned and left.

As the three women were filing out of the apartment and leaving Tim behind, Kris turned back to face his general direction with a sympathetic look. "I know exactly how you feel," she said.

Twenty

Miles outside the city, Dolan and Beth sat in the woods on the crunchy bed of dead leaves. Dolan hadn't ever spent much time in nature, in the loud silence of insects and birdsong, the oppressively crowded yet deserted fields: crowded with trees, devoid of humans. The trees were unthreatened, uninterested, unimpressed. There was something intimidating about trees, about the notion of living things you couldn't really manipulate in any way. Even if you cut them down, they wouldn't particularly give a shit. You could go fuck yourself, as far as trees were concerned.

Dolan watched Beth, though, and not the trees—or Farrah, as he still thought of her, even though he'd heard that brunette witch call her Beth. Was it possible that this hot, formidable young woman could actually be the same person as her broken-down pathetic mom that he used to kick around?

She sat cross-legged, her back straight. Though he was behind her and at an angle, he would guess her eyes were closed.

They were making slow progress through the woods, toward whatever their goal was; they walked slowly, and took frequent breaks. Dolan didn't complain. Thaumaturgically speaking, he'd never shown much personal potential, but he had been around long enough to know that Farrah was using their down time to dismantle or slip through some kind of barriers, barriers which did not apply to him because he didn't carry the kind of metaphysical baggage they were designed to block.

If it was taking Farrah (Beth) so long to get through those barriers, that could only mean they were headed for something well-guarded, and if it was well-guarded that could only mean it was valuable. Dolan told himself that was all he needed to know.

He wasn't trying to get in her pants anymore. If she wanted him, he would be her consort. For now he merely watched her. Watched her work; watched her do things.

Overhead, in the sky, some little birds, sparrows or whatever the fuck, were flying by. When they were over her head, they stopped; they zig-zagged above her a while; then all of them swooped down. For a moment it looked like they were going to kamikaze into her head, but instead they whipped around her like a whirlwind of which she was the calm eye. Dolan could make out the way the wind of their pumping wings stirred the strands of her red hair. After a few seconds, the birds zipped away from her, shooting overhead in a strange formation before they disappeared from sight, and from her zone of influence. From her current zone of influence, that was; he supposed it would continue to grow.

She was practicing. The last time they'd stopped, he'd been closer to her. Close enough to make out how the ants had formed a thicker and thicker column around her, marching in an obedient circle. He was certain that if he rose and went to her now, he would see the same thing—unless she had decided the manipulation of insects was beneath her now, and that she no longer had anything to learn from that.

Dolan had always been drawn to power. And if he was in a mood to be honest with himself, he would admit that "power" meant "safety." Because it took power to be safe. His thoughts drifted back to his childhood—they were never far away from it, and he revisited those days so often that he rarely even noticed the trauma of doing so.

He snapped out of his trance. A cat was approaching Farrah.

It had to be some pampered housecat that had gotten loose; no wild stray who'd been living out in the woods would sidle up to a strange human like this. Yet it wore no collar. And leaves clung to its matted fur, he saw, and its ribs were visible. And the more Dolan stared at the animal, the more the cat seemed dazed, somehow. Even though if you had asked him ten seconds ago how you could tell if a cat was "dazed," he would have shrugged and said you couldn't.

The cat walked toward Farrah. But it didn't look at Farrah, nor at him; it stared into space. Dolan was uneasily wondering what had drawn the animal here, when the squirrel launched itself.

Dolan jumped. Goosebumps sprouted over his body. The squirrel dropped down onto the cat from above, taking a bite out of its back with its big buck teeth. The cat yowled and swiped at the rodent, but its reaction seemed delayed and the squirrel got away. The cat didn't pursue, but remained rooted to that same spot.

Dolan was breathing harder. He felt sensations he hadn't known since his childhood. He looked at his companion, but she just sat there and stared straight ahead like she couldn't be bothered to even notice a squirrel attacking a cat.

A whole pack of squirrels started piling onto the stray. Almost too fast to follow with the naked eye, there were six, eight, nine squirrels circling the cat, dashing up and fearlessly biting at it despite each being a third its size. If something had been dampening the cat's reflexes before, that restraint was now removed—the cat slashed with vengeful, affronted claws, slicing three of its tormentors. They collapsed onto the ground, panting and bleeding.

Only, if the cat's reflexes had been restored to it, it nevertheless remained rooted in place by some force. More squirrels were scrambling down trees and madly throwing themselves at the cat. The cat's claws and teeth were enough to shred any one squirrel, and a lot of them were soon dead or dying. But numbers were on the squirrels' side. All of a sudden it seemed every squirrel in the goddam forest had gotten the call, and they streamed in from every direction, making Dolan flinch as they poured over his legs, in too big a hurry to go around him. (They gave Farrah a respectful berth, though.) The ground was a tidal carpet of fur, it was dizzying, it made a watcher feel almost as if he were the one in motion, the one rushing by out of control.

And then one couldn't see the cat anymore. Only a massive ball of squirrels clumped around something, as if there were a point of highly concentrated squirrel-specific gravity. It lolled, the thing within it struggling against the steadily growing weight, against the tiny claws and nutbreaker teeth. Dolan thought that under the squeaking madness of the squirrels he could hear a low suffering moan from the center of the rodent ball, but that was probably his imagination—he doubted the cat could still draw breath, because the layers of its attackers must be constricting its air passages and pressing in on its ribs.

As the now-unseen thing in the middle of that furious ball finally tilted over onto its side, Dolan felt a strange tingling nausea and wasn't sure if he was going to vomit or come. He'd always liked cats, more than he liked most things. A cat could survive in a city, a cat could live amongst people without ever needing to particularly give a shit about them. If Dolan had had to pick some animal to identify himself with, he would have liked for it to have been a cat, and it gave him a queasy feeling to watch this one be torn apart by its natural prey.

On the other hand, the squirrels were little things taking down a big thing. In his life, Dolan had often been the big thing; certainly he'd put as much energy as he could into being that. But he'd also been the little thing often enough that he got sort of hot watching the little things win the day for once.

Complicated though his feelings might be, when the squirrels were released and the survivors began to drop and limp away from the cat, wiping their mouths on their paws to try and rid themselves of the unfamiliar, disgusting taste of blood, there was nothing ambivalent about Dolan's compulsion to look away from the gory feline corpse that had been gnawed to the bone. His eyes fell on Farrah, and he was reminded that it had not, after all, been the little squirrels who had banded together against the big cat; it was the big witch who'd made them do it.

The void that had been left by Mannis was already being filled. Gazing at the redhead, Dolan reflected that she might be the most powerful person he'd ever met. All Dolan needed from his new mistress was that she tell him where to go and who to hurt.

Right now she was reaching her arms overhead for a luxurious stretch, as if waking from a nap. She turned to Dolan.

"Okay," she said. "Let's get moving again. That should be enough practice, for now."

Twenty-one

As far as Ann and Farrah could tell, the WASPish little town of Westmont betrayed no hint that it harbored some sort of mystical compound. But as they were cruising along its cute Main Street, Kris gasped in pain and said, "Pull over, please, pull over!"

"Why?! What happened?!" demanded Farrah from the backseat. Ann pulled over to the curb without hesitation. Leaving the engine running, she turned to Kris, watching her closely and awaiting the next cue.

Slumped low in her passenger-side seat, Kris held a quivering hand over her brow. She swallowed, and, a little hoarse, said, "I missed the warning posts. Because of my blinded mystical eye. Now we've come to the barrier walls, and I wasn't prepared. We'll have to wait here while I ask for permission to go any further."

"Do you need me to dial someone for you?" asked Ann.

"No, I'm not going to ask via phone." Kris sounded amused. "Let's just sit here a moment. I'm still weak, but they're looking at me now, so I won't have to muster a strong signal."

Farrah sat tight. Ann waited attentively. Farrah was surprised by how easily Aunt Ann was going along with all the mumbo-jumbo, regardless of whether she'd been levitated. It was like Ann could just tell that Kris was a serious person, and once she was satisfied of that she didn't need to know much else.

Kris's hand stayed on her brow but gradually stopped shaking. Her breath slowed and deepened, and it looked to the other two women like she had entered a trance.

They sat quietly for five minutes. Then Kris roused herself and said, "Okay, we're cleared." So presumably something had happened.

Ann put the car back into drive and they continued through Westmont. It didn't take long to go all the way through it. They headed up a winding road that led into the wooded hills.

The little back road grew narrower and windier. After long minutes of steady climbing, Kris said, "There ought to be a dirt road coming up on your left; take it." Startled, Ann looked over, checking to see if Kris's blindness had cured itself. It didn't seem like it had. She glued her eyes back to the treacherous road.

The dirt road appeared on the left. Little more than a path; Ann might have missed if she hadn't been warned. She took the turn.

For a while the road dipped down precipitously, at a steadily sharper and sharper angle. The ground fell away on both sides, and the road crawled along the crest of a ridge. Farrah assumed it couldn't be as dangerous as it seemed, because things simply weren't allowed to get that dangerous; then the car lurched as it slid a few inches across a patch of mud, and it came home to Farrah how narrow this road was, and how steep the drop on either side. Ann wrestled the car back under control, and the slope began to level out again. Then it started once more to climb. Soon they were grinding up a steeper and steeper incline. The road seemed to grow even narrower, although Farrah thought that might merely be the effect of the vegetation crowding in closer to the sides. Branches scraped and slid across the glass and chrome with spine-stripping squeaks.

Finally Farrah stopped staring out the window and closed her eyes. With the gravity pushing her back against the seat, she felt like she was strapped into a space shuttle blasting off in slow-motion.

The trees parted to reveal a large three-story red-brick house atop the plateau. Not a mansion, but it gave a mansion-like impression because of its majestic isolation, up here far from any population center. Farrah reasoned that there must be a more developed, paved road nearby. Otherwise she didn't see how the builders of the house could ever have gotten its materials up here.

She noticed that there was not just the one, big house; there was also a one-story house twenty yards past, on the other side of it from the car, and through the trees she spotted other red-brick flashes from still more structures scattered around the grounds.

When the houses had appeared, Ann had automatically slowed down. As the car crept forward she glanced at Kris for guidance. Though she didn't seem to have regained her eyesight, Kris could somehow tell or guess where they were and that Ann was looking at her. "They'll be out soon," she said.

Sure enough, a figure was approaching them from the trees. At first glance Farrah thought the person was wearing, like, a monk's robe and cowl, and she didn't know whether to laugh or be a little bit frightened. But as the person got closer she realized it was only a gray hoodie, and a long loose skirt. The chick had the hood pulled up and her hands shoved in the front pocket. Ann rolled down both front windows, because she expected the girl to tell them something. But the girl only took one hand out of her pocket to wave them toward a flat grassy spot in front of the main house. Ann followed the directions and parked.

As Ann cut the ignition, the front door of the house opened and a short, frumpy, frizzy-haired woman stepped out and made her way to the car. Ann and Farrah sat uncomfortably under the woman's stern gaze. It wasn't clear that Kris knew she was there at all.

Until the woman was nearly at the car. The crunch of leaves underfoot was doubtless enough to let Kris know *someone* was there; but she seemed to know exactly *who* it was, too, as she inclined her mouth toward the open window and said, "Hello again. I guess you told me so."

"Is that a joke?" demanded the woman. "Are you trying to joke around with me?"

"No." A moment ago there had been a sort of forced bravado in Kris's tone. Now she just sounded weary and resigned. "No, you really did tell me so."

"And you didn't listen."

"I didn't want to. What can I say. I was weak, and there's no excuse."

Someone else might have softened at the misery in Kris's voice. Not the frizzy-haired woman. "That's right. You were. There isn't. And now, there's going to be consequences."

Farrah and Ann were allowed to accompany Kris into the big house. No one spoke directly to them; the girl in the gray hoodie gave Kris her arm and led her, while Ann and Farrah trailed behind. They saw a few other women inside, ranging in age from twenty to sixty-five, or so. Everyone seemed to be calmly going about some business.

They were led upstairs to a room. There was a loveseat and a sofa and an armchair that weren't from the same set, and a couple of end tables. Soft, gauzy curtains that were almost completely open to let in the strong porcelain blue of the sky. The furniture was well-kept but bland. Earth tones and umbers predominated. A large tapestry covered the entirety of one wall. Its abstract design was so intricate that Farrah had to pull her attention away from it, lest it distract her too much for her to follow what was going on.

Farrah and Ann were guided to the loveseat and the frizzy-haired frumpy woman sat alone in the armchair, scowling at Kris, who was deposited all alone on the sofa. A teenage girl came in with a tray of tea things and started serving everybody wordlessly. She reminded Farrah of a fucking butler or something. Or a priestess doing a Japanese tea ceremony.

Kris sighed, still staring vaguely into space. "You know, I may be blind, but I can still feel how you're looking at me."

"The fact that you're here tells me that you know your friend is headed toward the Stone of Pellerian," said the frizzy-haired woman. "But I don't think you realize what will happen if she gets there."

"Of course I realize. That's why I'm trying to stop her."

"No. You don't. You think she'll just become a very powerful witch with a very dangerous weapon. What you don't realize is that the Stone will be a very dangerous weapon in the hands of a very, very, *very* powerful witch. We've been monitoring her progress all day, and the game has changed."

The frizzy-haired woman turned to Farrah, startling her. "That body of yours is truly incredible. No one guessed the depths of power it held. With its resources and your mother's training, she might wind up the strongest witch in North America. Or the world, for all we know. You really never felt the stirrings of its potential within you?"

Farrah shrugged helplessly.

The woman did not look impressed with her lack of self-knowledge. "Once you're back in that body you will come and stay here with us for a time. Even if we do fuse the wells of power temporarily shut during the transfer, you can't be sent out into the world with power like that without any training or preparation."

The frizzy-haired woman turned back to Kris. "You'll be able to feel the vibrations of her flexing her muscles, once you get your mystical sight back. Which I suggest you do as quickly as possible, if you hope to save her."

That last pronoun jolted Farrah. Considering that her mom was the one with all this amazing power, she'd expected the frizzy-haired woman to urge Kris to save "the world," or "herself," or something along those lines.

Kris shifted uncomfortably. "I'm working on it, as fast as I can," she said. "Meanwhile, I was hoping I could have the loan of some power, from the Sisterhood...."

"No. Not yet—at least, nothing more than a little something to tend your wounds. Any more would mean breaking *our* sacred vows, which would endanger our charter. And the work we do here must continue. It grieves me not to be able to offer you a less painful choice, but I'm afraid it must be *you* who breaks her oath."

"I don't give a damn about the Oath of Constraint. Or, no, I do ... this will mark the first time I haven't been true to my word. The first important time. That stings. But at this point all I want is to save my friend from herself, before she gets killed."

Now an element of sadness entered the frizzy-haired woman's face. No mercy, though. "You still don't understand," she told Kris. "You may have to save your friend *by* killing her."

Elsewhere, in the woods, Beth sat, introspecting, regarding the power within her with awe. It couldn't really be real, could it? Surely it couldn't be as potent as it *felt*. It felt like she could reach out, with her mind, and flick off the plane of existence any asshole she wanted. Maybe not *anyone*, maybe not *anywhere*— but she felt she could reach as far as Manhattan, or Brooklyn.

Well, maybe she ought to try it out and see if that was so.

Not on Kris. Not like that. And her mind whimpered away from the notion of vaporizing her daughter—sending Dolan after her had been one thing, but she didn't think she was ready to go that far, herself.

Now that her mind was in the vicinity of her daughter, though, she found that it suggested another target, by association. Beth threw back her head and laughed at the perverse randomness of it. Dolan scowled at her in confusion. She ignored him.

Stare at me like that, huh, asshole? You won't be staring at anyone else that way, ever again.

"What the hell does that mean?" demanded Kris.

"It means that her name will be written in the Black Book."

Kris sputtered, too outraged to get any words out. Finally she said, "Are you fucking crazy?!"

"An irrelevant question. As you know, it's not we who decide such things. The Council has sent word that's what's to be done."

"Fuck you! Her soul, imprisoned for all eternity?! For *what*?! Okay, she's fucked up. So punish her. Kill her, even. But not the *Book*!"

By the time she reached those last words, Kris was practically begging. Farrah felt a dread akin to that of a child at the sight of a weeping parent.

The frizzy-haired woman remained unmoved. "Your friend is about to attempt murder remotely, from a great distance. Any of us could kill from a few hundred yards, but we're talking miles. If she succeeds, she will be considered the most powerful agent of the Dark Powers in North America. *That* is what will warrant her inclusion in the Book. Word has come down."

"Then you've got to stop her," insisted Kris.

"*Excuse* me," burst in Farrah. "She tried to commit murder against me, didn't she? Her own daughter? How come *that* didn't warrant whatever?"

The frizzy-haired woman looked at Farrah like she wasn't supposed to be talking. "That was a mundane hit. People like us only get involved when there's magic in the mix."

Farrah hadn't thought it was very mundane, but she dropped it. She wondered how Frizzy had known about the attempted hit, anyway. Did this woman just generally know stuff?

Frizzy turned back to Kris. "Her name will go in the Black Book. It'll be spat upon by all those who are admitted to the Ranks, from here on until the great tapestry frays."

"*I've* spat on the Book! It'll be like I spat on *her!*"

"It'll be exactly like that. You should have stopped her before her crimes passed a certain threshold. Maybe you'll get lucky and there'll still be time. We'll know in the next few minutes."

"How can she be put into the Black Book? For killing just one person?! Someone she probably has a legit grudge against?! The Black Book is for people like Lefebre! For crimes like the Great Soul Enclosure, or the Screaming Thousand!"

"She will be placed in the Black Book in order to insure that every Warrior of the Light is her enemy. That none give her aid, that all join the fight against her. Because she is going to be so powerful, that that is what will be required. You're a grown woman, Ms. Bouts. Respect yourself and us by acting like it."

"You've got to stop her," Kris continued. "*Please.* I'll explain, to the Council, to whoever."

"They're not going to retroactively release us from our vows because you ask them to."

"Then cure me, goddammit! And I'll stop her! I'll stop her right now!"

"I'm sure you'd make a valiant effort, but it's not certain you could take her by yourself. Not even at full strength. I'm telling you, she really is quite extraordinary. What a waste. As for your recovery, curative waves have been directed at you ever since you entered our sphere of influence. We can accelerate the healing, but we can't effect it with the snap of our fingers."

"You've got to stop her. You've got to. Even if you have to kill her to do it." Then, with renewed hope: "Besides, she's about to kill an innocent person, isn't she? You can't just let whoever it is die!"

"You know perfectly well that we let people die all the time."

Farrah broke in again: "But, like, who is it? Who would she be trying to kill?" She feared that it was her, though hopefully all these witches were offering some sort of protection.

The frizzy-haired woman looked at Farrah. She closed her eyes, as if seeking a sight that lay behind her vision. Opening them again, she said, "It's someone you know, actually."

Eli had just been thinking about trying to text that girl he'd gotten lucky with the other night. Farrah. Not that she'd seemed very into him at the end there. He'd done like he always did—gotten shy and timid, till he'd been so scared of saying something stupid that he'd stopped talking at all, had just sat there like a lump. No wonder she'd eventually had to make it plain she wanted him to leave. Still, he should try texting her, just to see.

He was working up the nerve for it when his eyes started to itch. At first just a little. Then a lot.

A crowd gathered as Eli writhed on the sidewalk. People were shouting about epilepsy. Ten people were on their phones, competing to be the first to dial 911.

Eli's knees were banged up from having collapsed onto them as he'd clapped his hands over his face. But he didn't even notice that pain; it was nothing compared to the blistering agony in his eyeballs.

They felt like sulfurous red match heads being scraped across concrete. He let out a howl as he felt the heat's pressure build, and build, and build.... His palms pressing against his clamped eyelids seemed to feel the jelly give beneath them. As if his eyes were melting. Only imagination, surely; but a cold objective part of himself weighed the sensory data and judged that they were melting indeed. And Eli felt a hot prickling at each individual pore of his skin, and knew, in that calm place under the pain and horror, that while his eyeballs might go first, the rest of his body would soon follow....

Unbeknownst to him, in the woods many miles north, a redheaded woman gasped and shivered, abruptly aware of the cold sweat sleeking her down as her concentration broke and she returned to her physical body.

Back in Williamsburg, Eli continued to writhe and shriek a few more long moments, before he realized that the pain was gone, and that the only thing pricking him anymore was his own fear, and the pain's residue shivering along his nerves.

The frizzy-haired woman opened her eyes, looked at Kris, and said, "I have good news. Your friend failed to kill her target." Kris sagged in relief. "Don't get complacent," the woman warned. "She failed just now, but it's amazing that she had the strength to even try. And with every passing moment she's opening up those bio-thaumaturgic channels more and more. We're starting to think she may become *de facto* invincible if she reaches the Stone of Pellerian."

"Well, what the hell can I do to stop it?" demanded Kris. "I can barely even see. Quotidianly *or* mystically."

"Soon that'll be fixed. Meanwhile, I suggest you get out there. Your only hope is to head her off before she reaches the Stone, and pray you'll have mostly recovered by the time you arrive."

"Fine. But someone'll have to drive me out there. My eyes are getting better, but still, all I can see is a light blur."

Before Kris finished speaking, the frizzy-haired woman was already shaking her head: "No one from the Sisterhood may accompany you," she said.

"Just to drive me! Not to use any magic!"

"No. For now, the only help the Sisterhood is prepared to give you beyond the curative waves is advice. If you'd taken that when it was first offered, it would have been plenty."

Ann spoke up: "I can just keep driving her."

The frizzy-haired woman kept her expression impassive. Kris turned her head in Ann's direction. "It's dangerous, Ann."

"Sounds like it, yeah. I mean, it sounds like Beth *is* a danger, if I understand everything right. So somebody had better stop her."

"But you're pregnant, man," said Kris.

"I know. I feel like, before I was pregnant, I would have just decided it was somebody else's problem. But now that this is the world my baby is going to live in, I can't do that."

Kris turned back to the other woman. "You're going to let this civilian put herself on the line?"

Farrah worked up the nerve to speak. "Yeah, seriously?!" she complained, blustering through her fear. "I thought you guys were supposed to be these insanely powerful witches. And supposedly this is an emergency. And you're not even gonna help?"

Farrah's indignation failed to impress the woman. "I said we wouldn't help for now. It's not impossible that we will later. But there are conditions. The main one being need. That isn't up to us; we are constrained by several of our oaths, the very oaths that give us so much power in the first place, that allow us to draw from the Stone. We must refrain from giving aid in an outside struggle to any party that has not already exhausted her own resources. To anyone who has not proven her commitment by giving everything she has. Only to one who has given her all and still not succeeded, may we offer success in a worthy cause. And so on and so forth."

"In other words," said Kris, "they don't hand out loans to folks who ain't broke."

The other woman nodded, as if that were a fair summation. She signaled to a girl who stepped out of a corner—Farrah and Ann had had no idea she was even there. The girl said some chants over Kris and her eyes. To Farrah, the chants sounded Native American, or maybe just New Agey.

Ten minutes after that, they were being escorted back to the car.

Twenty-two

"Where are we going?" asked Dolan again.

She didn't answer this time, either. Beth didn't. The last time he'd called her Farrah, she'd snapped at him and demanded he call her Beth.

Dolan said, "Are you gonna start mind-controlling people the way you did those squirrels and birds and ants?"

At first she didn't answer, and when she did he heard uncertainty in her voice: "No. Probably not. Not unless I have to."

Sure, thought Dolan sourly. Probably turning people into mindless zombie slaves would be less fun than scaring them into obedience, than leaving their willpower intact and feeling them buckle under you anyway. He knew something about that.

"Where are we going?" he insisted. Something told him he ought to keep his mouth shut, but that alone was enough to egg him on.

"To our destination," she said.

Dolan gritted his teeth. Why couldn't their "destination" be someplace they could drive to? If ever there had been a city guy, it was Dolan—about the only times he'd been out of New York had been to go to Newark, and once to Baltimore on a trip for Mannis. He was sick of walking up this gentle but neverending slope. The carpet of crackling leaves and mulch sank treacherously under his feet with every step, and he was constantly afraid that some unknown thing was going to pop out of its thick cover at him. Like a fucking millipede or a rat or a snake or whatever. The whole goddam environment struck him as craven, sneaky, and dangerous.

He stopped and watched Beth continue on without him. When she didn't turn around, he said, "Hey, well why don't I just let you go on without me?"

She laughed and didn't stop walking. "Why don't you?"

He tried to think of something he might say that would make her turn and address him. But all he came up with was, "Why do you need me, anyway?"

"For muscle," she called over her shoulder. "But not for much longer."

Dolan remembered the cat and the squirrels, and had a hard time believing she would need him for that, at all. He said, "What's in it for me? What do *I* get?" There had been no more talk of fucking, and though he was still drawn to her, it wasn't exactly a sexual pull.

Finally Beth stopped. She turned and looked down at him. With something like a smile, she said, "You get to see what happens."

She faced forward again, and continued up the hill.

Dolan stared after her. *See what happens?* That was stupid. *Fucking* stupid. Whatever was going on, it had jackshit to do with him. There were big forces at play, and the safest thing would be to go back to the city and hole up somewhere. He knew all that.

He continued up the hill, following her.

As the three women rode along in Ann's car, the two mundanes quietly cast nervous looks at their blind, brooding witch companion. Kris was quiet too, till at last she grimly said, "I'm going to need every scrap of power I can get."

Hesitantly, Farrah leaned forward from the backseat. Clearing her throat, she said, "Uh, Kris? Uh, I know I said that the grimoire was gone, but...." She trailed off.

"But what?" demanded Kris, in a tone that brooked no shit.

"Well," said Farrah, "that was *mostly* true. But I did manage to save one page...."

"Do you have it? Tell me you still have it." Kris's hand was already thrust into the backseat area.

Farrah took the paper out of her pocket and handed it over. Kris carefully unfolded it and smoothed it out on her lap, running her fingers over it as if it were brail.

"I just assumed it wasn't any good anymore," Farrah said, trying to escape whatever trouble she might get into for having lied. "Does it still have any, you know, kick?"

"Oh, yeah," said Kris. She didn't sound any less grim, exactly; maybe she sounded more confident, but it was confidence in a fight she felt ambivalent about winning. "Not a lot. It all depends on what spell it is—I'll have to wait till I can see again to read it. But it's something, for sure. And like I said, every little scrap is gonna help."

With that, she refolded the piece of paper and put it in her pocket.

They continued on their way. Kris's eyes remained fixed straight ahead. But her gaze started looking very purposeful to Ann, who finally asked, "Can you see again?"

"Getting close. The Sisterhood's boosting me along, just like they promised."

"They're restoring your vision?" said Farrah.

"That, and lowering the barriers that stand between us and the Stone," replied Kris.

Ann didn't say anything, but she had the weird feeling that they were helping her, too. It felt like her car was flying along faster than the speedometer claimed. And she had the even crazier notion that, if she tried to find this curving stretch of two-lane highway on a map, she wouldn't be able to. There were no other cars.

"Coming up," said Kris after a while, in a flat voice.

"Where?" asked Ann, slowing down.

"Where I tell you," said Kris. "Just keep slowing. Be ready to stop when I say."

Ann obeyed, and soon was creeping along at five miles an hour. Kris sat very still, as if listening for something, until at a certain moment she said, *"Here."*

Ann eased her foot onto the brake. About five feet from where Kris had said "Here," the car came to rest.

"Back up, please," Kris said, politely but unapologetically. "About five feet." Ann gave her a funny look, but then put the car into reverse and did as she was asked.

"We have to get out of the car at this exact spot?" asked Farrah.

"I do," said Kris, as she unbuckled her seatbelt. "The Sisters have opened a gate for me. And it is straight and mighty fucking narrow."

"So if we tried to go some other way something would happen to us?" asked Farrah, looking up and down the road apprehensively.

"Not to you. To me. You two don't have enough thaumaturgical sensitivity." Kris stood up out of the car and looked around, blinking in the sunlight. "My eyesight's coming back. Fast."

Dolan sprinted to catch up with Beth, but slowed to match her pace before he quite did; instead of walking abreast of her, he was to the side and about four feet behind.

When she stopped short, though, he kept walking a couple paces before her pause registered and he stopped too. By then they were next to each other. Something had made her furious.

"They're helping her," she spat. "They're not supposed to meddle, but they're definitely helping her. Those goody-two-shoes bitches are *cheating!*"

They tramped along, struggling to keep up with Kris. Her legs weren't that long, and it wasn't like she was running, so Farrah couldn't understand how she could be going so much faster than the two women scrambling after her.

Farrah looked at Aunt Ann's red, puffing face. "Kris!" she called. Kris ignored her. "*Kris!*" said Farrah again, coming to a rebellious halt. Reluctantly, Kris paused and turned around.

Farrah indicated Ann's flushed, sweaty face. "She can't keep up." It was hard for her mom's beat-up old leathery lungs to squeeze out enough air for the protest. "I can't, either."

Kris nodded. "I'll slow down some," she said, begrudgingly.

She turned and started off again, not any slower as far as Farrah could tell. "Wait!" she said again.

Kris turned around again. "We're losing time," she growled.

"Aunt Ann is *pregnant*!" insisted Farrah, pointing at Ann, who seemed self-conscious. "Like, *super*-pregnant! She shouldn't even be here at all! We ought to send her back to the car."

Kris's face lost its dangerous edge. But it was still a firm look she gave Ann. "I'm sorry," she said. "But I may wind up needing you. And you did sign on."

"Need her for what?" demanded Farrah. "What can we mere mortals or whatever do? She could miscarry if she keeps pushing herself like this! Or what if you and Mom have your fight and there are weird radioactive magic waves floating around that might affect the baby?"

Farrah had only said that last bit to be an asshole. From the way Kris winced, though, she wondered if she might have hit on something.

Kris slid her eyes Ann's way. "What's happening is important, and I still might need your help. Even if it's just to pick me up and point me in the right direction, if I'm too injured to stand. You'll have to trust me."

Whereas Ann had been red a moment ago, now she was almost white. Farrah's comment about magical mutating waves had resonated. "I'm just starting to worry about my baby," she explained.

Kris nodded. "I understand. And trust me, the bond between a mother and a child is to me the most sacred thing there is."

The two women held each other's gaze for a long moment. Then Ann nodded and said, "Okay, then let's keep going." Before the other two knew it, Ann had passed Kris in her march up the hill. The other two women hurried after her.

For a while they walked in silence. Then Kris slowly came to a halt. Farrah and Ann waited, while she squinted into space. At last, Kris said, "Do you guys feel anything?"

Besides fear? Dumbly, Farrah shook her head.

Kris peered into the dense brown thicket and muttered, "She's there." Her hands came together and began to rub each other in what looked to Farrah disturbingly like a nervous gesture. If *Kris* was nervous, then Farrah was probably fucked.

Kris spotted a big tree in a clearing and pointed to it. "Let's go have a seat over there. That should do."

Do for what? As Kris headed to the tree, Farrah whispered to Ann, "We're just gonna *sit around?*" The idea that her mom might be within earshot frightened her.

Ann waddled after the witch, with no apparent need to ask why they should take a break. "Have a seat," Kris said again, then fished out of her pocket the folded scrap of paper that had been ripped from the grimoire. As she read the ancient ideograms, the sardonic twist of her mouth grew harsher and harsher.

Not wanting to distract Kris, Ann was almost timid as she asked, "Is that a spell you can use on Beth?"

"I don't want to," said Kris. "But that body she's in is so powerful, even if I break my vow and go whole hog, my personal bio-thaumaturgy may not be enough to take her out. And I think I'll have to try everything before...."

The women waited, but Kris didn't finish the sentence. "Before what?" asked Ann. Kris acted like she hadn't heard.

Farrah cleared her throat. "Are you going to hurt my mom very badly?" she asked, in a small voice.

Kris looked darkly up at her. "This spell you tore out of the notebook? This is an empathy spell."

Farrah frowned. That didn't sound serious enough to warrant the way Kris was acting.

Kris noted her skepticism. Another wry twist rippled through her mouth. "A specific sort of empathy spell," she went on. "A stereotypical Jewish mother's dream. A guilt spell. If you get hit with this, then all the bad shit you ever did, all the pain you ever caused, comes back around on you."

Farrah squirmed. Ann frowned and looked worried. Farrah said, a little defiantly, "Well, that doesn't sound particularly magical. People feel guilty all the time, don't they?"

"The pain you've caused comes back around on you *all at once.* And I use the word 'guilt' as a convenient shorthand. Guilt is just a phantom, a wispy hologram we conjure ourselves and that we could turn off any time we like, if only we weren't all so neurotic. What this spell does is recreate all the pain you ever caused, as if it had been stored all this while in some gigantic bucket of headache vomit, and force-feed it to you. If someone threw a tantrum when they were two years old and told their mom they hated her, they get to feel what their mom felt then, what she's felt every time she's remembered it ever since. Along with all the other heartache they ever caused, to anyone. It's enough to break the saintliest person." Kris passed another sour look Farrah's way. "I'm sure you've built up a long list of grievances over the course of your little life. Well, your mom's about to hear 'em."

Farrah's eyes stung. "Good," she said. "There's things I'm glad she's going to finally know about."

"Fuck you," said Kris. "You don't know what you're talking about." She rose, glancing in the direction in which she claimed to feel Beth's presence. "You guys wait here." With a second look at Ann and her belly, she added, "Try to hide behind this tree. But if you see the sky acting funny, like maybe lightning's about to strike, move the fuck away from it, fast."

The sky was a perfect clear blue. Neither woman protested, though.

Kris made her way through the woods. She stood straight and with her chin up, but one could read caution in the slowness of her pace. The folded-up piece of paper with the spell on it was in her hand. As Farrah and Ann watched her go, they were startled by the way that sheet of paper became hard to see—not invisible, exactly, but as if other, translucent realities had been overlaid on top of it, or as if the visual center of gravity were always a bit removed from it, or as if it were the center of some repulsing, anti-gravitational force, visually speaking. Or something like that.

They watched her go up the slope. Then there was a swell, where the ground rose at a greater angle. Kris continued up over the swell and down the other side, out of their sight.

Kris felt the leaves crunch underfoot. It was tempting, to open herself up to the sensory experience around her, take in as much as she could of the smells of the woods, the feel of the breeze, the quality of the beautiful light, since she knew that in a few minutes she might be dead and all of this lost forever. Also tempting, to go through her memories, to take one last look at her life. But she kept her mind on the task at hand.

Kris walked until the Beth-shaped humming in her mind grew very loud, then stopped. "Come on," she said. "I know you're there, Beth."

"I know you're there, too," came Beth's voice. She stepped out from behind a tree, and Dolan followed suit, hanging back behind her. The tree was way too skinny to have hidden them both, but Kris wasn't going to start getting googly-eyed over such a piddling level of illusionism. Beth could do shit now that would make that look like a two-dollar trick from a toy store.

Kris nodded toward Dolan. "Wasn't this guy Mannis's henchman? What, are you just taking his place now?"

"Stop trying to get my goat, Kris."

It was true, Kris was trying to provoke her in the hope she'd do something sloppy. That was a tactic she'd picked up from movies and comics, so it was no surprise that it didn't work. "I gotta bring you in, Beth."

"'In'? 'In,' where? To jail?"

"Back into the fold. Into civilization."

"What is it you're scared of?" Beth pointed up the hill. "The Stone of Pellerian is up there and right now there's no one between me and it. No one with any freedom of action—the Sisterhood's accepted so many bindings and constrictions in order to gain their power that they may as well have never bothered, for all the good it does them. Well, what makes you think I'm gonna wreak some big hideous evil if I'm the one who gets the Stone? You don't trust me any more than that?"

Kris ignored most of what Beth had said, replying only to the first bit: "*I'm* between you and the Stone, Beth."

Beth gave her a sad little smile and a warning shake of the head. "You don't get it, Kris. You have no idea the wells of power in this body. Seriously. I could bat you out of my way like a mouse, if that was what I wanted."

Kris nodded. "I know that you could," she said. "But I think you don't want to. And anyway, you'd better hope that I'm the one who manages to stop you, sweetie. Maybe it's true that no coven can get here in time to do anything. But they won't let you get away with it. And they'll put your name in the Black Book."

Shock and fear flickered across Beth's face. All she said, though, was, "You really believe in that shit? There's nothing beyond this life."

Beth's impiety bruised something deep inside Kris. "And then there's your daughter. That's her body, you know. Do you know how much you've meant to me all these years? How could you have let yourself turn into someone who would do this?"

"I *explained* to you how this happened!"

"And then you explained to me how you were going to put things back. That was before you tried to kill her." It was hard to speak past the sandpaper lining her throat. "Before you tried to kill your own kid."

Beth's arms thrashed out, her fists clenched. For a second Kris felt a thrill of fear as she thought her friend was prepping an attack spell, but no; the movement was just the spasm of bottled rage with nowhere to go. "And what do you think that goody-goody Sisterhood will do, if I give Farrah the body back the way it is now?! With all this power coursing through it, and her not knowing how to control it?! She'll be a threat! The Sisterhood'll come gunning for her, and she won't know how to defend herself!" Beth took a step toward Kris. "If I can get to the Stone, I can sort of arrange things so that she'll be safe, once I *do* transfer back. I haven't figured out exactly what that arrangement will be, is all. But once I've got the Stone, I'll have enough breathing room and leverage to sit down and work out a real plan."

Pretty big jump to that, from trying to assassinate her, thought Kris. She felt guilty for how pathetic she found Beth right now, and the irrationality and injustice of that guilt made her angrier still. She said, "The Sisterhood will bring Farrah in. They'll direct her training."

Beth barked a laugh. "Yeah, right."

"They will. They said they would. And you know how they are about sticking to what they say."

"If Farrah gets dumped into this body without learning how to control it first, she'll blow the roof off that compound of theirs."

"They're going to fuse the wells shut during the transfer." Assuming Kris could subdue Beth and bring her in, that was. "It's reversible. As Farrah goes through the training the wells will naturally open."

Beth stared, suspicious. "That's a lot of interference, by their standards. You got them to go along with that? How?"

"Just trust me."

Beth shook her head, like Kris was an annoyance who wouldn't listen to reason. Turning back toward Dolan and in the direction of the Stone, she said, "I don't have the time...."

"Beth, wait!"

Beth paused, heaved a sigh. Turned back to Kris, broadcasting her impatience.

Kris let all of her hurt, all of her disappointment press out to the surface of her face. "Don't you trust me, Beth?"

The rigor of Beth's anger slipped. One could see the memories spooling by behind her eyes: their childhood together, Beth's mother; and also more recent memories, of how Kris had come all the way back from Europe to try to help her, and had left the grimoire where Beth could find it. And also the realization that, thanks to Beth, Kris had gotten so entangled with unauthorized magicks that she'd certainly blown her shot with that coven.

Instead of continuing uphill toward the Stone, Beth took a step in Kris's direction. Holding out a tentative hand, she said, "Hey, Kris, I trust you...."

During this vulnerable moment, the notebook sheet flung itself back into existence in Kris's hand as she blasted its empathy spell Beth's way.

Kris's hand moved so fast it was hard to see the blur— she'd always been one of the quickest draws around. But the combination of Beth's new powers and her taut nerves meant that Beth's hands were springing up in a warding mudra even before her eyes had registered Kris's move. *"Pahz'vell!"* she cried, with an uncanny voice; in the ancient tongue of Borrindath, that meant "Deflect!"

The spell's energy bounced off her hastily-conjured invisible shield. Before bothering to check where the energy had gone, she snarled and extended her arm and snapped her wrist, also with supernatural speed; Kris went flying back, hit with a telekinetic blast. She tumbled to the ground twenty yards away, behind the swell in the hill, and Beth could hear her body as she rolled down the slope on the other side.

Beth huffed and quivered, too angry to breathe, too angry to move. Kris had tried to play her! Kris!

You couldn't trust anyone. No one. Even the people who were supposed to love you would fuck you over. Especially them. Beth started walking, to go finish Kris off. But a raggedy howl stopped her.

That cry chilled her. There was nothing directly supernatural about it; yet she would never have believed that so much pain could have been communicated by mere mundane means.

She turned, and walked back to Dolan.

He was doubled up on the ground, writhing, moaning his agony into the rotted vegetation and heedless worms. Electric blue sparks of residual thaumaturgic charge crackled over him. A new kind of horror trickled into Beth's blood as she realized this was what Kris had intended to do to *her*.

Gradually she realized that Dolan's roaring and howling was intended as some kind of speech. Listening closely, she realized he was trying to cry out, "I'm sorry! I'm sorry!"

"What did she *do* to you?" demanded Beth.

"I'm sorry!"

She started to understand. "An empathy spell?" she hazarded. "Are you feeling regrets for some bad things you might have done?"

"Yes! Oh God! God, kill me!"

197

"How's your wrist?" she asked, remembering the feel of his fist clamped around her own. His was twisted and clenched, as if coursing through it were all the shrieking nerves of all the wrists he'd ever twisted, compounded by all the times he'd done it.

He yelped, as if her mentioning the pain made it even worse.

She pounced onto her hands and knees next to him, her fingers curling into the dirt. "You feel all the shit you did to me?" she hissed. "All the little slaps and shoves? All that fear? All that shame?"

"Please." He looked out at her from under a well of tears, snot, and pain. *"Please. Please* forgive me."

She spat in his face. He was hurting too much to notice. She scrambled upright and kicked him. He howled anew. "Take it!" she shouted, and kicked him again. *"Take* it, bitch!" The noises he made as she kicked him grew less and less human. "Take it all! I give it all the fuck back to you!"

"Momma!" he howled. *"Momma!"*

"Fuck your momma!" she said, and kicked him again.

Meanwhile Kris had picked herself back up and checked to make sure she had no broken bones. From the commotion up the hill and beyond the rise she figured out that her spell had gone awry; she couldn't help but be glad. From the way she was shouting at Dolan it sounded like its effects were keeping Beth occupied, at least.

Kris still had to take her out, since if Beth made it to the Stone her name would go in the Black Book, her soul frozen for all eternity in the Black Ice beyond the Weft. She circled around the swell, trying to be quiet but mainly concentrating on speed.

Her hand hung at her side, palm up; above the palm a swirling globe of reddish energy was coalescing. A pure blast; Kris hoped it would be enough to stun her friend, and leave her vulnerable to a freezing-spell, or a hell of a binding spell. It would take all her power, but so be it. *After all, the lady said the price would be everything I have....*

Kris smirked. *Who are you kidding? You know what she meant.*

Although that henchman was still howling, Beth's tirade had ceased. Kris figured that meant she'd turned her attention back to finishing Kris: showtime. She crept swiftly back up the hill via a curving trajectory, coming around behind the rise. She diverted a bit of sorcery from the energy ball she was mustering in order to muffle the crackling noise of her steps.

Coming back around that swell of earth, she spotted Beth from behind, peering down the slope, looking for her. It was the best set-up Kris was going to get. Again she snapped out her hand, flinging the ball of energy Beth's way.

But Beth's reflexes had become uncanny to the nth degree. Somehow she felt that ball hurtling at her back, *before it was even launched*, and had enough time to spin around and whirl her right hand in a warding mudra that exploded the ball into harmless droplets of energy, while with her hand sinister she made a plucking gesture in Kris's direction and in a voice like a thousand oaks splitting in a huge cave cried, *"Krohng!,"* which in the ancient constructed sorcerers' tongue of Kirt translated literally as, "Back from whence!"

Even if Kris had had time to process what was happening, she never would have been able to fight the field of power snapping her into its folds, yanking her into the air and sending her flying head-over-heels. She had less than a second of disorientation before the magic slammed her into the big tree she'd started from, her body traversing all those many yards like a line-drive hit by a giant.

When Kris slammed into the tree she was moving so fast that Ann and Farrah barely had time to perceive her approach; at the impact they both shrieked and scrambled away, then crawled back. Not too close.

Kris's wide eyes stared blankly. Blood trickled from her mouth. Clothes and flesh were in tatters from the branches she'd flown through. Her neck was at a strange angle, and it had a great bump in it, mottled by the blood spreading under the skin. It looked broken.

"Oh God," squeaked Farrah. She looked at Ann, who kept her eyes riveted on the broken woman. "Oh God, she killed her."

Something told Farrah that if Beth had been willing to kill Kris, there were no limits to what she might do.

Ann got her breathing under control, more or less. She started looking around, back toward where Beth was, back the way they'd come, at other random points. Farrah didn't know the rhyme or reason of her gazes, but it sort of looked like she was trying to form a plan, which was good because Farrah sure didn't know what to do.

Eyes darting in the direction Kris had come flying from, Farrah hissed, "She could be *coming*. She could be coming *now!*"

Ann was powering through her brief near-panic. "Okay, listen," she said, keeping her voice reasonably calm. "Here's what we're going to—"

She yelped. Farrah jumped, looked down; Kris's bloody hand had gripped Ann's forearm. Farrah yelped too as Kris's other hand grabbed her own arm, pulling on it as if she were trying to haul herself up.

Kris glared up at Ann, teeth bared with pain and effort. She wasn't looking at Farrah, probably because whatever was wrong with her neck kept her from turning her head that way. "*Help* me," she hissed.

Ann did, pulling her upright by the arm. Farrah recovered enough to follow her example. Ann said, "We thought you were dead!"

"I *am* dead," growled Kris, as if it were obvious. "That's why I need your help."

Beth slumped on the ground in front of Dolan. The air seemed cooler now, there was a coldness that leaked up from the ground and into her body through her backside. Dolan continued to moan and howl. It was less wild than before, but only because his ravings had weakened him physically; his thrashing had exhausted him, his throat-flesh was so inflamed and swollen from screaming that his breath wheezed as it passed in and out. So he was quieter. But one could see that the same pain still roiled inside. It would until it killed him.

Beth stared at him with dull eyes. *All that was meant for me.* She reached out and patted him twice on the shoulder. "There, there." She struggled to her feet and started trudging back up the slope. May as well keep going after the Stone. What else was there?

But she hadn't taken many steps before she frowned. She was trying not to notice or think about anything, because there was nothing that wouldn't remind her that she'd just killed Kris. But an awareness of the funny way the sky was acting finally seeped in.

And then she became aware of something else, something more important. A sense, a smell, a one-of-a-kind vibration in the nearby air.

With a grin, she turned around. "Kris?!"

Ann and Farrah got Kris on her feet and got her leaning back against the big tree. Once she was upright and relatively stable, she waved her hands and rasped, "Okay. Now get away."

The other two women hesitated. Kris looked like shit, and they were loath to leave her on her own. Plus the sky overhead was filled with a weird swirling darkness all of a sudden. Both Farrah and Ann instinctively wanted to stay close to Kris, the one person who might be able to explain things and protect them from whatever was going on up there.

But Kris was insistent: "Get the fuck away from this tree!"

This time her urgency got through, and the women hurried away. Looking up, they saw that what was darkening the sky overhead was not a sudden mass of storm clouds; it was more like the air had gotten thick, more opaque, almost like there was a slowly whirling pool of heavy liquid suspended up there.

On the other hand, in some ways the phenomenon did act like a storm cloud. For instance, that bright spark forming and swelling in its center right above the tree wasn't really much like lightning; but it wasn't totally unlike it, either. Farrah and Ann broke into real runs.

Kris, her last reservoirs of power sputtering out with the drain of reanimating her own corpse, couldn't look up because of her

201

broken neck. She could feel the power sent by the Sisterhood gathering, though. Good to see that the landmark she'd chosen had proven acceptable to them.

Neither Farrah nor Ann were watching when the power came coursing down, following the path of the tree trunk to find and upload itself into Kris; they saw how the bright flash of it turned the whole woods orange, though, and then the shockwave hurtled them face-down. Ann twisted her body so that she landed on her side, bringing her knees up to protect the baby.

Kris was flooded with light, with wild, strong, stern power. It was impersonal, and yet it bore the stamp of a very definite identity: it was the coordinated might and magery of the Sisterhood, crowding and shoving its way into her, crying out for release, screaming at her mercilessly for it. All she was now was a gun, and they the ammunition; the last task she was called upon to perform with the remaining dribbles of her life-force was to aim.

So she did. She'd thought that it would be hard to keep herself from dwelling on exactly what she was doing, on her betrayal of Beth; but there was no question of "dwelling" on anything; it was all she could do in the midst of those shrieking panic lights to accomplish her one job, that of focussing her attention on Beth, so as to provide an arrow, a path for the Sisterhood to follow.

Please, I hope they don't kill her. That was the last conscious thought she managed before the raw power overwhelmed her and quashed all sense of personal identity.

Beth had started in Kris's direction to try to help her. The irony of that hit her when she saw the spark forming in the sky, for she had an inkling what it might be; then the light hit her, knocking her onto her back, enveloping her, blinding her, cutting her off so completely from all sensory input that she might as well have been transported into some other dimension.

She struggled, fought; with her will, with all the power she had available; she kicked, bit, clawed, metaphysically speaking.

No good. No single one of the Sisters could have defeated her, but she was no match for all of them bound together.

Fingers, worms of energy that felt like matter, pushed their way into her mouth, into all her orifices; into her eyes, into her pores. Inside her there was a melting and a shrinking, a drying up that felt paradoxical given the liquid-like surging within her.

They were *inside her*. She tried to thrash, tried to wriggle; maybe her physical body out in the world moved, but she had no clue; she was too overwhelmed by this sorcerous attack to be able to pick any sensory data out of the mundane world. What mattered was that she was powerless to stop their encroachments in her spiritual body. The struggle was exhausting, and served as an engine that amped up her own desperation even more. She would have liked to stop, to let whatever was going to happen happen, she was almost impatient for them to defeat her completely so she could finally stop, rest, die.

The screaming light filled her nose, mouth, throat, swelling like a physical presence, leaving her no space, forcing her out, out....

But then all grew calm. Silence. Darkness. Maybe she was dead.

Except it wasn't silent: there was birdsong, there were leaves rustling in a breeze. It was just that the sudden departure of that howling chorus from her head made the sounds of the normal world seem like silence by comparison.

She was freed from the attack. Released. The cessation of pain was so delicious that she started to weep.

Not that she was free of *all* pain. There were aches, which were very familiar and yet which she felt she hadn't noticed in quite a long time. In fact, in a way she found their presence so usual and ordinary that it struck her as odd that they should now seem strange.

Her eyes fluttered open. Though her vision was bleary, she was relieved to discover the light had not blinded her. She sat up. Cautiously, she placed her open palms flat on the ground, and blinked at her surroundings. Somehow it didn't seem she was still in the same spot as before she'd been attacked; then again, woods were woods. She couldn't understand why her arms should feel odd somehow, why the torso they were holding up should feel odd. And the slope here was gentler than it had been a few minutes ago, she was sure of it.

Turning around, she let out a silent gasp of air that would have been a cry if she'd had more strength to put behind it. Kris's body was crumpled at the base of a big tree maybe thirty yards away. Blood ran from her nose, mouth, ears, and eyes, and her neck looked broken; yet as she stared, she realized that Kris's chest was moving, and a steady pulsing wheeze was coming from her mouth. Still alive. Beth hurried to get up, only to collapse back onto the ground.

As she was trying to puzzle out why her body seemed not to be responding the way she expected, she realized that her sister-in-law Ann was here, too. She was getting to her feet. Brushing the leaves off her clothes, holding her big belly protectively, she heaved toward Kris to check her out. Along the way she glanced at Beth, with a bland expression as if she only meant to look and confirm Beth was there (though why Ann would expect her to be there, Beth couldn't imagine). Then Ann did a double-take. She leaned forward, squinting at Beth, peering at her closely.

It made Beth nervous. "What?" she demanded.

Ann gasped, like a giant spider had appeared on Beth's face. She staggered back, almost losing her balance and grabbing a tree to steady herself.

Beth sat up straighter and started patting herself down to pinpoint what was the matter—and as she did so she caught sight of her own arm. It was both intimately familiar and not at all what she'd expected. Ah, she realized, after one last spurt of terrified adrenaline had squirted itself into her system—she'd been transferred back into her own flesh. Duh.

A spike in the volume of Kris's wheezes brought her back to the here-and-now. She crawled as fast as she could to her friend. Out of the corner of her eye she saw how Ann tensed, still gripping that tree, holding herself motionless as if Beth were a dangerous animal that hopefully would move along if Ann didn't attract its attention.

As Beth got closer to Kris, as she blinked her dazed vision clear, Kris looked worse and worse. More than the raggedy cuts in her clothes and body, more even than the blood fleeing through every exit of her face, it was that wrenched swelling in Kris's neck that frightened her. Yet the small, struggling, obstructed bellows of her lungs continued to noisily work, and her blood-pinkened eyes locked onto Beth's with definite, conscious awareness.

Beth reached Kris, held her face only inches away from her friend's. "Kris," she whispered, in a tone like a frightened child's whose mischievous prank has gone wrong. Whatever was wrong with Kris's neck, it looked nasty enough that Beth didn't want to touch her until the paramedics arrived.

But then Kris rasped, "I hung on ... to say goodbye...." and Beth realized the truth, that Kris was using her very last traces of personal magic to bind her life force to her ruined body. In that case it didn't matter what physically happened to Kris anymore, and Beth rushed to gather her friend in her arms and squeeze her close.

She propped her up, bringing Kris's face up higher and lowering her own. All that power she'd had only minutes ago, and now that there was something worthwhile to use it for, it was gone. Not that she could have kept her friend alive indefinitely—but even if it were only a few more seconds of life.... "Kris," she said. Then, "I'll try to contact the Sisterhood somehow. Maybe they'll...."

Beth trailed off, for lack of a believable way to end the sentence. The smirk on her friend's face told her that Kris agreed about the odds of help from that quarter. "Those bitches ... charge ... a heavy price...."

"Sh. Rest."

"Will ... soon...."

Tears stung Beth's eyes. She kept them inside; she didn't want to make Kris watch her cry.

Kris's hand jerked up and gripped Beth's sleeve like a claw. She drew in another rasping breath, and said, "You ... need to be a ... better soldier...."

"I will," said Beth. "I will." After she said it the second time, she realized she was talking to a corpse. A real one.

For a long moment she continued to clutch Kris's broken body. Without hope, she tried to will life back into her, but it was no good. Probably no witch, mage, or sorcerer on Earth could have managed it at this point. And she was nothing anymore. Her wells were completely cut off. Once more she could feel the scar tissue clogging her channels of power.

A sudden thought pulled her out of her grief. Her eyes shot back up to Ann, still standing there, flinching under her stare. Ann knew what she'd done, Beth thought, and she felt a shame so strong it was fear.

Her eyes flashed past Ann, further up the slope. It wasn't only Ann who was here with her in these woods. And now that she listened, she could hear the weeping groans of Dolan drifting from beyond the swell, not so far away at all.

And if *he* was near, then Farrah must be, as well....

With a whimper of fear, Beth flung herself back on the ground, staring over Ann's shoulder and up the hill. She scooted back a few feet on her rump before managing to get to her feet, then she turned and fled, running crazily through the trees and not stopping.

Twenty-three

Ann stood in the living room and watched Tim as he walked by her without making eye contact. Her impulse was to follow him, to make him pause by touching him, but she wouldn't let herself.

"Don't you want to be here when Farrah shows up?" she asked. After five weeks of silence, Tim had gotten a voicemail from his niece today. She'd said she was calling from the Sisterhood's compound, and that they had decided she was ready to handle a day trip into the city, though they wanted her to return before nightfall and continue living up there a few more months.

Tim had been sullen for weeks, but the voicemail had sent him over some kind of tipping point.

He opened his middle drawer, took out a stack of shirts, and carried them back across the room to his open suitcase. Still without looking at Ann, he said, "You'll be here. Why should I be, too?"

"You're her uncle. You're her blood relative."

"To hear you talk, that kind of thing doesn't matter."

"I never said that."

Tim was rustling through his suitcase, making sure he had all the clothes and supplies he'd need for a while. "You guys are the ones who had this big crazy experience together in the woods. It didn't involve me."

Finally Ann broke down. She stepped forward and, saying "Tim," placed her hand on his shoulder.

He shook it off. Then he paused, catching his breath. When he spoke his tone was almost conciliatory, but he still wouldn't make eye contact with his wife. "I can't help it," he said. "I've tried. But my sister was always so fragile, and you sided against her, and once you beat her she ran into the woods and nobody's seen her since."

"Don't think about it like I sided *against* her, I just.... I mean I was just trying to help Farrah. Doesn't that count for anything? She's your family too, you know."

"Instead of taking sides I wish you'd stayed out of it."

"Tim, please...."

"I can't help it," he said, latching the suitcase. "I can't help how I feel."

Ann huffed a sigh. She had too much pride to beg him not to go. "Where will you stay?"

"A hotel, I guess. At least at first. I don't have any friends I know well enough to crash with."

He was heading toward the door. The baby in Ann's belly felt very heavy. Her due date had already passed. As his hand touched the knob she stepped forward, pride buckling. "*Tim,*" she said again.

He paused at the door, but didn't turn around.

"I did the right thing," she pleaded.

He turned his head a bit, but not enough to look at her. "I know," he said. "But that just doesn't matter." He opened the door and left, closing it behind him.

On the southern tip of Manhattan, at Battery Park, Farrah leaned against a rail gazing out at the Hudson. A clutter of piers and authorized-only constructions hid the island's natural shore.

The Sisters had given her today as a field trip, a day off. Her first. She had learned not to hate them. They'd come for her that day as she lay in the woods, staring up at the sky, running her hands over herself, unconvinced that her spirit was not on the verge of being flung out of her body yet again, this time not to reside somewhere else but only to career through the void forever. Somewhere someone was sobbing.

They'd come for her just as she was realizing that the sobbing was nearby and was coming from that man who had tried to kill her. The women had shown up in their hoodies;

among them had been that grumpy frizzy-haired boss-lady from the compound.

Farrah let them pull her to her feet and start gently, firmly leading her off, all without saying anything. But then, as they moved her away from the black guy's crying, she tried to twist around to get a look at him. The women holding her, who were quite strong, didn't want to let her turn. "What's going to happen to that guy?" she asked.

"We'll put him out of his misery," said the frizzy lady. "Only humane thing to do, after a spell like that."

Before they'd even reached her, while their magery was flooding Beth out of the body, they'd fused shut its channels of power. Whatever that meant. But apparently the effects of such an operation were only temporary. Now that the wells had opened once, they would inevitably open again. She supposedly had great power, and it was going to reappear.

During the first week at the compound, Farrah had the feeling they were watching her, waiting for her to pass some test. Despite the gruff distance of the Sisters, she felt that there actually was warmth there for her; but it was warmth held in abeyance, waiting to see if it should be redirected elsewhere and not wasted on her.

No one said so, but she had the impression that if it looked like she was going to fail this test, the Sisters would kill her.

Whatever this test was, it had something to do with this power she could feel *pushing* inside her. As if there had been crevasses in her interior whose fleshy edges had been fused together by a blowtorch, and now there was pressure building behind those thin new walls of meat. Farrah didn't think that the Sisters were actually testing for anything very specific. She suspected they were simply waiting to decide whether or not she was a shithead. If it turned out that she was, she guessed it would be too dangerous for them to let her stay alive once that power started to break through its shell and she gained access to it.

By the time she was able to move small objects with her mind, it seemed like they'd decided to let her live. At first Farrah hadn't been sure she was grateful. She'd never been particularly comfortable in this body, but now it was torture; not even for a second since her transfer back had she felt at ease in it; she couldn't shake the sense that the frail link between her and her flesh might be broken at any moment. Even if it wasn't, there was still the new awareness that the link was entirely contingent. There was no special reason for her to be who she was, instead of anyone else.

But maybe a state of existential despair over the reality of her own identity was not a bad starting point from which to reinvent herself. And the Sisterhood wanted nothing less than a reinvention. They were willing to let her live, willing to allow this unbelievably powerful body to continue its existence in this unsuspecting world. But only on the condition that that body not continue to belong to the same old needy, neurotic, frivolous girl. The exercises they were leading her through taught her how to *do* things, yes: how to stack blocks one atop the other neatly, for instance, without ever lifting a finger. But they were also shaping her spirit. They wanted her more serious. They wanted her somber, even. And she was starting to get the idea that they wanted her loyal to the Sisterhood.

That would probably be fine, she thought. It might feel good to be loyal to something.

She turned from the water to lean back against the fence and look across the park. Idly her gaze picked through the people milling about. There were business people and finance types, out on their lunch breaks. A homeless skinny black man with a decayed shopping cart into which were piled mountains of plastic bags filled with soda cans. Some old-timers, oddball New York types who maybe had bought apartments in this neighborhood way back when regular humans could afford to do such a thing.

And another homeless person, way on the other side of the park. A woman. Walking with her head hanging and her jaw slack, not from drink or drugs but from perpetual horrified disbelief. Leading with her shoulders as she lurched along, her arms dangling straight down, a zombie gait. Red hair.

Farrah took a step away from the rail, quivering. "Mom?" she said.

There was no way Beth could have heard her from so far. Yet she jerked to a halt even so.

Farrah was in motion, her feet carrying her forward. "Hey, Mom!" she cried.

Her mother looked over, stricken—she was too far away for it to be true, yet Farrah could have sworn she could make out the blistered whites of her mom's eyes. Then Beth turned and bolted.

"Hey!" shouted Farrah, and took off after her.

Beth was running out of the park, toward the street. "Mom!" shouted Farrah. Was her mother running out of shame and humiliation, or because she was afraid Farrah wanted revenge? Would she have been right to fear that? Farrah didn't know. "Goddammit, Mom, fucking stop!"

To look at her a second ago you would have thought Beth was falling apart, and that there was no way she could outrun her young healthy daughter. But those dirty feet sure were pumping. Battery Park was a wide enough expanse that even from this distance Farrah could keep Beth in sight. But, though the gap between them was narrowing, Beth now put on an extra burst of speed and flew out of the park and across the road, into the city. Farrah put more oomph into it, really racing now, keeping her eyes on her mother till she disappeared around the corner of the first intersection she reached.

Farrah didn't slow down. She had faith that, even though her mom was temporarily out of view, she'd catch sight of her again just as soon as she looked round that corner, herself.

But once she did reach it, and then skidded to a stop, all she could do was stare around wildly. The street wasn't that busy; there weren't even that many stores along it for Beth to duck into. No sign of her mom, though. Farrah could keep hunting. But she knew she wouldn't find her. She'd melted back into the city, back into the anonymous world.

Bitter tears built up pressure behind Farrah's eyes. Her face was a pink, puckered wound, passed over unnoticed by the crowd.

It might feel good, she thought. *To be loyal to something.*

ALSO FROM SALTIMBANQUE BOOKS:

IRONHEART, by J. Boyett

Part H.P. Lovecraft and part *Alien*, *Ironheart* is the story of what happens when the mining ship *Canary* comes across a strange derelict on the edge of the galaxy—a derelict occupied by a strange and seemingly immortal woman....

THE UNKILLABLES, by J. Boyett

Gash-Eye already thought life was hard, as the Neanderthal slave to a band of Cro-Magnons. Then zombies attacked, wiping out nearly everyone she knows and separating her from the Jaw, her half-breed son. Now she fights to keep the last remnants of her former captors alive. Meanwhile, the Jaw and his father try to survive as they maneuver the zombie-infested landscape alongside time-travelers from thirty thousand years in the future.... Destined to become a classic in the literature of Zombies vs. Cavemen.

DAUGHTER OF THE DAMNED, by J. Boyett

Before Carol was born, Harold ruined her mother's life. Now Carol's out for vengeance, with the help of the bounty hunter Snake.

But her quest has set off a trap left by her mother. And Carol and her mother's old enemy will have to team up, if either wants to get out alive.

THE SEXBOT, by J. Boyett

The AI Revolution has come, and it ain't easy for a single dad to find a decent job. Most things a human can do, a computer can do better and cheaper. So Brad provides for his kids as best he can, using virtual reality to remote-control a sexbot in a brothel. Male, female, straight, gay: Brad the anonymous operator does it all. A man's got to provide.

But even the brothel gig is barely enough to scrape by on. So when his kids' guidance counselor Duane shows up as a customer, Brad wonders if he can use this chance encounter to build a better future for his children?

COLD PLATE SPECIAL, by Rob Widdicombe

Jarvis Henders has finally hit the beige bottom of his beige life, his law-school dreams in shambles, and every bar singing to him to end his latest streak of sobriety. Instead of falling back off the wagon, he decides to go take his life back from the child molester who stole it. But his journey through the looking glass turns into an adventure where he's too busy trying to guess what will come at him next, to dwell on the ghosts of his past.

STEWART AND JEAN, by J. Boyett

A blind date between Stewart and Jean explodes into a confrontation from the past when Jean realizes that theirs is not a random meeting at all, but that Stewart is the brother of the man who once tried to rape her.

THE LITTLE MERMAID: A HORROR STORY, by J. Boyett

Brenna has an idyllic life with her heroic, dashing, lifeguard boyfriend Mark. She knows it's only natural that other girls should have crushes on the guy. But there's something different about the young girl he's rescued, who seemed to appear in the sea out of nowhere—a young girl with strange powers, and who will stop at nothing to have Mark for herself.

I'M YOUR MAN, by F. Sykes

It's New York in the 1990's, and every week for years Fred has cruised Port Authority for hustlers, living a double life, dreaming of the one perfect boy that he can really love.

When he meets Adam, he wonders if he's found that perfect boy after all ... and even though Adam proves to be very imperfect, and very real, Fred's dream is strengthened to the point that he finds it difficult to awake.

BENJAMIN GOLDEN DEVILHORNS, by Doug Shields

A collection of stories set in a bizarre, almost believable universe: the lord of cockroaches breathes the same air as a genius teenage girl with a thing for criminals, a ruthless meat tycoon who hasn't figured out that secret gay affairs are best conducted out of town, and a telepathic bowling ball. Yes, the bowling ball breathes.

RICKY, by J. Boyett

Ricky's hoping to begin a new life upon his release from prison; but on his second day out, someone murders his sister. Determined to find her killer, but with no idea how to go about it, Ricky follows a dangerous path, led by clues that may only be in his mind.

BROTHEL, by J. Boyett

What to do for kicks if you live in a sleepy college town, and all you need to pass your courses is basic literacy? Well, you could keep up with all the popular TV shows. Or see how much alcohol you can drink without dying. Or spice things up with the occasional hump behind the bushes. And if that's not enough you could start a business....

THE VICTIM (AND OTHER SHORT PLAYS), by J. Boyett

In *The Victim*, April wants Grace to help her prosecute the guys who raped them years before. The only problem is, Grace doesn't remember things that way.... Also included:

A young man picks up a strange woman in a bar, only to realize she's no stranger after all;

An uptight socialite learns some outrageous truths about her family;

A sister stumbles upon her brother's bizarre sexual rite;

A first date ends in grotesque revelations;

A love potion proves all too effective;

A lesbian wedding is complicated when it turns out one bride's brother used to date the other bride.

Made in the USA
Middletown, DE
31 July 2020

14171111R00126